KATYA'S WORLD

"It's a highly effective, thought-provoking novel, and it left me looking forward to the next volume."
Philip Reeve, bestselling author of Mortal Engines

"A really well imagined world, detailed and utterly believable, a great mix of technical detail and breathless action."
Charlie Higson, bestselling author of the Young Bond *series*

"A wonderful writer and storyteller."
The Huffington Post

JONATHAN L. HOWARD

THE RUSSALKA CHRONICLES I

KATYA'S WORLD

STRANGE
ChemISTRY

STRANGE CHEMISTRY

An Angry Robot imprint
and a member of the Osprey Group

Lace Market House
54-56 High Pavement
Nottingham
NG5 1HW
UK

www.strangechemistrybooks.com
Strange Chemistry #5

A Strange Chemistry paperback original 2012
1

A catalogue record for this book is available
from the British Library.

ISBN: 978-1-908844-12-5
Ebook ISBN: 978-1-908844-14-9

Set in Sabon by THL Design.

Printed in the UK by CPI Group (UK) Ltd, Croydon, CR0 4YY

To Katharine, a better friend than I deserve.

I AM LEVIATHAN.
I come to you in blood
And lie in shadows.
My heart is a sun,
And my nerves sing with lightning.
I have come to kill you.
All of you. Each and every one.
Every man,
And every woman,
And every child.
As you huddle in families,
Or hide alone.
I shall not let any of you live.
For I am Leviathan.
I come to you in blood
And sleep in shadows.
My heart is a sun,
And my mind...
My mind...

PROLOGUE

RUSSALKA

One hundred and fourteen years ago, humanity first touched Russalka.

It was a cold, machine touch, a robot probe that arrived in orbit and observed the tempestuous surface of that storm-wracked world. The robot and dozens more like it had been sent out in a great wave of expansionist hope. Earth was past the point of saturated population growth. The solar system had been explored and exploited, offering almost everything but what the humans really wanted – a new world to call "home".

The robot deployed its faster-than-light communications array and relayed the data it was gathering about the world, a world then known only as RIC-23. Yes, its atmosphere was breathable. Yes, its temperature was bearable. Yes, its gravity was acceptable. What it couldn't offer was the simplest thing. RIC-23 was an ocean world. But for its polar ice caps, there was not even a square meter of dry land on the whole planet.

Disappointed, the humans left the robot to continue its survey while they turned their attention upon other more promising worlds in the region.

The robot dropped a lander from orbit that fell on gossamer drogue chutes through the angry storming skies and fell into the ocean, communicating its discoveries back to Earth via the robot above. Earth looked at the analysis with growing astonishment. RIC-23 was rich in rare minerals dissolved into the oceans. Perhaps it was not the most glamorous planet they had discovered, but it was certainly one of the most useful. If a colony was founded there, it could supply the other settlements in the sector.

A colonisation project was mounted. In common with all such projects, the colonists were all taken from a single ethnicity. Previous experience had shown that, in the stressful environment of a new world where disasters may occur at any time, people look for others to blame and ethnic differences were frequently where fracture lines formed. The RIC-23 project drew its personnel purely from an area spanning Moscow to New Petrograd.

The first act of the thousands selected was to name their new home. They looked to folklore and chose the name *Russalka*, after a race of mermaids, beautiful and mysterious. If they had looked deeper into the myth, they might have changed their minds – a Russalka was a predator that would use her charms to draw men to the water, to be drowned and fed upon.

The humans found Russalka a difficult world to love. The storms that scoured the surface rarely quietened, the seas rarely grew peaceful. Still, it had never been the plan to live on the surface. The ocean depths were where the minerals were, and the storms could not touch them down there. Using their advanced technologies, the colonists located submarine mountains and ridges, and melted tunnels and caves into them with fusion cutters that burnt as hot as a star. They sealed and drained these new cave systems, covered the bare rock with corridor walls and floor gratings, installed lighting and heating. The settlements started to spread, named for countries and cities lost to the sea on distant Earth – Atlantis, Lemuria, Mologa, and dozens more.

On the surface, the technicians built floating platforms for the handful of aircraft they maintained, and the shuttles needed to reach the few short-range starships parked in orbit. These they would use to maintain trading contacts with the other nearby colonies, close neighbours only a few light years away.

The first phases of the colonisation effort were not without their difficulties and setbacks, but they passed largely as planned, and the Russalkin – as they now called themselves – waited for further supplies and colonists to arrive from Earth. They waited, and they waited, and they waited in vain.

There had been tensions on Earth when they left, and even rumours of war, but the Russalkin found it hard to believe that it could ever really come to that. They listened for any FTL signals from Earth, but heard nothing, only from the other colonies saying that they too had heard no news.

Years passed, decades, generations, and Earth remained silent. The ships the colonies had were incapable of travelling the vast distance to Earth to investigate, and they lacked the technologies and knowledge to build such a ship. They could only guess at what had happened, that war had indeed broken out, and that terrible weapons, whose very threat had always proved sufficient before, had finally been armed and sent to evaporate cities, countries, whole civilisations.

Earth was dead and gone.

A century passed, and the colonies had become well established. The colonists felt at home on their worlds, and none still considered themselves Terran. Life was hard, more so on Russalka than most, but the Russalkin developed a deserved reputation for toughness and pragmatism, and that pleased them. It was dangerous living in purely manmade environments with a hostile ocean on the other side of every airlock; it was hard sometimes going years without even seeing the sky, travelling between the settlements in submarines.

True, there were always the crews of the surface platforms who weathered the storms with a coolness that perturbed even the hardy submariners. The platforms travelled together in a fleet, and the crews came to call themselves the Yagizban, a private joke they didn't care to share with those who lived in the depths. The Russalkin shrugged and ignored such Yagizban eccentricities. After all, the fleet – the Yagizba Enclaves, they called it – was where most of the planet's cutting edge technologies were developed. If anybody could rediscover the secrets of long range star travel, it would be they.

As the colonists went into their second and third generations, it became apparent that some sort of unifying organisation would be necessary to keep all the settlements working in harmony, to deal with disagreements and even the occasional crime. The Federal Maritime Authority had been founded early on to handle submarine traffic control and, as it had a presence in every settlement, its officers were given a broader remit, to act as peacekeepers and police when necessary. It was never envisioned that the FMA would ever become military in nature, but then, nobody can tell what the future will bring.

One day, without warning or fanfare, the Terrans returned.

A great, hulking Terran warship entered the atmosphere and settled into the angry sea, the waves crashing against its hull. FMA vessels surfaced and hailed the ship, identifying themselves as representatives of the people of Russalka and welcoming the Terrans as long-lost relatives. The Terrans were in no mood for speeches and celebrations. Bluntly, they demanded that the FMA be dissolved and control of Russalka be given immediately to Terran governors. Earth had suffered a century of troubles, but those days had passed. Earth was under a new unified government, and now they were reasserting their grip upon the colonies. They didn't care to hear about Russalka's claim to independence, based on a hundred years of hard-fought building, all done without aid from Earth. The FMA commander told them that Earth was no longer home to him and his people, that Earth had no claim on Russalka.

The Earth ship considered this for a moment.

Then it opened fire.

Two FMA subs were lost in the first salvo before they even had a chance to dive. The rest, ill-equipped to engage such a foe, launched torpedoes more in desperation than expectation. Their luck was good, however. One struck a killing blow, and the Terran ship was badly holed. Amid fire and explosion, it sank. Any sense of jubilation on the part of the Russalka was lost in the astonishment of such unjust demands from the home of their ancestors, and in the sure knowledge that there would be retaliation for their defiance.

The Russalkin worked desperately for a year, building new ships, preparing orbital defences, conscripting as many as they could into the FMA to be trained, drilled, prepared to fight to the death to protect their world against the invaders from Earth they knew were coming.

The war, when it came, was short, brutal, and inconclusive. The Terrans arrived, and attacked immediately.

First they destroyed everything the Russalkin had in space – their starships, defence satellites, and the irreplaceable FTL communications array, severing the world's last link with its fellow colonies. Then the war moved from space into the seas. The Yagizban floating aerospace platforms were hunted down and destroyed within hours, and the Yagizba Enclaves were forced to flood their emergency ballast tanks and hide beneath the waves.

The FMA fought hard against a foe they barely understood. They outnumbered the Terrans, but the Terrans had brought with them advanced technologies that made up for their lack of troops. Settlements were destroyed with horrific losses of life. The Russalkin had prepared evacuation shelters where their children were to wait out the war; the truth of how many of their parents and older brothers and sisters were dying in the battles and massacres was kept from them. To the Russalkin, the Terrans ceased to be human at all. They were merciless, degenerate killers. Dirty landgrubbers, come to wipe out the colony and take their world, grubbers who murdered and wrecked without hesitation or pity.

Then, after a little over a year, the war simply petered to a halt. The Terrans had given up, seemingly unable to maintain such a ferocious campaign over such a vast distance from their homeworld. The Russalkin watched the skies fearfully for months, and then they started to rebuild.

War leaves scars, though, and even ten years after the last shots were exchanged, the scars remain obvious. Almost a whole generation was lost, and the next generation found its childhood cut short as they were trained to take the places of their dead or missing parents, brothers, and sisters. The fear of a new attack runs deep, and the FMA has never stepped down from a war footing. New warboats were built, drowned settlements resealed and pumped out, martial law maintained. In the chaos of the aftermath, criminality broke out here and there, culminating in pirate attacks on civilian transports. It seemed that Russalka had fought off an enemy from without, only to find a new one within.

This is Russalka now.

Wounded. Isolated. Proud.

This is Katya's world.

ONE

JUDAS BOX

The locksman took Katya's identity card, looked at it briefly, and handed it back. The whole time, he never stopped chatting with her uncle.

She took it back feeling slightly cheated. She must have looked at that card a hundred times since it had arrived from the Department of Matriculation, reading and rereading the fine print. Her family had been so happy for her, Uncle Lukyan especially. "Now you're an adult, Katya!" he'd said, picking her up under the armpits like he'd been doing since she'd been born. "Being an adult isn't a matter of age. It's a matter of responsibility. And this card shows you're ready for that!" There had been a little impromptu party and everything.

And now nobody seemed to care. She hadn't been expecting fireworks, but she'd hoped for a friendly nod from the locksman, an acknowledgment that she was entering a great fellowship. Instead she was being ignored, standing to one side as the locksman and Uncle Lukyan – she mentally pulled herself up – *Captain Pushkin* were gossiping like old women while they went through the boat's documentation and journey plan.

Suddenly, the locksman turned to her. "Going to Lemuria with your uncle, eh?" he said. He didn't quite say "little girl" but the sense of it floated around. "Seeing relatives or doing some shopping?"

Katya looked at him blankly. This wasn't going properly at all. She was just trying to come up with a reply that made her sound grown-up when her uncle cut in. "God's teeth, Mikhail, didn't you even look at her card properly? She's an apprentice. This is her first voyage in a crew chair."

The locksman had the decency to look abashed. "I'm very sorry," he said to Katya, "may I trouble you for your card again?"

This time the response was much better. "A navigator?" he read and looked at her. "Difficult discipline." He was still looking at her but the words were clearly meant for her uncle.

"Not for my niece," said Uncle Lukyan with visible pride. "She has the brains for it. You should have seen her examination results. I think the examiner thought she'd been cheating. 'Well, Captain Pushkin,'" he imitated the examiner's wheedling tone, "'they are remarkably good results. *Remarkably* good.'"

The locksman laughed. "Durchev thinks people need crib sheets to put on their boots in the morning."

Katya watched them chat and thought, one day I'll be able to talk like that, to know everybody. There goes Katya Kuriakova, the best navigator in the water, they'll say. She concentrated on trying to make her blue eyes steely, her chin determined, her nose... Her damned nose. She was just going to end up looking sweet and, in all likelihood, adorable. It always happened. She could drown a hospital

and they'd still let her off for being in possession of a but-
ton-nose. She stopped trying to look heroically competent
and concentrated on just not looking chronically winsome.

"Straight light haul to Lemuria, two seats full of electronic components," her uncle was saying, going through
the folder containing their itineraries and permissions.
"Sergei will ride shotgun in a passenger position while
Katya takes the co-pilot's seat. Show her what it looks like
from the sharp end."

"Is she going to draw your plot?"

"Yes, I am," said Katya, tired of them talking about her
as if she wasn't there.

The locksman looked at her uncle with a question he
didn't want to say out loud. Lukyan laughed again. "Yes,
she can do it. I'd trust her to give me a plot through the
Consequentials, never mind an easy haul like Lemuria. She's
got talent, real talent." He ruffled her short blonde hair
affectionately. "She's the family genius." He closed the folder
and put it back in his documents case. "We'd better move
or we'll miss our departure slot. Come on, Katya."

Katya had been aboard the *Baby* several times, but always
back in the passenger seats. "Don't step over that line,"
her father had once warned her, pointing at the yellow
line that split off the pilot and co-pilots' positions from
the rest of the cramped interior, "or Lukyan will have you
swimming home." He had only been half joking. Safety
aboard was always a primary concern and breaking the
concentration of the crew was absolutely taboo while the
controls were live. That yellow line might as well be a
steel bulkhead.

Now she found she still couldn't step over it. Lukyan

was already in the left-hand seat and strapping himself in when he noticed she hadn't joined him. He looked at her, his eyes gentle. "I'm sorry. I forget how important this is for you." He cleared his throat. "Apprentice Kuriakova, please take the co-pilot's position."

"Aye-aye, captain," she said, too nervous to smile. She stepped past him, over the yellow, and slipped into the co-pilot's seat. It seemed enormous: all shaped plastic and restraint mountings. As she struggled to get the seat's safety systems to adjust to her shape and to remember her in future, a dour face appeared around the open lock door.

"Who's that little snot in my chair?"

"Hi, Sergei," said Katya. She pressed the memory button on the chair. Instead of remembering her settings, it reset them back to Sergei's. She swore mildly.

"Cursing already," said Sergei, stepping forward. "One minute at the con and she's Captain Ahab. Here." He pressed the memory button and another unmarked one lurking nearby. The chair finally acknowledged the new settings. "It's not very intuitive. Just one of those little things you don't learn from simulators." He plumped himself in one of the two empty passenger seats, the two opposite him being folded up and the space taken with plastic wrapped boxes, their cargo for Lemuria Station. "Experience. It's a grand thing. Learning by getting your hands dirty. Loads more fun than the classroom."

Katya prickled slightly. Was he getting at her? She'd always been good in school. She slid a look at Lukyan but he was checking his wristwatch against the *Baby's* chronometer.

"Ten minutes before MTC will let us out. Might as well use the time." Lukyan waved his big slab of a hand at the three screens ranged in front of her beneath the forward viewport. "How similar is this to your simulator?"

For her answer, Katya reached forward and tapped the screens one after another. They immediately glowed into life. She looked briefly at each and said over her shoulder, "Is this your set-up, Sergei?"

"Yes. Why? Are you going to tell me I've been doing it wrong all these years?"

"No," she said lightly, "I was just going to congratulate you for doing it exactly as per the textbooks." She heard him grumble under his breath and smiled; he'd probably reprogram it the first chance he got now rather than do it the way the schools did. He was almost pathetically proud of being self-taught.

She pointed out the screens to her uncle. "Navigational, waypoints. Sonar returns. Navigational, plot. Shall I write up a plot or pull one from memory?" She quickly added, "Sir." It was tricky to remember that, for the time being, her big friendly bear of an uncle was her captain and was to be treated with respect.

"You'll learn nothing by using an old plot. Draw up a fresh one, *apprentice*."

Katya barely had time to shift the data from the right-hand multi-function display onto the more convenient and larger middle one when they were hailed by Maritime Traffic Control.

"Petrograd MTC to RRS 15743 Kilo *Pushkin's Baby*." Uncle Lukyan responded and Control continued, "Please hold until advised."

"What?" Lukyan bridled. "What's the problem, Control? Don't tell me we've been bumped?"

"No problem, Lukyan. Please hold." Traffic Control

broke the link before Lukyan could ask for clarification.

"No problem," he said, seething. "No problem. That means there's a fat problem." He looked apologetically at her. "I'm sorry this isn't going to plan, Katya. Today of all days."

"These things usually don't," said Sergei from the back. "All part of the learning experience. Lesson one: expect to get screwed over for the convenience of others on a regular basis."

Uncle Lukyan looked back at him and then at Katya. He shrugged. "He's right, unfortunately, miserable bilger that he is. Well, we might as well make the best of a bad lot. You know your MFDs. How are you on the rest of the instruments?"

Katya looked at the banks of instruments. They had never looked quite this threatening when reduced to computer graphics on a simulator panel. Her wan smile told Lukyan everything he needed to know. He pointed at a box mounted up and to the right. "Judas box. That's got all your warning lights on there and a couple of telemetry monitors. Should always be a healthy green like it is now. If it starts getting spotty, you're in trouble. The closer to the top of the display the light is, the more vital the system."

"But isn't this stuff on the MFDs?"

"It is," said Sergei, "if you can be bothered to page through to find it. The point is that the Judas box is always in the same place. You want to know your system status, you look right there. Fast and easy."

"Same goes for these other instruments," agreed Lukyan. "You need to be able to find this information quickly." He tapped another display. "Depth gauge. If the figures are green…"

"Then you're safe," finished Katya. "If they're yellow…"

"Amber," muttered Sergei.

"…it means you're below your test depth and if they're red, then you're beneath your crush depth."

"I've only seen them amber a couple of times," said Lukyan. "That was during the war. I've never seen them go red outside an instrument test. I hope to God I never see them do so otherwise."

Katya looked at him with interest. He rarely spoke about his experiences in the war. Like many, he regarded it as a penance the world had suffered to remain free. "Why did you dive so deep, uncle? Sir?"

"Dodging a torpedo. We were already beneath the thermocline so there were no thermal layers beneath us to dive for. Our last hope was to lose the fish in the geography of the sea bed. Find a canyon to hide in or a spire to duck behind. You could hear the torpedo's active sonar pinging off the hull. It sounds nothing like a boat's sonar. High and fast. If we could drop a noisemaker and move into cover at about the same time, we might be able to fool the torpedo into attacking the wrong thing. A few metres above the gully we found, the depth gauge went amber. By the time we were safely in cover, the hull was groaning. Not much, but the torpedo had already put a powerful fear of death in us. Hearing the boat's ribs creak just about put the jam on it." He shook himself slightly, bringing himself back to the here and now. "Anybody who says war is glorious is a damned fool, Katya."

"But you managed to dodge the torpedo, didn't you?"

"No," butted in Sergei. "It hit them and they all died horribly. That's why he's here to tell the story."

"Thermal layer detector," said Lukyan, ignoring him. He pointed out a vertical display. "There's not many torpedoes to dodge these days but a thermal layer will still mess up your sonar, so you need to know where they are. They can make life very difficult when you're prospecting with high intensity sonar pulses or surveying charges." He waved at the instruments. "Even with all this, travelling through the seas of Russalka is like running through clouds of teargas. *Everything* makes navigation difficult. The thermocline is...?"

It took a moment before she realised he was questioning her. "Uh. The thermocline is the layer of water heated by solar energy. Not much of that gets through the storm clouds on Russalka, so it's not as deep as on some other worlds. As you get deeper, it gets colder, the water gets denser..."

"...and it screws up your sonar," commented Sergei.

"Then there's the halocline. As you get deeper, more mineral salts are dissolved into the sea water, making it denser..."

"...and it screws up your sonar," repeated Sergei.

"There's the pycnocline, which is a combination of the effects of the minerals and the temperature. Oh, and there's the rusocline, which is unique to our world. That's a sort of halocline but caused by the mineral spouts in the seabed."

"And guess what it does to your sonar?" said Sergei.

The communicator bleeped into life again. "Petrograd MTC to RRS 15743 Kilo *Pushkin's Baby*." They actually heard the controller sigh. "I'm really sorry about this, Lukyan. You've got visitors."

"Visitors? Who?"

There was a banging on the hatch Sergei had sealed after himself. Uncle Lukyan's face grew dark with anger. "Sergei..."

"Yeah, yeah." Sergei had already unstrapped himself

and was moving aft. "Tell them we don't want any." They looked back as he opened the hatch and stepped out. They heard voices for a minute and then Sergei stuck his head inside. "You'd best step out, captain. It's the Feds."

Lukyan's temper cooled slightly. It never helped to antagonise the Federal Maritime Authority. He quickly unstrapped himself and left the *Baby*, Katya following close behind.

On the lockside, Sergei was standing talking to a man in a Federal Security uniform. Actually, thought Katya, "man" was probably putting it a bit strongly. He only looked two or three years older than her. He was neatly turned out in the utilitarian black jumpsuit, short peaked cap and combat boots of the Authority, but his crop of acne damaged the overall effect. What presence he had was mainly the result of the large handgun in his belt holster; a standard issue maser. It took her a moment to notice there was another man standing a couple of metres back from the officer. She realised with a shock that he was handcuffed.

"What's this about?" Uncle Lukyan demanded of the officer. He jerked his thumb at the man in the handcuffs. "Who's *he*?"

The officer held a piece of paper in Lukyan's face. "FMA business. I'm commandeering your boat."

Lukyans's eyes bulged. "You're *what*?"

"You are to transport me and my prisoner to the FMA penal facility at the Deeps with all dispatch."

"The Deeps? That's nowhere near our…"

"Failure to comply with the terms of a Federal warrant is a criminal offence. Do you comply?"

Katya had never seen her uncle so angry. His clothes

almost seemed too small for him as his muscles bunched with fury.

"Listen, you officious little snot, I didn't fight a war just so the likes of you…"

"*Do you comply?*" shouted the officer in his face. Katya would almost have been impressed with his bravery except for the gun. She had noticed the officer's free hand move down to rest on the pistol grip and it looked as if Lukyan had seen it too.

"Give that here," snapped Lukyan and snatched the paper from the officer's hand. He made a great show of examining it, but Katya knew that he had already lost. If her uncle wanted to keep his master's license, his boat and his liberty, he really had no choice but to obey. Finally, he folded up the paper and gave it back. "Academic, anyway. We don't have sufficient space for two passengers."

That took the officer aback, the first time his careful façade of authority had wavered. Katya reckoned he probably spent hours in front of the mirror, practising being cool and official.

"Your boat's rated for two crew and four passengers."

Lukyan smiled. "Half the passenger space has been given over to cargo and we're carrying three crew today. It's all in our itinerary and manifest. Nice and legal."

"You don't need three crew for a bucket like that."

Lukyan's smile faded quickly. The officer didn't notice; he was pointing at Katya. "What does she do?"

Without being asked, Katya snapped out her card and held it out to him, open. "I'm the navigator."

"You?" The Fed didn't even try to conceal his disgust. "You're just a kid."

"Not in the eyes of the law." They all turned to look at

the prisoner in surprise. He was somewhere in his late thirties, thin rather than lean, with dishevelled light brown hair worn at collar length. He was wearing loose clothing, a baggy shirt, a long jacket of some light material. Katya had never seen anybody dressed like that, couldn't even remember ever seeing clothes like that. They were soiled and dirty; he had plainly been in a fight recently. One lapel and shoulder of the coat were speckled with blood from an untended cut on his forehead. He spoke again, quiet and controlled. "She's rated as an apprentice navigator, which is about equivalent to a junior commissioned rank in the FMA. That should be good enough for you, officer. After all, you've got a Federal ID, which qualifies you as some sort of crime-busting hero rather than the chimp in a uniform that you first appear."

Katya had no idea what a "chimp" was, but it didn't sound like a compliment to her. It apparently didn't sound like one to the officer either. He drew his baton in one smooth move and slammed it across his prisoner's thigh so hard that she wouldn't have been surprised to hear the bone snap. The prisoner grunted and fell to the floor. The Fed stepped up to kick him where he lay when Sergei cleared his throat.

"Ahem," he coughed theatrically. The Fed stopped and looked at him. "Officer, educate me. Aren't there regulations about the handling of prisoners?"

The Fed's face was pale with anger, which only served to make his acne stand out. "He... he was... Allowances are made for subduing prisoners."

Sergei nodded sagely and cocked his head on one side to look at where the prisoner lay on the floor clutching his thigh. "Subduing. Right. Seems fair enough. He looks pretty subdued now, wouldn't you say?"

The Fed scowled, grabbed the prisoner by the arm and pulled him back to his feet. "You," he said to Sergei, "are you the usual navigator?" Sergei nodded. "Then she stays behind. We don't need two navigators."

Uncle Lukyan still didn't look happy, but she knew that he had no choice. She was already braced for the bad news when he turned to her. "Katya. I'm so sorry– "

"Miss your first voyage in a crew position?" butted in Sergei. "I don't think so. It's not a long trip to the Deeps. You can head straight to Lemuria from there and be back here halfway through third shift easy. I'll sit it out."

Katya could almost have kissed him. Almost, but not quite. Instead she made do with a grateful smile.

Leaving Sergei on the dry side of the lock, they trooped back into the *Baby*. Katya and Lukyan strapped themselves back into their seats as the Fed secured his prisoner in the passenger position behind Katya. Then he moved forward, blithely stepping over the yellow line to lean on the crew seats. Lukyan glared at him, but the Fed was utterly unaware of the faux pas. He watched as Katya laid in a new course that would take them to the FMA facility. After a few seconds he snapped, "What are you doing?"

Katya bit back the sarcastic comment she was dying to make and tried to be helpful and friendly. "I'm plotting a course to the Deeps, as you wished."

"You're deliberately wasting time. Why isn't the course direct? Why this detour? Explain yourself!"

Katya couldn't believe it. Were there people who really believed that the quickest route from A to B was always a straight line? "If we go there directly," she said slowly, as if talking to an idiot, "we will have to go through this volume. See? This bright yellow place on the map? That's amber for caution. That's the Weft, a volume of random currents. Russalka has lots of places like that."

"Is that area dangerous?"

Katya realised that the Fed truly knew nothing about submarine operations. He was thinking in two-dimensional areas, not three-dimensional volumes. She fought down the urge to lecture him on that subject; the Weft was clearly going to be hard enough to explain.

"No, but the *Baby* doesn't have the big drives of a military boat. If we get caught in a tow, it could put hours on the journey while we break free. Believe me, it makes more sense–"

"Use a direct course. That's an order."

"You," said Lukyan, quiet and dangerous, "do not order my crew. I'm still captain here."

"Then tell her to set a direct course." The officer moved aft without waiting for a reply and strapped himself in.

Katya looked to Lukyan. He plainly had murder in his heart, but crushed it down by effort of will. He nodded.

As Katya scrubbed her previous plot and started inputting the insane new one, her uncle hailed Traffic Control to explain what was happening. "Tell Lemuria they'll get their parts a few hours late," he finished.

"We'll try but the comms hardlink is down, has been for a week. I'll try to get a slot on the long wave array but I don't fancy the chances. The weather-buoys have been squawking all day about an electrical storm up top. Not too choppy for a change, but there's a lot of interference."

Lukyan heaved a sigh. "Today's not been easy so far. I can see it's not going to improve. Do what you can, please, Control. Katya, how's the plot coming along?"

She leaned back and spread her hands in disgust. There was no art and precious little science to a straight-line plot. It had taken her perhaps twenty seconds to complete it, most of which had been for the Petrograd departure and the Deeps approach waypoints. It was impossible to dignify it as "navigation".

Uncle Lukyan looked at it for a moment, sighed in sorrow and relayed it to Traffic Control's computers for the records. After a moment, the controller spoke. "You're going straight through the Weft," he said in a careful monotone.

"Not my choice or my navigator's. Our Federal commodore here ordered it."

"Does he know it will take you off the FMA patrolled routes?"

"I don't think he cares very much. I could ask, if you like?"

"Would there be any point?"

"None. Are we cleared for departure?"

A pause. Then, "You're cleared for departure, RRS 15743 Kilo."

"Thank you, Control. Opening lock now." Uncle Lukyan reached up and toggled a switch. Ahead of them, a crack of dim light appeared in the pitch darkness. Katya watched it widening in expectant silence until her uncle ordered, "Wake her up, Katya."

"Aye-aye, captain," she said, almost light-headed with excitement. Despite the change in plans, the idiotic Federal officer and his prisoner, and the insultingly simple course she'd had to lay in, this was still her first time out and it would never be repeated. This was the first time she'd prepared to leave dock and she wasn't about to mess it up. "Sonar to passive. Check. Wayfinder online. Check. Trim adjusted. Check." With each "Check," the

Baby's computer marked off another box on the list. "Navigational lights, on." She flicked the switches and the inside of the lock suddenly illuminated. Just beyond the port, she could see plankton floating, so close she could have reached out and touched them. "Check. Status lights..." She looked up at the Judas box. All its lights glowed a reassuring green. "Check. We're clear to disengage, captain."

"Thank you, Katya." He swept his gaze over his own screens. "Confirmed. Disengaging... now!"

With a dull thud of metal on metal, RRS 15743 Kilo *Pushkin's Baby* was seaborne, moving out of the docking lock under her own impellers. Within moments, Petrograd Station was lost in the submarine gloom behind them.

TWO
GHOST RETURN

Uncle Lukyan gave Katya the helm until they reached the first waypoint. She steered the little submarine cautiously, very aware of the responsibility the steering yoke gave her. The Federal officer made impatient noises from the back but they both ignored him. The prisoner, apparently seeking another beating, asked the Fed – with great concern if little sincerity – whether he was feeling ill?

When they reached the waypoint, the officer insisted that they go to automatic pilot. Katya regretfully gave up control to the wayfinder. Now that the boat's computers were in charge, there wasn't a great deal to do except monitor systems that were automatically monitored by other systems anyway. Every time she'd been aboard the *Baby* in the past, switching onto automatic pilot would have been the cue for one or other of the crew to unstrap and come back for a chat or a game of chess. With the compartment full of passengers and cargo, that would have been difficult. With the stifling presence of the Fed, who seemed to carry the full powers of the FMA around with him like a bad

31

smell, it was impossible. Katya and her uncle were reduced to reading checklists off to one another until that got boring. Then they lapsed into an uncomfortable silence. The trip to the Deeps couldn't be over fast enough for either of them.

The prisoner, on the other hand, kept trying to start conversations with everybody. He asked Lukyan how long he'd owned the *Baby*. He asked Katya what her favourite subject had been at school and why she'd liked it. He even asked the Fed what the interview for the FMA officer's job had been like as he was considering applying himself.

"Shut up," said the Fed.

"Just wondering. Once all this misunderstanding is sorted out, I was wondering what I might do for a job and then I thought, *don't just go for a job, go for a career. It's a man's life in the FMA*. Since you and I have been acquainted, Officer Suhkalev, I've become very impressed with the FMA. Specifically its low standards. I thought to myself, well, if *he* can get in…"

He stopped suddenly with a cough of pain. Katya looked back to see him doubling up; Suhkalev had elbowed him hard by the look of it. "Hey!" she called back. "Cut that out!"

"Don't tell me my business, girl," the officer snapped.

"How about I do?" said Lukyan. The officer was silent, his expression resentful. "You've got your gun on your right hip. You're sitting to the left of your prisoner. Did it ever cross your mind that he can reach your gun at least as easily as you can?"

Suhkalev glared at Lukyan, but he drew his gun and put it to his left all the same.

"Damn," said the prisoner, "I was looking forward to

getting that. Oh," he added in a different tone, "I'm very sorry but I seem to be bleeding on your deck."

"Hell, that head wound has opened again," growled Lukyan. "Katya, could…"

But Katya was already out of her seat and taking down the first aid kit from its locker. She looked around for somewhere to rest it while she opened it and the prisoner indicated his lap. "Put it here, it'll be handy."

"I didn't say he could be treated," said Suhkalev.

"You don't need to," replied the prisoner. "It's in FMA regs on the treatment of and conditions for prisoners. You ought to read it sometime."

Katya rested the box on the prisoner's lap and opened it. "How do you do?" he said, peering over the raised lip of the lid as she pulled on surgical gloves and located the necessary medications. "We haven't been introduced. I'm Havilland Kane."

Katya looked up sharply. Had he just said… "Havilland Kane?"

He smiled, amused. "My infamy precedes me."

"You're the… pirate?" It couldn't be? This bedraggled, painfully polite man couldn't be Kane.

His eyebrows rose. "Am I? Perhaps I am. I've been accused of so many nonsensical charges it becomes difficult to keep track." His smile broadened but – and perhaps it was just Katya's imagination – seemed to grow colder. "And your name is?"

She didn't answer, instead busying herself with a swab. She cleaned his wound quickly but carefully. He barely winced though the cut was deep and was already showing some signs of a mild infection. "I'm going to close it up now. I've put in some antibiotic matrix," she said, carefully neutral, "but it needs seeing to properly. Make sure the medics at the Deeps know about it."

"You're an angel," he said, but so quietly that she doubted anyone else heard it. Then he hissed slightly with discomfort as she used the suture pen to bind the edges of the cut together.

"Have you finished?" muttered Suhkalev. Katya didn't even look at him. She closed up the kit and stowed it in its place before returning to her seat.

As she strapped herself in, she thought she heard Kane say, "Thank you, Katya Kuriakova," but it was hard to be sure over the hum of the *Baby*'s systems.

The journey continued in a strained silence apart from the quiet curses of Uncle Lukyan as they entered the Weft. As predicted, the random currents were not their friends. The boat started to go off-course almost immediately and Katya and he had to wrestle the controls around before extemporising some new intermediate waypoints to try and get them out of the cross current that had them. They succeeded in that but ran quickly into a lazily twisting vortex that turned them around again and again. Lukyan was concerned that the extreme manoeuvring might upset their inertial guidance; Katya could see the strain on his face as he watched their coordinates like a hawk, waiting for a telltale lurch in their apparent location. After the vortex, they hit a head current that the *Baby* forged against with agonising slowness. "One hour it would have taken us to go around," hissed Lukyan loudly enough for the Fed to hear. "We'll be lucky to get out of here in five at this rate."

Finally, the going became easier as they reached the centre of the system of complex currents. It was only a respite;

things would become difficult again when they tried to leave, but at least they had a few minutes' peace.

Katya spent the time thinking about their handcuffed passenger. She couldn't believe it: Havilland Kane sitting right behind her. She didn't know whether to be excited or scared, and settled on faintly worried. Kane had been all over the news bulletins for the last six months. Commerce raids, drone intercepts, the disappearances of any vessels in the region had all been put at his door. There had been talk of crews murdered, too. The FMA hadn't had an image to show, given any background on him, or even provided a reliable description, and the idea had grown in her head that Kane must be some sort of monster. She'd envisioned him as ugly and hulking, unshaven, with eyes devoid of the faintest glimmer of mercy. Now it turned out that he looked just like anybody else. If she'd passed him in a corridor, she'd have thought he was a tutor or a researcher. She frowned to herself. Maybe the FMA *had* messed it up. Looking at Officer Suhkalev, it was difficult to believe that they were infallible.

Any further reflections were blown away by one of the *Baby*'s automated alarms. It wasn't one of the danger alerts – she knew well enough the difference between a status alert and the urgency of a failing major system alarm, but it made her jump all the same. Not nearly as far as Suhkalev, though.

"What's that?" he blurted. "What's happening?"

Lukyan had already switched his largest multi-function display to show a sonar map of the seabed. The computer represented it as interconnecting triangles of dull blue and red light drawn against blackness.

In the centre of the display, the seabed rose up to form a

hump described in triangles that dimmed to orange where they joined the ocean floor. *Pushkin's Baby* was, like many other private submarines, a jack-of-all-trades. Its insect-like yellow hull contained and carried many different types of equipment, allowing it to do many jobs from geological survey to cargo carrier to salvage vessel. Katya knew the display was relaying data from the geological sensor array, but she had no idea what the hump was or why it was worth an alarm. She started to ask her uncle, but she saw the expression on his face and the question died. He had a rapt, focussed expression, like a man who has seen the merest hint that all his dreams were about to come true.

"Katya," he said slowly. "We might be very, very rich."

"A deposit?" she said. Russalka was rich in minerals, one of the reasons the Grubbers wanted it so much. Submarine mining, however, was difficult. Finding large deposits of ore just lying on the seabed wasn't unknown, but it was very rare, and the savings meant the discoverer of such a deposit could more or less name their price. Katya read the scale information from the nuclear magnetic resonance display and felt her own eyes widen with disbelief. It was *huge*.

Lukyan brought the *Baby* to a halt and adjusted the active sonar, increasing the frequency of the pulses to get a better picture.

"What? What are you doing?" the Fed spluttered in his outrage. "We have a *prisoner* to deliver here! We don't have time…"

"*You* don't have time. I've got all the time in the world for a beautiful sight like that." Lukyan tapped the screen. "I can't run a business running errands for the FMA. This is a once in a lifetime opportunity."

"You'll be recompensed for your journey," said

Suhkalev, perhaps realising that he should have mentioned payment earlier.

"Oh, yes. An FMA scrip that will take years to be honoured, if it ever is. You can hold your water for a few minutes. Look at this, look at this!" He studied the sonar returns. "The signal's good. No, the signal's excellent. There's a mound of ore down there. A hill of the stuff! It must be, I don't know, a hundred and fifty thousand tonnes. If it extends beneath the bed, maybe quarter of a million. Katya, arm a probe."

Katya turned back to her controls, trying to look efficient. Although munitions and ordnance were among the co-pilot's jobs, she'd never even studied the systems outside a training manual. She checked the launch tube's inventory and found they were, indeed, carrying a couple of geo-survey probes. Getting them from their magazine into the tube was another matter. Her mouth felt very dry as she tried to work out how to do it quickly. The silence in the submarine drew out, punctuated only by the wheedling survey alarm. She felt they were all watching her make a mess of it and blushed, which just made her feel even more embarrassed.

Then Uncle Lukyan lost his patience, leaned across and hit the right keys and switches to load and arm a probe, completing her humiliation. She just sat there feeling childish and useless as he returned to his own console and fired the device off. The hiss of the compressed air driving the stubby cylindrical torpedo out of its tube resonated through the hull.

"Survey probe away," reported the computer primly.

Lukyan settled back in his seat, very pleased with himself and insensitive to Katya's burning face. "On its way.

Man alive, even if the quality's poor, there's so much of it, it's as makes no difference. You're crew, Katya, you get a share too. What do you..." He turned and saw her expression. He seemed surprised for a moment and then his face fell as he realised how he'd inadvertently humiliated her in front of the Fed and Kane. "Oh, Katya. I'm–"

The computer interrupted. "Probe link lost." Lukyan's attention was back on the sensor readouts in an instant.

"What? But it's right on the scope."

But it wasn't. The probe had vanished. And, quickly, before their startled eyes, so did the ore deposit. The great mound simply seemed to flow back into the seabed, flattening out in seconds. The polygons that it had been drawn in faded from the brilliant gold they had been a moment before to dull reds and blues, indistinguishable from the rest of the submarine landscape.

"That's..." said Lukyan, "...that's just not possible."

"Maybe it was methane," said a voice from the back. Kane. "Perhaps it was methane gas from rotting plant matter caught in a mat of sunken vegetation. You punctured it with your probe and it just..." he shrugged, "deflated."

Lukyan turned slowly in his chair, his surprise and disappointment turning to sneering anger. "The only gasbag around here is sitting in handcuffs. The NMR was lit up like a birthday cake, that thing was magnetically aglow. Methane..." He turned back to face forward, still muttering angrily. "Methane, he says."

"Whatever it was, it's gone now. Maybe we ought to get moving," said Kane. Suhkalev looked at him suspiciously.

"You seem to be in a big hurry to get to a holding cell, Kane."

"I just don't like..." Kane shrugged and laughed lightly. "I just don't like hanging around under three hundred metres of water in the middle of the Weft. It's a bad place to be."

Katya didn't need to look back at Kane to know there was something else bothering him. A submariner of his experience must know that the Weft was a nuisance but certainly no danger. That laugh had been altogether too mannered and a little strained.

"No," said Lukyan, his disappointment still evident in his voice. "We're going nowhere until I've run a diagnostic analysis of the sensors. I've never seen a ghost return like that. If they're feeding us garbage data, then we're blind. Worse than blind. I'm not risking going through the rest of the Weft until I'm happy."

Predictably, Suhkalev was *not* happy. "You've wasted enough time here, captain. Get us under way!"

"No. My authority over my vessel is absolute in matters of operational safety. You can't tell me to go anywhere until I'm happy with the operation of this boat."

"He's right," said Kane. Suhkalev shot him a dirty look. Kane grinned unapologetically back. "It's no good getting shirty over it with me. It's in the maritime regulations. The *FMA* maritime regs, that is. Like I say, you *really* ought to read them some time. Gripping stuff. I laughed, I cried."

Katya tried to ignore them. Why did Kane keep provoking Suhkalev? All it would get him was another beating.

Abruptly, another alarm sounded: the proximity alarm. Now it seemed the *Baby* thought there was danger of collision with something. She toggled the alarm off and nestled her headset on more comfortably.

Lukyan watched her silently while she – her hearing younger and more acute than his – listened carefully through the submarine's ears. In the *Baby*'s hull were mounted highly sensitive microphones. When relayed to a human listener, they provided a stereophonic sound image of the marine environment. She sat in absolute silence, her eyes shut as she concentrated entirely on what was coming through the headset speakers.

"Hydrophones are picking something up," she said finally, eyes still shut. "Can't make it out. Very low frequency."

"Manta-whale?" asked her uncle.

"No, nothing like a manta. There's no song. Just a hum, slight pulse." She dipped the hydrophones' active frequencies so they translated sounds normally too low to be heard by the human ear up into the audible range. "Really quiet. Almost silent, but it's there."

Kane said, almost to himself, "We really ought to go," but everybody ignored him.

Katya's eyes fluttered open, her expression confused like somebody waking from a cryptic dream. "I thought I heard cavitation. Just for a moment."

"A sub?" said Lukyan, his frown as puzzled as his niece's. Cavitation was the sound caused by water travelling swiftly over an imperfectly streamlined surface. It developed into tiny water vapour-filled bubbles that hissed in the water and sounded clearly through audio sensors. It had long been the bane of war submarines; the faster you went, the greater the cavitation noise. In submarine warfare, silence is life. A loud boat is a dead boat.

Lukyan had fought before and he knew that golden rule. Katya seemed to be describing the barely-detectable sound of a war sub. Lukyan knew that an opening torpedo tube door, the gap in the hull flawing the otherwise perfect teardrop design, could have caused the momentary sound of cavitation.

Perhaps he was being paranoid, but he'd rather be paranoid than dead.

"Nobody make any noise," he whispered as he switched off the impellers that were holding their position, the sound relays, even the ventilator fans. *Pushkin's Baby* drifted freely, silent and – Lukyan fervently hoped – invisible to hostile hydrophones and passive sonar.

"Pirates!" hissed Suhkalev at Kane. "Your crew, no doubt?"

"I said *quiet*!" whispered Lukyan, only keeping his voice down with a massive effort of will.

Kane said nothing. He just sat looking at the deck, his hands clasped in front of him. Katya was meanwhile trying to get more of an idea of what they were dealing with, or at least where it was. About the only thing she could think of that might work in this situation was a complex technique called integrated coordination. This combined simple triangulation with examining the Doppler shift in any sound data. It usually needed so much data drawn over such a long period that it was of very limited use when dealing with a moving target. It could, however, at least give an idea of range.

Lukyan looked at what she had pulled up on her main screen and nodded approvingly. The seconds ticked by, turning into minutes.

Katya was lost in concentration, only faintly aware of the increasing tension in the three men who watched and waited for her to perform her mathematical magic. She needed a decent frequency shift, she thought, as target and listener moved relative to one another. Just a few millihertz, she wasn't greedy. When the *Baby* drifted into a tendril of the Weft and moved smoothly away from the target for a few seconds it was all she needed.

"I have an IC resolution," she whispered, gently tapping the numbers into the workpad. Then, her normal voice sounding like a shout after the quiet, "Oh no! 800 metres! Closing rapidly!"

Both submarines had seen each other simultaneously.

The time for stealth had gone. "Navcom!" barked Lukyan at the computer. "Evade! Evade!"

The impellers whirred into life as the navigational computer started running the evasion programs that had been standard on every Russalkin boat since the war. "Evading now," it reported. Then, "Multiple contacts in the water, closing one two zero knots."

Katya couldn't believe it. "*How* fast?" She'd never heard of a torpedo that could beat a hundred knots. To go faster meant using very loud drives and – she listened intently through the hydrophones – she could just hear some faint cavitation noise. The torpedoes were almost silent.

"We're not at war, are we?" asked Suhkalev from the back in a shaky voice.

"Uncle?" said Katya as she pulled off her headset, "I'm not picking up any active sonar pings. What kind of torpedo doesn't use active sonar?"

Lukyan wasn't listening; he'd opened communications channels. "Mayday! Mayday! Mayday! This is RRS 15743 Kilo *Pushkin's Baby*. We are under attack! Repeat, under attack! Requesting urgent assistance."

Katya was horrified. The chances of anybody being within range when Suhkalev's orders had taken them so far off the recognised lanes were minimal. Her uncle must know that. With a sense of cold sickness deep in her belly, Katya realised how desperate their situation was.

"Mayday! Mayday! Mayday! This is RRS 15743 Kilo

Pushkin's Baby. We are under attack! Repeat, under attack! Requesting urgent assistance. We are..." He paused as the sensor screens suddenly filled with red emergency light. The impact-warning klaxon sounded. "Oh, no..."

Katya couldn't believe how quickly the water came in. It was as if a spar of ice had punched through the *Baby*, stabbing clean through her metal and plastic hull and then instantly turning back to liquid. By the time she thought *we've been holed* the water was already up to her knees.

It all became confused then; too many stimuli, not enough time to examine each of them. She saw her uncle punch the emergency surface control and felt the *Baby* lurch, as her trim weights were dumped and her ballast tanks were blown empty with compressed air. The depth gauge stopped falling, even rose for a couple of metres, but they'd taken on too much water and started to fall again. She heard her uncle shouting "Locks! Locks!" but that made no sense. Then she felt the water rise cold and deadly over her hands and was shocked by how high it was. She reached down and tried to release her harness but it wouldn't unlock. She thought she really should have asked Sergei about the seat's eccentricities and she'd make a point of asking him next time.

Then she thought, *except there won't be a next time because I'm going to die before the next time.*

She tugged at the seat's webbing until she realised the water was up to her neck and she ought to worry about breathing. Then something happened – she guessed that the *Baby* had lost trim and rolled – and she was completely underwater. She fought with the straps a bit more but it was no good, they simply weren't going to let her go. She looked up and saw the Judas box. Almost all the lights were red, especially the ones across the top row. Hull integrity, motive power, life support – all her favourite green lights had gone red and that saddened her as the cold water leeched the life out of her.

She couldn't care anymore. She couldn't concentrate enough to care. She couldn't even feel her fingers anymore.

She looked across at her Uncle Lukyan and found he was looking right at her. There was an expression of such horror on his face. For a moment, she thought he was afraid to die, but then she realised that he was horrified that she was going to die. She wished she could have hugged him, told him it was all right, that she couldn't care anymore, but the straps held her firmly into her seat and she couldn't care about that either. Then the power failed and they were in darkness. She watched the lights on the Judas box flicker out and wondered if the Judas box had a Judas box indicator on it. She guessed not, or else there would be a lone red light burning there now, to tell them that the Judas box was broken.

In the darkness, Death snuggled up close to her. She realised that she was still holding her breath and wondered why she was bothering, now death had finally showed up to embrace her. She tried to hold her breath a little longer just to show she could, but death wanted her to come with him. She didn't want to be impolite. The stale air bubbled out of her mouth and nose. Liquid flooded in.

She thought, in the brief moment before the darkness claimed her, that it was a shame she'd died just before her sixteenth birthday. There was going to be a party. It would have been fun.

THREE

NOVGOROD

If Russalka had a global religion, it was atheism.

Colonising a new planet had given the settlers a long-range perspective on the workings of religion and it all seemed so distant to them here; so irrelevant, so faintly childish. Religions were still studied, though, if only as mythologies, and as a way of understanding some aspects of Terran politics and history.

But nobody was very interested in knowing much about the past of that distant world now, anyway. People had much more important things to worry about.

Katya was raised as an atheist from birth, but she knew about angels. When she died, she was slightly surprised to find herself taken to Heaven by one.

The angel carried her upwards through the darkness of space, leaving Russalka behind. Higher and higher they rose, until she saw the distant lights of the Celestial City.

She wondered how she was going to apologise to God for being wrong all the time about Him. Still, she wouldn't be being taken up in rapture from her worldly existence unless He was a forgiving God; the vengeful version suggested in other comparative religion files would have left her in Limbo or worse. No, she was sure He'd be able to accept an apology in the spirit in which it was meant and they could start afresh. She wondered if He played chess.

Then the light grew bright and she flew strongly and happily towards it, borne by her angel. They struck it and the light shattered into a thousand million fragments, scattering around her, droplets of Heaven falling back into the sea.

The sea.

The sea?

Where she had been in rapturous certainty a moment ago, now she felt panic and confusion. She wasn't in Heaven at all. There was no God waiting for her with the chess pieces already set out. There was only the sea and the lightning flashing spasmodically across an angry sky. Was this Hell? Was she still on Russalka? Were they – the thought flittered momentarily and vanished before she could settle upon its intimations – the same thing?

More lightning, distorted through water drops on plastic. She realised she was wearing goggles, but how..?

She was wearing an emergency respirator pack, but she could not remember putting it on, nor could she remember escaping the *Baby*. She couldn't even remember managing to undo her seatbelt. Her tongue felt strange in her mouth, impeded somehow and she suddenly realised her mouth was full of liquid. She moved to tear away the respirator pack's mask but a hand restrained her. She spun around in the water and found herself face to face with Kane.

His emergency respirator mask made him look insect-like and sinister. Part of the breathing mechanism itself was clear and she could see a green fluid inside. She cursed herself for her stupidity. The whole near-death experience suddenly made perfect, if humiliating, sense.

He gestured to her to follow and swam towards a beacon-buoy floating a few metres away. With a sick feeling, she knew it was the *Baby*'s beacon, automatically released when all else had failed, and she knew what it meant. The *Baby* was gone, and Uncle Lukyan was dead.

They clung to the side of the small buoy as the waves slapped half-heartedly at them. The weather report had been right; the sea wouldn't go out of its way to drown them. It didn't have to; Russalka's electrical storms were notoriously disruptive to communications. They'd be lucky if anybody detected the distress signal the buoy was transmitting for hours. They'd be dead from exposure long before then.

Kane hooked his arm around a stanchion on the buoy, closed the respirator's valves and took it off. The green fluid ran from his nostrils as he vomited up the fluid that was in his lungs. It wasn't really vomiting – lungs simply aren't equipped for dumping liquid contents like stomachs – but it allowed him to breathe the thick Russalka atmosphere.

When he'd got about as much out as he was likely to under the circumstances, he helped Katya to do the same. It was an ugly sensation; she'd grown used to the feel of the liquid in her throat and lungs since she'd come around. Feeling cold air flooding her mouth and trachea right down inside her chest was uniquely unpleasant.

"Are… are you all right?" asked Kane, coughing up more of the fluid.

"My uncle, what happened?"

Kane looked away from her, out across the choppy sea.

"I'm sorry. I could only try and save whoever was closest to me. That was either going to be you or that worthless FMA bletherskite. I couldn't have got to your uncle in time."

"He tried to save me," said Katya. She wanted to cry, but something seemed broken inside. She could only talk, she didn't seem able to feel anymore. "He was shouting about the Lox packs." She touched the emergency respirator. Its trademark name was a LoxPak, Lox supposedly meaning liquid oxygen. It was a misnomer and unpopular among mechanics who dealt in the real thing; real liquid oxygen would kill anybody who tried to fill their lungs with it, an agonising death as their throat and chest froze solid. In contrast, the green fluid in LoxPaks was merely saturated in oxygen, releasing it directly into the lung tissue.

The fluid also scrubbed nitrogen rapidly from the blood, vital if a victim of a submarine disaster was to stand any chance of surviving a rapid ascent from a few hundred metres down to the surface. She wasn't in agony, blind or dead, so at least she knew her LoxPak had saved her from the worst symptoms of decompression sickness. The worst symptoms, but Katya now realised, not *all* the symptoms.

One of the lesser symptoms was the "rapture of the deep". Hallucinations. Katya knew she'd suffered from them now. Her guardian angel bearing her to a better place had been a notorious pirate taking her to the surface, where she could die more slowly. She laughed out loud, surprising Kane, but the laugh finished with her bringing up more Lox liquid and by the time she'd stopped coughing, the opportunity to ask her what she thought was so funny seemed to have passed.

They floated in silence for some time. Then Katya said, "What happened to your handcuffs?"

"They were an inconvenience," said Kane. "I got rid of them." He caught Katya's expression. "I'm sorry, that sounded fatuous, but they *were* a nuisance. While you were tending to the cut on my head, I borrowed a probe from the medical kit. FMA cuffs really are primitive. I could teach you how to pick them in ten minutes."

"You've practised?"

"Of course I've practised. The Feds might not be the brightest intellects in the universe but even the stupid get lucky sometimes. I like to be prepared."

Another minute passed. "How did they catch you anyway?" asked Katya.

"You ask a lot of questions," replied Kane.

"I can't feel my feet."

Kane looked at her seriously, and she knew why. Hypothermia would be setting in soon. The sea was freezing and slowly leaching the heat from them. They needed to concentrate and talking might be the thing to give them a few more minutes.

"How did they catch me," repeated Kane. "It wasn't brilliant detective work, put it that way. It was the reward money that did it. I was informed on." He noted Katya's blank expression. "I was grassed on. Done up like a kipper." None of this seemed to be getting through. He tried again. "Sold out?"

Katya finally seemed to understand what he meant, so he continued. "Did a bit of business with a man who I'd have thought would know better, walked out straight into three officers waiting for me with masers drawn. That's the trouble with this planet; all the criminals are such amateurs.

How is Russalka ever going to get a real criminal underworld going if anybody will grass up anybody for a fistful of small change? It's divisive."

"You're not from Russalka?" She'd thought not. Not with that name and that accent. She'd met people from other colonies before. Now they were all trapped on Russalka since the Grubbers had attacked and destroyed their few starships.

"No, I'm not from Russalka. If I could leave tomorrow, I would, too. This place is a dump. Why did anybody ever decide it was a good idea to colonise a planet with no dry land at all?"

"Minerals."

"I know. I was talking rhetorically."

"So if you hate it so much, why did you come?" She knew Russalka was considered a freak world to colonise. No land to speak of, just one great global rolling ocean with a couple of icecaps. Nothing had ever evolved to grow on them though. The ocean teemed with life, but the icecaps and the sky were dead. Everybody else from the Grubbers – the Terrans – through to the other colonies had land to stand on. Out of all the colony worlds, Russalka was unique and difficult, and the Russalkins were proud of that.

"I didn't want to. Circumstances dictated it."

Katya wondered what he meant by that, but something in his tone warned her off, and she didn't press him for an explanation. "Well, you're stuck here for a while then," she said.

During the war, all Russalka's space assets had been destroyed; her communication, navigation and meteorological satellites, the launch platforms and the handful of starships had all been wrecked by the Grubbers to deny Russalka any line of defence from orbit out to the transition shelf where starships entered the star system.

In the end it had all been for nothing – the war had just stopped. The Grubbers never sent any diplomats or anybody to explain why they weren't going to fight anymore, they'd just stopped coming. One morning Russalka woke up and there were no new incursions, no more targeted asteroid hits, no more robot hunter/killers splashing down. The war just stopped. As far as it went, Kane was right about organised crime on Russalka being a bad joke, but that was true of everything. They'd lost a lot of people and a lot of technology. Thankfully Russalka was a mineral rich planet with a lot of energy to be had; they would rebuild, but it would take time.

There was a lot to do before Kane could leave Russalka for somewhere more suitable for a career criminal. New launch platforms would eventually have to be built, new starships constructed to be launched from them, new satellites put up to feed the ships the accurate astronomical data they needed before hitting the transition shelf and initiating quantum drive. It would take a lot of effort, a lot of will, a lot of money and, worst of all for Kane, a lot of time.

"I heard Lyonesse was building a platform," said Kane conversationally. A wave rolled over him and Katya waited until he'd finished coughing before answering.

"I heard it was just for sub-orbital transports. Nobody's interested in space at the moment, Kane. We've got enough problems on planet without worrying about what's overhead."

"What if it's the Grubbers who are overhead?"

"Then…" Katya paused. She was glad her uncle wasn't here to hear her say this, but she believed it all the same. "We should surrender."

Kane made a point of getting eye contact before he replied. "Do you really think so?"

"Yes," she said without hesitation. "If they attack again, they'll kill us all. Let them bring their stormtroopers. They can't be any worse than the FMA."

"I wouldn't bet on that. The FMA are light entertainment compared to stormtroopers."

"It doesn't matter. The travel time is what will do the trick. It takes a year to get to Russalka; it's not a cheap trip to take. Anybody they send will end up going native, just like we did. They won't be sending occupiers, they'll be sending new colonists."

"Interesting thought. I think you underestimate the Terrans, but you're right about surrendering. If they can scrape together the resources for another invasion task force, this world's in no shape to resist." He looked up at the tip of the buoy's spire, a metre above them. Upon it, a brilliant white light flashed rhythmically.

They watched it in silence for a minute or so. Katya was beginning to feel very tired. It was so cold in that sea, and she knew it was killing them slowly. She tried to wedge her arm into the spire's frame so if she fell unconscious, she wouldn't simply slip under the waves. The spire's supports were too close together, though, and she couldn't manage it. She looked at the dark sea beneath the sullen sky, and death felt all too close. "Do you think somebody will save us?" she asked.

Kane thought for a moment as if working out an exact answer, but then only said, "Maybe. At least whoever put that hole in the sub didn't come after us to finish the job."

"Who do you think that was?"

"I don't know," replied Kane, a little too quickly.

Katya had no intention of dying with questions unanswered. She was about to ask him again when her mouth stopped in mid-syllable, and she was left with a foolish expression. Kane looked at her oddly and then followed her line of sight.

Perhaps five hundred metres away, the sea had begun to boil. As they watched, the commotion grew more focussed, more kinetic, and Katya realised it was coming closer. She also realised what it was.

"It's a bow wave! There's something headed right for us!"

"I'm glad you worked that out for yourself; it saves me having to explain it," said Kane. "Survival tip, Katya. Take a deep breath just before it hits us. That should be enough, but keep your LoxPak handy in case."

The mound of angry sea was almost upon them. "In case of what?" she screamed as the roaring of the waters grew deafening.

"Oh, you know," said Kane, looking straight at the mound, which was quickly turning into a mountain, "stuff."

The front of the great pile of sea charging towards them seemed to tear and sheer away as the great muzzle of the object was finally exposed. With a hideous, shuddering whine, the muzzle split into three equal jaws – one below and two opening up and away to the left and right. The waters, thrashed until they were milky, sluiced violently over them and back into the sea. The jaws devoured Katya, Kane and the distress buoy all, slowly closing again as the monstrous thing sank back into the ocean. In a few seconds, there was no sign that they had ever been there.

The petty officer who opened the airlock into the salvage maw was only expecting to find a distress buoy. The furious fifteen-year-old girl and the bedraggled man were definitely a surprise.

"What was that?" spat Katya in a fury, waving her arms around to take in the maw and, by implication, the whole process of being swallowed by a submarine. It wasn't very pleasant in there. It was cold and wet – if not as wet as it had been before the bilge pumps drained it – and dark but for the flashing light on top of the buoy and a dim maintenance light over the door. The maw was like being in a tall conical room that had fallen on its side. Its use was simple: it opened wide, swallowed anything the boat's captain wanted to look at and then clamped shut. They were also never used in rescues as there was too great a chance of a survivor slipping between the edges of the jaws as the maw shut and, regrettably, being snipped in half. "What did you think you were playing at? You could have *killed* us!"

Kane was weighing up the petty officer's uniform; it seemed that an FMA vessel had picked them up. He decided, all things considered, that he'd prefer not to be taken back into custody. If they wanted to know who he was, they'd have to work it out themselves. The petty officer turned to the bulkhead and snapped open the cover on an intercom.

"Deliav to bridge!"

A voice replied almost immediately. "Bridge. What's the matter, Deliav? Is the buoy damaged?"

"No, captain! At least, I don't know, I haven't checked

it yet. Captain! We picked up survivors! They must have been hanging onto the buoy!"

As the sailor and his captain talked, Kane leaned close to Katya. "Do you believe in paying your debts?"

Katya grimaced and narrowed her lips. She'd been wondering how long it would take him to get around to this. "Yes, I know you saved my life. Don't worry, I won't tell them who you are. Then we're even, okay." It wasn't a question.

"Okay," said Kane, leaning away from her again. She thought he seemed oddly disappointed, as if she'd said the wrong thing.

The captain sent a small party down to get Katya and Kane, taking them first to the sickbay where the boat's medic spent half an hour checking each for signs of nitrogen narcosis sickness, hypothermia, and shock. When they were warm in fresh, dry clothes – Katya was glad she was quite tall and fitted the smallest uniform one-piece they could find – they were taken to the captain's cabin for "debriefing". She didn't like the sound of that at all.

"It's just questions," the doctor told her when she asked. That still didn't make her feel any better. How could she explain what had happened without dragging in the fact that Kane had been a prisoner aboard?

If Captain Zagadko had appeared at an audition for a production about the war, he'd have been turned down for looking too stereotypical. He was grizzled, lean, and his eyes had the distant look of a man who has seen things he'd rather forget. He oozed competence and professionalism and, if Katya hadn't been so worried about having to lie to him, she would have felt his presence reassuring.

He offered them coffee from the pot on his table and began the debriefing.

"Firstly, I'd like to welcome you both aboard the shipping protection vessel RNS *Novgorod*." Katya had heard of the *Novgorod*. She was a big boat, perhaps four hundred metres in length and the pride of the shipping protection fleet – the "pirate hunters" as they were popularly known. Kane seemed to have fallen out of the frying pan into the fire and then climbed back into the frying pan. "I'm truly sorry that you were brought aboard in such an unconventional manner. I'd made the assumption that there would be – forgive me – no survivors. I'd also assumed that whoever was responsible for this outrage would still be nearby, which is why the *Novgorod* made the quick grab at the surface. It appears I was wrong on both counts. I can only ask your forgiveness."

"Nothing to forgive, captain," said Kane. "Any competent captain would have made the same assumptions."

"I agree," added Katya, feeling quite grown-up in this conversation. "Please accept our thanks for rescuing us. Also, please extend my apologies to Petty Officer Deliav for anything unpleasant I may have called him when he discovered us in the salvage maw."

Zagadko smiled. "I'll do that. But, to business. Do you have any idea what sank *Pushkin's Baby*?"

Of course, Katya realised, this was bound to be about what happened to the sub, not about who was aboard and why they were there. Perhaps she could avoid talking about Kane at all. Any relief she felt at that was quickly overwhelmed by remembering the *Baby*, and her uncle's fate.

"Not pirates," said Kane with certainty.

"Oh? Why not?"

"There was no warning, no shot over the bows, nothing. They just came up and put a hole clean through us. It doesn't make sense for pirates to sink a vessel. They're after cargoes, not wrecks."

The captain nodded and turned to Katya. "I understand you were the co-pilot, Ms Kuriakova?"

She nodded. "My first trip. I'd only just been rated."

"You were in a good position to see the controls. What do you remember?"

Katya concentrated. "We had just given up on a survey. A ghost return. It looked as good as a mountain of gold for the few moments it was on screen. My uncle wasn't happy about it turning out to be a mirage and he wasn't happy that we were trying to cross the Weft with unreliable sensors–"

"The Weft?" interrupted Captain Zagadko. "What were you doing in the Weft?"

"We had a passenger, one of your lot, actually. FMA." She became aware of Kane tensing slightly in the chair next to her. "He had some business at the Deeps and wouldn't listen to reason about how much the Weft could slow us down. He insisted we go through it."

"What business?" said Zagadko. Katya could have sworn his eyes flickered over to look at Kane when he said it.

Katya wondered if she should just tell him that Kane had been Suhkalev's prisoner. Then she thought of Lukyan.

Once he had made some silly promise to her when she was a little girl and she had laughed and said he was lying. She remembered his smile dying a little, and that had sobered her. "Little Katya, a man is only as good as his word. A man whose word is worthless is a worthless man.

If I promise a thing, I will do everything in my power to keep that promise." And he had, going halfway around the world to get her some silly little trinket for her birthday.

Now she had given her word, or as good as. Uncle Lukyan was dead; she knew that. She owed it to him to keep her word.

"I'm not sure," she replied. "He talked to my Uncle Lukyan outside the lock. When my uncle came back in, he had a face like thunder. I think the Fed… the Federal officer had pulled a commandeering order on him or something."

"Indeed." Captain Zagadko turned to Kane. "That must have been very inconvenient for you, sir?"

Kane flipped a hand dismissively. "Not so bad, captain. It was only a short diversion or, at least, it would have been. Going into the Weft was a mistake, but the officer was just a kid and a corridor rat at that, by the look of him. He didn't know any better."

"You're a submariner yourself, Mr Kane?" Katya was partially appalled that Kane had given his real name and partially relieved that she didn't have to remember any alias he might have thought up.

"In years past. I'm happy to be a passenger these days."

Zagadko narrowed his eyes. "Do I know you, Mr Kane?"

The intercom popped and barked into life. "Captain to the bridge!" They all heard the urgency in the voice. With one last curious glance at Kane, the captain stood and ran out into the corridor.

Kane stood and looked at the open door. "Thanks," he said. "I appreciated that."

"I won't cover for you indefinitely."

"You won't need to. He's a wily one, that Zagadko.

He'll work out soon enough who I am. Whether he gets a chance to act on it is another matter." He stepped towards the door.

"What do you mean?" Surely he didn't mean to kill Zagadko?

Kane paused to look back at her. "Why do you think the captain's been called to the bridge so urgently? Whatever attacked us... it's back."

FOUR

LEVIATHAN

The bridge was busy when they arrived. Deliav was just saluting the captain. "I've recovered the data card from the distress buoy, captain."

"Hold onto it for the moment, Deliav. We have more pressing business at present."

"Permission to enter the bridge, captain," said Katya crisply. She knew enough about the military not to go barging around on their boats as if they were on a pleasure trip.

Zagadko shot them a look. "I'm afraid not, Ms Kuriakova. We're in a state of battle readiness. There's no place for you here. Go to the ready room, please."

Kane cleared his throat. "With respect, captain, Katya was at the controls when her boat was attacked. If you may be engaging the same foe..?"

Zagadko was not the sort of man to dither. "Point taken. If you could stand just over there, Ms Kuriakova, and endeavour to stay out of the way." They made a move towards the bulkhead the captain had pointed at, but he stopped them. "Not you, Mr Kane."

Kane blinked with surprise. "But, captain—"

"You weren't at the controls, were you? Unless there's something you're not telling me?"

The two men looked at each other for a moment. It was Kane who broke eye contact first. "I'll be in the ready room if you need me," he said and walked out with what dignity he could.

Zagadko watched him go. When the hatch had closed behind Kane, he said to Katya, "You and I are going to have a conversation when Mr Kane isn't present. Count on it." He turned away from her, leaving her feeling guilty and worried.

"Range to the wreck?"

"Three thousand metres."

Katya started. They'd been hunting the wreck of the *Baby*? The captain noticed her surprise when he turned back. "I wasn't about to leave her lying there for pirates to pick over, Ms Kuriakova."

"Captain!" Zagadko turned to one of the sensor technicians. "I have something on hydrophones. Low, really low."

Katya remembered the ghostly sound she'd picked up herself over the *Baby*'s hydrophones. She watched as the operator dropped the frequency translation range, just as she had done. This was a military vessel; she wondered how much better the *Novgorod*'s sensors were in comparison to the *Baby*'s.

"Sonar?" demanded Zagadko.

The sonar operator sat hunched over his screen, looking carefully over every square millimetre of it. "Nothing, sir. Nothing on passive."

Zagadko humphed. "Pulse."

"Sir?" It was the first officer, a thin, dark man with heavy-lidded eyes. "We'll give away our position."

Katya thought that was a redundant thing to say. Zagadko was a veteran; of course he knew sending an active sonar pulse would be like lighting a match in a dark room. They would be able to see better, but everything else would be able to see them all the more easily.

"They already know full well where we are, Petrov. Active pulse, sensors."

The sonar pulse rang through the hull as it emanated out from the *Novgorod*. The *Baby*'s sonar had made a chirpy little *ping*. It had sounded somehow friendly to Katya. The *Novgorod*'s pulse, however, was a dull, mournful beat of sound that seemed to buzz inside her bones long after her ears had ceased to hear it.

The sonar officer checked his screen again. "I don't understand it, sir. We're picking up some sound; we should be able to get a passive lock on it." He waited for the sonar echoes to return. He seemed to wait a long time. "No bounce from the pulse, sir. I'm trying for an IC resolution – it's giving me a range of a thousand metres but won't give me a full solution. It's like hunting a ghost."

Katya remembered her own encounter. She realised that she was sweating. The *Novgorod* was a hundred times bigger than the *Baby* but she still had a horrible feeling, squirming in her gut, that history was about to repeat itself.

The hydrophones operator looked up. "I'm getting something… Cavitation noise, captain!"

Katya blanched. "Oh no," she said in a desperate little voice. Captain Zagadko looked around at the sound and was surprised to see her almost hugging herself in fear. "Cavitation," she said in a whisper. "Then it attacks."

Captain Zagadko was obviously becoming quite sick of this mysterious foe. He didn't like the way it was avoiding detection, he didn't like the way it had moved into an attack with none of the usual preamble of submarine combat, and – very especially – he didn't like the way it kept being referred to as "it" all the time.

He was sure it was a submarine, and a submarine is a "she," just like any ocean-going vessel. There was an atmosphere on the bridge as if they were facing some mythical sea monster and he wasn't having it.

"Petrov!" he barked. "Sweep the external cameras, floodlights on!"

"Aye-aye, captain." The first officer moved to the salvage controls. "The water's not too bad," he reported as the cameras flicked into instant life. "With enhancement running we should be able to see anything within a thousand. Nothing in the forward quarter, searching…"

"Incoming!" called out the sensors operator. "Single contact. Eight o'clock high. Fast, very fast."

"Eight o'clock high!" snapped Zagadko at Petrov. Petrov started swinging the lights and cameras to look that way. Zagadko was already standing over another crew member at her position. "Weapons! Two torpedoes on a reciprocal, forty-five degree search cones, three minute dry. Helm! Hard to port, dive for the isotherm, flank speed."

"Torpedoes away, launched and running. Noisemakers, Captain?"

"Yes, and wait for my signal. Petrov, have you..?"

But Petrov was looking at the main viewing screen on the forward bulkhead with sheer astonishment. Zagadko looked too and was struck dumb himself for several long seconds. All across the bridge, the crew paused to look up from their stations. Katya didn't want to look, but she really couldn't help herself.

"What," said one of the crew in blank disbelief, "is *that*?"

On the screen, a shape, a massive shape, loomed out of the dark, the smallest part of it illuminated by the *Novgorod*'s searchlights. It was unbelievably, shockingly huge, dwarfing the *Novgorod*. Smooth and almost featureless, it was impossible to say whether it was a machine or a creature. It swept gracefully by them, almost silent and invisible to sonar, and it never seemed to end.

Kaya heard a voice in the silence, speaking so quietly that she was sure she was the only one to hear it. "Leviathan." She looked sharply at the speaker.

It was Kane, standing by the hatch. Before she had a chance to speak, an alarm klaxon suddenly started bleating raucously, shattering the awful moment.

"We're taking on water forward!" called an officer.

"What?" Zagadko was bemused. "With no detonation?"

"No explosion, sir," reported the hydrophones operator, "but there was a lot of hiss, a little cavitation. It reminded me of the steam bubbles rising from a volcanic vent, very similar sound."

"Sonar? Are you getting anything?"

The sonar operator shook his head. "I don't know what's going on, captain. That contact I took to be a torpedo of some sort made a close pass and then pulled away. It's returning to... *that* thing – whatever it is – now. And," he looked embarrassed and confused, "I've lost our torpedoes. They just... disappeared."

"Damage control, what's the flooding situation?"

"Much faster than the pumps can deal with, captain. We're taking about four tonnes a minute. We're losing trim."

"Can we surface?"

"No, sir. We're already too far gone."

Zagadko stood a moment in deep thought, rubbing his earlobe. Every captain loves his vessel almost more than life itself, but every captain has to be ready to abandon that vessel at a moment's notice if there is no alternative. "Where's the hostile now?" he asked.

Neither the hydrophones nor the sonar operator could find any trace of the huge shape that had attacked them. "It's gone, captain. It's just vanished."

"This is very calculated," said Captain Zagadko. "It hurts us just enough to sink us and then withdraws. What's it up to?"

Katya was wondering about that too. "Captain?" He turned to her with a mild expression of surprise and she realised he'd forgotten she was there. "Captain, when it attacked us, we had multiple contacts. The *Baby* never stood a chance.."

"She's right," said Kane from the hatchway. "I was conscious throughout. It really laid into us."

"I thought I told you to go to the ready room, Mr Kane."

"Yes, you did. It was rather dull so I came back again."

"You are not helping," said Zagadko, his irritation starting to show. "Leave my bridge and–"

"What's the point, captain? We're sinking and you can't stop that. There's nothing out here but the Soup. We really don't stand much of a chance."

Just when she thought it couldn't get any worse, it did. "We're over the Soup here?" she said, pleasing herself by keeping a waver out of her voice.

The Soup was one of the great mysteries and attractions

of Russalka. In the deepest parts of the world ocean, beneath the crush depths of all but the strongest hulls, a thick mineral solution formed lakes and submarine seas. It was far denser than water, but still liquid, and it existed in standing bodies all over the planet. Little was known of it. A few small experimental samples had been taken and these showed the Soup, as it quickly became known, was rich in metallic salts including some of rare elements.

Simply put, the Soup was worth a fortune to whoever worked out a way of extracting it. Many rich men had tried and left poorer. Many poor men had tried and their bodies had not been recovered. The sheer density of the Soup was one of the things that made it so difficult to manipulate and the depth at which it existed made for a very dangerous working environment. Even a vessel capable of diving to great depths like the *Novgorod* could not hope to enter the Soup and survive. Every litre of Soup weighed – depending where in the world it had been gathered – as much as twenty kilograms, twenty times denser than water. Diving five metres into the Soup was like diving into a hundred metres of water. The few boats that could dive that deep were already past their test depth if they reached the surface of the Soup. A few metres down would send the pressure rocketing past the crush depth equivalent and the submarine would be crumpled like a paper boat in a giant's hand.

Unless they abandoned ship immediately, they would soon be too deep for LoxPaks to save them. Then they would have no choice but to ride the stricken vessel down into the Soup, where they would be crushed in a moment.

Kane coughed. "If anybody's got any bright ideas, now would be a good moment to share them."

Katya had an idea, but it was so stupid, she debated sharing it for a moment.

"Blow tanks!" ordered Zagadko.

The hull thrummed as water was driven out of the ballast tanks. "That's helping, sir," reported the steerswoman "We're still sinking but nowhere near as fast. The nose is heavy but we can pull it up a little on the hydroplanes."

"Not enough," murmured the captain, watching the depth gauge. "Navigator!" Katya looked up, but he was talking to his own navigator. Of course, thought Katya, don't be stupid. "Can we make Lemuria?"

The navigator stabbed at some controls – Katya was once again impressed by how much better the *Novgorod*'s technology was than anything she was familiar with. On the main screen, a map of the area appeared with the stricken sub in the middle. "At our current rate of descent, we will make it," a red circle appeared on the map, "this far." The red circle was nowhere near large enough to encompass Lemuria Station.

The captain stepped up closer to the display. "All right, so we can't hope to reach Lemuria. Anything else in the area? Research bases or mining encampments? Anything?"

The navigator checked his files and shook his head. Captain Zagadko swore under his breath.

So, that was that. They were all going to die and, it struck Katya, that even if she did make a complete idiot of herself, there would be no witnesses soon enough.

"Captain? Does the *Novgorod* carry any ship's vessels?"

"A couple of EVA pods and that's about it. I'm afraid we don't have enough to evacuate the whole crew."

Great, thought Katya, now he thinks I'm a coward and

just want to grab a pod. "I was thinking of reconnaissance vehicles. Flying reconnaissance vehicles."

The captain was confused now. "Two CG craft, but we have to be surfaced to launch them. I don't…" His eyes lit up. "Great gods! Yes, I do! Tokarov!"

Lieutenant Tokarov had already seen what Katya was getting at. "On my way, captain!"

As he left the bridge at a dogtrot, Zagadko said to Katya, "Go with him, please, Ms Kuriakova. Take a flyer each." Katya didn't need a second bidding.

She caught up with Tokarov raiding a storeroom. "Here," he said, tossing her a spool of metal tape. "You'll need a crimping gun too. Ever used this stuff before?" She shook her head. "It's very easy. The trick is to keep the stuff taut. Loaded up? Let's go!"

He led the way through bulkhead door after bulkhead door until they found themselves in the section directly behind the salvage maw. She'd remembered the dark shapes up in their cradles when Kane and she had been taken from the maw to the sickbay. She was glad she'd been right about what they were.

Tokarov climbed up onto the hull of the starboard contra-gravity craft. It looked like a long surface boat with heavy outriders, which she guessed contained the forward drives. They wouldn't be needing those, only the powerful lift units. Tokarov fed a length of tape around the craft and its cradle, and crimped it shut. Katya climbed onto the port craft and started doing the same.

"These cradles have clamps on them. Won't those be enough?"

The lieutenant shook his head as he laid a second length

of tape further down his craft's hull. "They're just to stop the flyer falling out of the cradle in harsh conditions or during extreme manoeuvres. What we're doing is something else again. How are you doing?"

Katya had just managed her first binding and didn't think the crimp sealing the tape into a continuous loop looked very secure. "I'm doing okay," she replied, promising herself that the next one would be better.

Tokarov had the benefit of experience and longer arms and had his craft almost cocooned in the silvery tape before Katya was even a quarter done. He came over and helped and soon both craft were fastened to their cradles as thoroughly as was possible without getting out welding gear. Tokarov went to the intercom and hailed the bridge. "Ready when you are, captain."

"Do it now, lieutenant," snapped Zagadko's voice in reply. "Time is wasting."

The lieutenant clambered quickly up into the cockpit of the starboard craft, Katya doing likewise for the port flyer. "Ever flown one of these, Ms? It's simple. Power is just like a minisub's." Katya sought and found a bank of switches like those she'd used to fire up the *Baby* just a few hours before. It seemed impossible that things could have changed so dramatically and so awfully in so little time. "That's good. Lift controls are the ones under your left hand, the slide control. On my mark, move it forward *slowly*. Ready? Three, two, one, mark!"

Katya gently slid the control forward. As it moved, the status screen showed the amount of mass the contra-gravity units were now ignoring. "Approaching parity," she reported. It was a phase she'd heard some pilot use in a drama about the war once. She guessed it meant that the craft now effectively weighed nothing. It sounded calm and professional and, if she'd got it wrong, at least Tokarov had the decency not to laugh at her.

"Check," he replied. "Keep going. Watch the tolerance meter. You want that to go through yellow into a deep orange. Not red, or this has all been for nothing."

Katya pushed the control slowly further still. Now her craft weighed less than nothing. She noticed the tapes running across the flyer's predatory nose growing taut as it tried to lift from the cradle. The tolerance meter was changing colour so achingly slowly that she wasn't sure what it was from moment to moment. What if it changed so subtly that what she thought was a very deep orange was actually red? What if she fried the flyer's CG units because she couldn't tell?

"I'm pulling four gravities and that's as far as I dare take it. What are you up to?" asked Tokarov.

Ah, blessed numbers, Katya sighed with relief. Numbers were nice and reliable and unambiguous. "Three point seven, eight, nine... four gees!" She locked off the controls without being told to and climbed out. Tokarov jumped from his craft's cockpit and landed in front of her. "Will it be enough?" she asked him.

"Only one way to find out," he said. "Come on."

The bridge was still quiet and Zagadko was grim. "Good work," he said. "Good idea, Ms Kuriakova. Effectively cancelling out the reconnaissance flyer's weight and giving us more buoyancy to boot has reduced the rate of descent significantly."

"But we're still sinking, sir?" asked Tokarov, his disappointment evident.

"We're still sinking. You've bought us some more time, though, and that's bought us more range." He pointed to the screen and the new larger red circle showing how far the *Novgorod* could go before hitting the bottom. "At least we'll clear that Soup lake. No chance of making Lemuria, still."

"Captain, if I might make a suggestion?" said Kane. He was still standing at the hatchway. He wouldn't enter the bridge without being invited and the captain seemed adamant that he wouldn't get such an invitation. Katya fumed inwardly; grown men behaving like children. She wished Uncle Lukyan were here. He'd have banged their heads and made them work together.

The captain clearly didn't want to hear it, but under the circumstances had little choice. "What is it, Mr Kane?" he asked in a tone of deep disinterest.

"Over there on that mountain," he pointed vaguely.

Zagadko glared at him. "Get on the bridge, man, and point it out properly."

"Thank you so much," said Kane with politeness so perfect, it was deeply insulting. He walked over to the screen. "This mountain, there's a mining base in it."

Zagadko shot a glance at his navigator who was already checking his files again. "There's no base listed, sir," he said finally.

"You won't find it on the active base lists," explained Kane. "It was decommissioned five years ago. The miners have long since gone."

"With no crew there, how are we supposed to negotiate the locks? Blast our way in?"

"You can if it makes you happy, captain, but it really isn't necessary. It has a moon pool."

Katya could see the captain considering. A moon pool was a harbour inside a base, the water kept at bay by air pressure. A boat need only swim along a short submerged tunnel and surface at the quayside. No locks needed to keep the ocean out, no crew needed to man the locks.

"How big?" asked Zagadko.

"Big enough. It used to handle ore carriers at least as large as this boat."

"Good enough. Navigation, set a course for the abandoned mining station." He turned back to Kane. "Thank you, Mr Kane," he said with evident distaste.

"Always pleased to help the FMA in its little troubles," said Kane, and smiled back with at least as much feeling.

With the *Novgorod*'s course set, her engines running at full power and the contra-gravity units of the two reconnaissance craft holding up well, there was little to do but wait and think.

Petty Officer Deliav had finally got to hand over the data he'd removed from the *Baby*'s distress buoy: the little boat's last half an hour of instrumentation readings and control settings. Captain Zagadko and Lieutenants Petrov and Tokarov watched the recreation of the events on the *Novgorod*'s computer while Katya talked them through it.

"There seems little doubt that this huge ore deposit that so mysteriously vanished was actually the vessel that then went on to attack you," said Petrov. "Its stealth capabilities are astonishing. I wonder why it had them all deactivated when you first detected it lying on the seabed?"

"We don't know it is a vessel," said Tokarov. "It doesn't behave like any submarine I've ever encountered or heard of."

"Of course it's a vessel," scoffed Petrov, "what else could it be? Or are you suggesting it's some sort of sea monster?"

"Leviathan," said Katya to herself.

"What was that, Ms Kuriakova?" Zagadko's hearing was apparently as sharp as his intellect.

"Oh, uh… nothing," she replied, flustered. "Just a name I heard. My father once told me that Russalka has no myths or legends yet, but it would grow them because people needed them. He told me that Earth's history had been full of monster legends and we'd follow suit."

"Fond of Earth, is he?" asked Petrov tartly.

"He died in the Battle of Lyonesse, fighting the Terran marines." Tokarov shot Petrov a dirty look. Petrov bit his lip. "I hardly remember him. Just little things. He taught me the names of the Terran monsters and I remembered them at first because they were fun to say. Then I remembered them because they reminded me of that day." She spoke the names softly like a prayer. "Kraken. Scylla. Leviathan."

Zagadko broke the uneasy silence that followed. "Ms Kuriakova, what do you think we're facing?"

She realised with a small shock that the captain of one of the most powerful warboats on the planet was asking *her* opinion. Petrov still seemed embarrassed by his gaffe, but Tokarov also seemed interested in her views. She thought carefully and said, "I think it's a machine. But I don't think it's a submarine, at least no sort of boat that has ever come out of our shipyards, and I don't know how it got here. Maybe it was here all along."

"Aliens?" said Petrov, but he wasn't scoffing now. Humanity had always half-hoped and half-feared to discover other intelligent life out among the stars. Up to now it had been half-disappointed and half-relieved to find none.

"Maybe," she conceded, "but then, wouldn't *we* be the aliens?"

"No, that's not possible," said Petrov. "No signs of intelligent life having been here before us has ever been found."

"But the whole planet hasn't been fully mapped," pointed out Zagadko. "We have no idea what lies beneath the Soup. Sonar just bounces off it."

Katya remembered how close to a Soup lake they'd detected the "ore" deposit. In her mind's eye, she could see that great bulk now crawling from the lake, slowly, painfully, until it had collapsed exhausted in the middle of the Weft. Then along they'd come and...

"It was defending itself!" she said suddenly. "Of course, I've been so stupid." She looked at the officers. "We shot a probe at it. How was it to know we weren't attacking? It cloaked itself somehow and fell off our sensors, killed the probe and retaliated." The realisation only served to depress her. Uncle Lukyan was dead because of a misunderstanding.

"That may be so," said the captain slowly as he weighed up the implications, "but it doesn't account for its attack on the *Novgorod*. We didn't attack it. We didn't even see it."

"Besides," said Tokarov, studying the *Baby*'s frantic last seconds on the computer log, "its tactics are completely different. Look at this. There are four or five small contacts out there and the hull damage report issued to the distress buoy's memory in the last moment before it was launched show multiple breaches. Hmmm, still no explosions on the hydrophones. Against us, there was one contact and damage control reports one, possibly two holes in the salvage maw and that's it, the limit of the attack on us. It doesn't make sense."

"It makes perfect sense."

Zagadko whirled in irritation towards Kane, who had spoken. "If you're going to join the conversation then kindly do so, Mr Kane. I, for one, find your habit of hanging around at the edges deeply annoying."

"Very well." Kane got up from the seat he'd taken without permission and stepped closer to them. "I said it makes perfect sense." When he was sure he had their attention, he continued. "The *Baby* was destroyed quickly because it was perceived to be a threat. This vessel, entity, whatever you want to call it, Leviathan is as good a name as any, thought it was being attacked and defended itself. Now, it punches a couple of holes in a much larger boat and then runs away. Why? Any ideas?"

"It didn't intend to sink us," said Tokarov.

"You're quick. That's right. Why didn't it want to sink the *Novgorod*?"

Katya thought Kane sounded like a maniac teacher. Who knew why the Leviathan – the more she used the name, the more fitting it seemed – had only damaged them? They'd just limp off to dry dock, get fixed up and come straight back out, looking for a fight. What could it possibly gain? Then Katya thought through that sequence again and suddenly knew.

"It wanted to see where we'd run. It wanted to know where the *Novgorod* called home."

"Lemuria." Zagadko was grim. "It wanted us to lead it right to Lemuria so it could… Gods' teeth, if it hadn't hurt us more than it had intended, we'd have led it right there. What would it have done?"

"I think we can make a pretty good guess," said Kane. "That thing against an almost undefended base... They wouldn't have stood a chance."

"But that means," said Petrov, "it's out there, right now, tracking us."

FIVE

ENVIRONMENTAL CONTROL

Katya had known it intuitively, even if consciously she had elected not to think about it. Of course the Leviathan was probably after them; it would hardly have attacked and then just swum off, giving them grace to lick their wounds. Of course it wanted to know where they would run. The only "of course" she could not supply was what it would do when it realised that they had made a bolt hole of an abandoned mining base. She doubted it would just give them up as a bad job and go off to harass somebody else.

She'd watched the *Baby*'s distress log four times before the captain had decided that she was past the point of analytical interest and well into obsession. "There was nothing you could have done," he'd told her, not without kindness. Of course there wasn't. Of course he was right.

Of course.

It was difficult to take one's gaze away from the main screen, which still continued to show the *Novgorod*'s course and maximum range. The centre of the map was still the submarine herself; the map updated thirty times a second and she got closer and closer to the abandoned

mine with every minute. The red circle grew smaller each
minute too, but the mine stayed within its circumference.
Just, only just.

The lack of a safety margin obviously vexed Captain
Zagadko so much that he was even prepared to listen
to Kane.

"Have you ever flown a fixed-wing aircraft, captain?"
asked Kane.

"I've flown CG craft, but what's your point?" Katya
noticed Petrov give Kane a very suspicious look as
Zagadko answered.

"The point is, you're going to have to treat this boat like
an aircraft on the final approach. A fixed-wing aircraft
doesn't handle anything like a CG, believe me. You've got
a source of thrust – propellers, jets, whatever – and that's
it. The aircraft develops lift through its aerodynamic lifting
surfaces. You can't slow down to think things through,
you fly on gut reaction and experience."

"Sounds dangerous."

"It is. That's why everybody uses contra-gravity; it's
much more forgiving. Usually, a sub handles like a CG aircraft but, with this steady sinking, we're behaving more
like a fixed-wing aircraft at the moment. She's constantly
fighting going down and crashing."

"I ask again, what's your point?"

"We've got a good head of speed up at the moment. That
can make us climb if we use the hydroplanes like the wings
of an aircraft."

"And that's it?" said Petrov dismissively. "You think we
don't already know that?"

"Oh yes, you know it intellectually. But you don't know
it in here." Kane tapped his chest over his heart. "You're

going to try to translate too late and we won't climb far enough or too early and we'll stall."

"Stall?" said Zagadko.

"If you burn off too much speed, you'll sink like a brick and it'll be 'next stop, crush depth'."

"Let me understand you. Are you asking to be at the helm when we make our approach on the mine?"

Kane smiled. "I've done something similar in the past. I can do this. Trust me."

Zagadko didn't hesitate. "You'll have the helm at a thousand metres off the mine."

Petrov's jaw drooped with incredulity for a moment. "What? Sir?"

Zagadko looked at him steadily. "I hope you're not intending to debate your captain's command, lieutenant?"

He clearly wanted to do just that, but discipline overrode it. "No, sir. Of course not."

"Good." Then to Kane, "The helm position uses a perfectly standard yoke. You might want to run a couple of simulations before the real thing to get the feel of the vessel."

Kane, who'd apparently been expecting some argument at least, was almost as taken aback by Zagadko's agreement as Petrov. "Yes. Yes, that would be helpful. Thank you very much, captain."

Only Katya saw the captain's expression when Kane turned away to set up a simulation and she didn't like it at all.

Kane, on the other hand, was too focussed on the work at hand to pay much attention to anything else. It was the work of only a couple of minutes to set up a simulation of the *Novgorod* approaching the mine from a range of a thousand metres, engines at full power and the nose pulling down harder than the rest of the sub could lift back. The one unknown was the exact proportions of the mine's moon pool. "We don't have time to model it anyway," Kane told Tokarov who'd assisted in setting up. "I'll concentrate on hitting the outer entrance and then make up the rest as we go along. Going from full speed to a dead stop in perhaps a couple of hundred metres is going to be quite a party trick in itself."

"What if the entry tunnel is shorter than a couple of hundred metres?"

"Then we'll be making a dead stop no matter what I do. Ready?"

Tokarov checked a display and nodded. Kane pulled on a headset, braced himself in his seat and nodded. "Let's go, then."

Katya stood behind him as the screen flared into light and movement. *Novgorod* was running fast and noisy; there was no possibility that the Leviathan could not detect them. Indeed, it was probably right behind them at that very moment. With stealth no longer a concern, the captain had given Kane leave to use active sonar on the approach. A little more noise would hardly make a difference. He'd set up a tight cone of rapid pulses to give high resolution to the imaging sonar. In the same way a terrestrial bat would build up a picture of its surroundings in pitch darkness by using sound pulses, the *Novgorod*'s computers would be using the sonar returns to make a model of the mountain and the tunnel entrance.

On Kane's display, the rocky finger of the underwater mountain thrust up from the seabed six kilometres below. Four hundred and fifty metres below the sea surface, high on the mountain, the tunnel entrance stood out in pulsing red. The *Novgorod*'s current depth was one and half thousand. Kane immediately paused the simulation. "I know we're at flank speed, but is that *flank* flank, or is there a little bit held back for special occasions?"

Tokarov shook his head. Kane nodded. "Okay. This is going to be difficult." He toggled the speed display from kilometres per hour over to knots and started the simulation again.

The mountainside flew towards them at shocking speed; Kane was like her uncle in preferring to work in knots but Katya was a kph woman herself. She did the calculation in her head quickly and grimaced. The *Novgorod* was doing one hundred and ten kph. They would cover the thousand metres in a little less than thirty-three seconds. Kane immediately started pulling back on the yoke, making the hydroplanes dig and the boat climb. They would have to climb over a thousand metres in a thousand metres of forward travel. Katya didn't need to delve into sines and cosines to know that was at least a forty-five degree climb. She looked around her, looking for a bulkhead she could sit against when the deck tilted up like that.

The simulated *Novgorod* climbed quickly and smoothly, but its velocity was withering away with every metre, faster than she would have believed possible. As her speed dropped, the intercept time drifted upwards from thirty-three seconds. At forty-six seconds, the *Novgorod* stalled, her forward speed no longer enough to make the hydroplanes bite. The nose went down and she ploughed into the mountainside fifty metres below the entrance.

"Only a first attempt," said Kane, a little unsteadily. "I'll do better next time."

"You don't have a next time," said Zagadko stepping up

beside him and looking at the display with disgust as the virtual *Novgorod* scraped down the virtual mountainside with her virtual nose crumpled and her virtual crew dying. "In one minute, you have the helm." He went to his command chair, swivelled it forward and clamped it. As he strapped himself in, he ordered a collision warning.

"All hands secure! Brace for impact!" squawked the usually placid computer voice throughout the boat.

Tokarov found a vacant seat for Katya and put her there when he saw her making to sit on the floor. "We're likely to hit something pretty fast and pretty hard," he warned her. "If you're not strapped in, you'll smash your brains out on the far bulkhead." She didn't need a second warning, strapping herself in quickly and efficiently just as Sergei had shown her. She hoped she wouldn't need Kane to get her out again in as much of a hurry as last time.

"Twelve hundred metres. You might as well have the helm now, Mr Kane. Good luck," said Zagadko, his voice carefully toneless as if he was handing down a death sentence.

The "active" light on Kane's console turned to green. The sonar image on his screen was now the real thing and Katya imagined how very useful it would be if the "pause" control still worked, freezing the boat in the water while they worked out something cleverer than simply flinging themselves at the side of a mountain.

Kane pulled back on the yoke, but nowhere near as violently as he had in the simulation. The deck started to tilt back as the *Novgorod* began to climb towards the surface. He didn't want to kill their speed so badly this time, but now he ran the risk of not climbing far enough in the short distance they had. The hull thrummed with the water rushing rapidly over the hydroplanes, angling back further and further.

"Eight hundred metres," read off the navigator. "Depth thirteen-fifty."

It's not going to work, thought Katya, not with numbers like those. We're not going to do it.

Zagadko clearly thought the same. "Weapons," he ordered, his voice tight, "dump all the torpedoes. Don't bother arming anything; just get them out of the tubes."

"Aye-aye, sir," replied the weapons officer. A warship has to be in a tight position before it will willingly disarm itself, but nobody could argue that things weren't desperate. Even the lightest of the weapons weighed several hundred kilos and that might make the difference.

The hiss of torpedo launches sounded again and again as the autoloaders shoved every weapon from the magazines into the tubes. Katya winced at the thought of all that live armament drifting down into the depths. Kane was already pulling the yoke back much harder. The *Novgorod* was climbing rapidly, but she was losing speed just as quickly.

"Four hundred. Depth six hundred."

Katya stared. How was that possible? Then she saw the attitude indicator had drifted far past forty-five degrees. They were on course to hit the docking tunnel but at this angle they would blow into its ceiling and the journey would end abruptly and fatally.

Suddenly, Kane shoved the yoke forward. What was he doing? In her mind's eye, Katya saw the *Novgorod* start to tip nose down while her depth... what? Of course, a boat as big as this would carry vast amounts of inertia – she couldn't hope to manoeuvre as tightly as a little sub like the *Baby*. The boat would get an even keel even as she continued to climb for a brief second or two. And in that time…

"Zero! Depth four-fifty!" The navigator was almost shouting. On the main screen the mine entrance swept towards them and then out towards the edge of the display as it engulfed them. "We're in!"

But they weren't out of trouble. The very inertia that Kane had used to perform a vertical skid still existed in their headlong rush. "Full astern!" snapped Zagadko. "Forward cameras! Overlay on the sonar image!"

The main screen flickered and they were seeing through the *Novgorod*'s eyes as it hurtled through the tunnel. The walls shot past them as if they were falling down a well. Suddenly, they broadened and they were out in the internal lake of the mine's moon pool. The far wall rose up ahead of them.

It would be an unfair irony, thought Katya, if they'd saved themselves from being smashed on the outside of a mountain only to be smashed on the inside of one. She'd hardly noticed that she'd dug her heels in against the floor plating as if she could bring the submarine to a halt by sheer force of will.

"Beaching ramp to port!" called Kane and wrenched the controls over. Many such pools had beaching ramps where boats could be pulled out of the water for routine mainte- nance. Usually, the boat rode up on a custom-built wheeled cradle, all prim and pampered.

The *Novgorod* hit the ramp with her bare belly and ran up, screaming every centimetre of the way. A four hundred metre long vessel can build up quite a bow wave, espe- cially with her hydroplanes in the vertical position to act as water brakes. The wave was three metres high when it hit the quayside and broke, running tonnes of water across ground where nobody had stood for five years. It hit the front of the empty traffic control offices and stove in the thick glass sheeting. Katya watched all this on the boat's cameras. She wondered if somebody was going to have to pay for all this damage.

"Engines, all stop!" commanded Captain Zagadko. "And kill that damn sonar!" With the sonar grids out of the water, they were just making a fierce wittering tone that echoed around the pool's cavern. On the quay, the backwash of water from the bow wave gushed back into the moon pool.

The engines died. The sonar died.

The silence was beautiful.

"Damage report," demanded Zagadko as he unstrapped himself, standing up and testing the skewed angle of the deck with his feet.

It wasn't as bad as it could have been. Structurally, the boat was intact. There were any number of minor pieces of damage, but they were largely unimportant to the operation of the vessel or easily fixed. The greatest problem was the actual physical situation. The *Novgorod*'s first quarter was out of the water and there was no possible way of getting her back into the pool without heavy equipment. "She'll swim," the damage control officer concluded, "but she'll need help to do it."

Tokarov was at the environmental controls. "Captain, I've taken a sample of the air in the mining base."

"Is it breathable?"

"It's not just breathable, it's at maintained levels. They must have left the environmental systems running when it was abandoned. Perhaps they thought somebody would be going back to finish stripping the place and it never happened."

Zagadko nodded; there was an excellent chance that was exactly what happened. A typical failure in communications between two work crews hired through different contractors and both under the impression that the other would be the last ones out. With no personnel left there to put a strain on life-support, it could tick over quite happily on its fusion cells for ten or twenty years.

"That's something, at least. We're going to have to get a message out somehow. Put together a party, Lieutenant Tokarov, and see if there's any communications gear still in place. Even the bare terminals of a transmitter array will do – we can provide the rest." Tokarov saluted smartly and moved off to put together a landing party.

Zagadko pursed his lips and grimaced. "Which leaves me with one last unpleasant duty." In a single smooth action, he drew his sidearm and clapped the barrel against the back of Kane's skull as he sat at the controls. "Hands clear of the yoke, Mr Kane. I have no desire to kill you so please don't make it a necessity."

Kane slowly raised his hands. He didn't look at all surprised. Katya, on the other hand, was outraged. "What are you doing, captain? He just saved all our lives!"

Zagadko shot her a sideways glance. "I don't deny it, Ms Kuriakova. But the fact remains that I have reasonable grounds to believe Mr Kane here is an agent of a foreign power. I'd be failing in my duty if I didn't take him into custody. Which reminds me – Mr Kane, by the authority vested in me by the Federal Maritime Authority and by the Russalkin legislature, you're under arrest."

"So I gather," replied Kane. He seemed faintly amused by it all. Katya couldn't see anything funny about having a maser pistol tight against the back of your skull. "May I ask under what charge?"

"Suspicion of insurgent activity, acting against the interests of Russalka, farting in a confined space... does it really matter, Kane? There's something wrong about you and I intend to find out what it is. Specifically, I intend to hand you over to Secor and they can find out."

"But–" started Katya.

"I'm fully aware of the service that Mr Kane has afforded this vessel, Ms Kuriakova," Zagadko interrupted her. She saw he was becoming angry, and shut up. "And I'm not unappreciative. I shall make that clear in my report. The fact remains that he's said enough things that make me think he's a Terran. That's enough reason for me to arrest him and more than enough for you to accept it."

"Don't argue with the captain, Katya," said Kane softly. "I'd do exactly the same in his place."

Katya fumed. Why did they insist on talking down to her like this? "How can you be so calm? Do you know what Secor will do to you?"

Secor was the popular name for the FMA Security Organisation and was the only popular thing about it. Nobody liked to think about what went on in Secor establishments or what its agents did with the carte blanche they'd been given by a desperate government during the war. Now, ten years later, the government seemed too terrified to withdraw those powers.

Kane smiled. "Sensory deprivation, psychotomimetic drugs, RNA stripping, the usual. They're quite old fashioned in their ways, bless them."

Zagadko had Kane taken to the brig by a couple of marines. He seemed embarrassed to have Kane present on the bridge for any longer than was necessary, Kane's calm acceptance of his arrest unnerving him somewhat.

For her part Katya watched him go with very mixed emotions. He was a ruthless pirate, a murderer who had saved her life. He was probably a Terran, a Grubber, one of the filth who had killed her father and thousands more, yet he had also saved the *Novgorod* and everybody aboard her. Katya didn't know what to think. She couldn't bring herself to hate him, but she certainly couldn't like him either. That only left her the option of indifference, and Kane was a hard man to be indifferent about. She settled on something like grudging respect, but that just made what Secor were going to do to him feel all the worse.

Tokarov arrived back to report he'd put together his party. "Shall I have weapons issued, sir?"

The captain looked at him as if he was mad for a second, but then his brow clouded and he nodded. "Yes. Yes, that would be wise. I don't like the way Kane knew so much about this place and the way the life-support has so conveniently been left running. We may not be alone here."

Katya watched the party troop up the deck, restlessness growing in her. She didn't care to be trapped in the *Novgorod* with the likes of Captain Zagadko. She'd known Kane was a criminal, but Secor? They'd tear his mind to pieces looking for Grubber conspiracies, and leave him a hollowed-out wreck. She'd heard too many ugly stories of what Secor agents did to amuse themselves, from friends and from Sergei in his darker moments. If even half of what they said was true... Why couldn't Zagadko just have said he'd hand Kane over to the normal law enforcement agencies?

"Captain," she began.

"Request denied," replied Zagadko blandly without even looking away from the damage report he'd just been handed.

"You don't even know what–"

"You were going to ask permission to go ashore." He finally favoured her with a look. "Weren't you?"

She had been, but she just glared at him as her answer.

"Well," he continued without giving her any more time to speak, "that's impossible. I'm not convinced that this mining site is nearly as abandoned as Mr Kane tried to suggest."

"What?" said Katya, anger making her incautious and impolite. "You think the Terran army is hiding here?"

The captain ignored the venom in her voice. "Criminals tend to associate with criminals, greater and lesser. I think our Mr Kane is the former, and that he will associate with the latter. Pirates, perhaps? People who have little to lose by working for somebody like him."

"You're making a lot of guesses, captain."

The captain's face hardened. "With all due respect, Ms Kuriakova, you know nothing." The grimness of his voice indicated that she was due precious little respect, from him at least. "The war was only ten years ago, not even a generation, and you know nothing of it."

"My father–"

"Died in it? Lots of fathers died in it. And mothers. And sons. And daughters. You dishonour their memory. The first strikes were against our air arm. Remember that much?"

"The Andrev Platform was destroyed. Of course I–"

"And what kind of aircraft were destroyed there? Eh?"

Katya couldn't answer; she had no idea. Her mouth opened and closed a few times until the captain lost patience.

"Contragravitic craft, girl! CG craft just like the ones in the forward compartment! They were all we had; ideal for lifting from a submersible platform. How then," he leaned close and she could suddenly feel the weight of that war on his shoulders, all that loss and agony expressing itself in the cold fury of his glance, "did Kane have experience flying fixed-wing aircraft? Those are Terran!" He spat the word out like diseased phlegm.

He drew himself up and took a long calming breath. "No Russalkin could have saved our lives in the way that he did," he finished quietly.

SIX

DECK SWEEPER

Katya sat at a table in the otherwise deserted junior officers' ward room and wondered how so much could go so wrong in so little time. The memories kept running around her head in a jumbled mess: clinging to the distress buoy; that idiot Fed Suhkalev; getting dressed that morning, putting her navigator's card so carefully in her pocket; the ghost return from the "ore mountain"; torpedoes in the water. Most of all, she remembered her Uncle Lukyan. He'd survived the war only to die on some stupid milk run. It wasn't right and it wasn't fair. It was not fair.

"Theoretically I'm not allowed in here without an invitation." She looked up. Lieutenant Petrov was standing in the doorway, his hands on the top frame, looking speculatively around. "I'm the first officer," he continued, "so I'm not really a junior officer anymore. Tradition says I don't go any further without being asked."

Katya looked at him for a long second. She wasn't sure she liked him; she still remembered the look on his face when Kane had made the slip about aircraft that had condemned him. If the captain hadn't picked it up, she was sure Petrov would have informed him of his suspicions. But, like so much else, it was duty. Duty and tradition. Traditions from old Earth, strangely enough – the world they cursed in one breath and held in grudging respect the next. "Come in," she said.

Petrov looked too tall to be a submariner, she thought as he folded himself through the door and slid with practised ease but little grace into the seat opposite her. With his close-cropped hair and his cold grey eyes, he was almost a parody of the stereotypical Secor officer. A Russalka spider-crab made human.

He sat in silence, regarding her for a moment. Then he opened his breast pocket and reached inside. "I have something for you." He slid her navigator's card out and put it down on the table in front of her. As she took it, he added, "It was in your clothes. I thought you'd like it back."

Katya was looking at her picture on the card. There she was looking so seriously back out at herself and Katya thought *that was taken eighteen days ago. Why do I look like such a child?* "Thank you." She put the card away. "You searched my clothes?"

"Of course," said Petrov, unsurprised and unembarrassed by the question. "You came aboard with a criminal. I wanted to make sure your story, at least, was true."

She felt oddly complimented. Petrov hadn't thought *she's just a girl;* he'd thought she might be a desperate criminal. He was the first person the whole day who had treated her like an adult. No, that wasn't quite true. "Have you heard anything from Lieutenant Tokarov yet?"

"No. Not yet. These tunnels will play havoc with communications though, so that doesn't necessarily signify anything untoward."

"But you're worried?"

He raised an eyebrow. "What gives you that idea?"

Katya shrugged. "I don't know. Perhaps the way you're so keen to explain away the fact he hasn't reported in yet."

Petrov looked at her blankly. Then he smiled. It didn't light up his face and seemed as if it rarely had many opportunities to show itself, but it was a smile nonetheless. "Your prodigious talents extend further than just navigation, I see. A student of human nature too."

"Prodigious?"

"I read your card, remember. Your scores are excellent. With more experience you could walk onto any boat in the ocean and they'd be pleased to have you. I haven't seen such impressive scores since, well, my own. I was something of a wunderkind too, you see." The smile flickered briefly again.

Katya's gaze seemed distant, and Petrov wondered what she was seeing. Then she looked him in the eye and said, "My uncle's dead."

She said it flatly, as if the words and their meaning had become disconnected in her mind.

Petrov's smile instantly went. "Yes. I'm sorry."

"What I don't understand is, why don't I care?" She shook her head. "I loved him. He was there for us right after papa died, has always been there. Why can't I cry for him?"

"Perhaps," said Petrov, "because he's always been there. You know he's gone but, part of you, a very great part of you does not believe it. You expect him to walk through the door at any minute."

She looked at the door, an open door on a boat Uncle Lukyan had never set foot aboard in his entire life. Yet somehow, she could see him in her mind's eye, stepping around the frame, looking up and seeing her, that slightly prepossessed air that he usually carried turning to the great smile he'd reserved for her ever since she'd been born. She willed him to be there, for the whole thing to have been a dreadful mistake or a stupid joke. No Leviathan, no attack, no drowned corpse strapped into the wreck of the *Baby*. She couldn't do it. She knew she could never do it. Finally she started to cry.

Petrov stood, unfolding himself easily out from the confinement of the table and chair and left her silently to her grief.

Some time later the speaker in the wardroom's bulkhead burst into life. "Battle stations!" barked the captain's voice, tense with anger. "All crew to battle stations! Prepare to repulse boarders!"

Katya's head jerked up. She'd been drifting in a shallow sleep, exhaustion finally catching up with her. For a moment she had no idea where she was or how she'd come to be there. Then it all came back in a sickening flood. She might have sat there in indefinite despair if the captain's words hadn't finally sunk in. Her eyes widened.

Repel boarders?

The gangways were in frenzy when she stuck her head out of the door. Ratings and officers were hurrying back and forth, and she realised with a shock that they were all carrying weapons. Not just the sidearms that the senior officers wore but longarms – maser rifles, close-assault guns, even a flamer pack.

She followed the flow of personnel to the bridge and found it almost empty. The top hatch was open and she could hear shouting going on outside, the voices echoing around the great cavern of the moon pool. Then the shooting started.

She had no idea how far away the firing was between the echoes and the sound coming down the hatch but it didn't sound that close. There was the sporadic *krak!* of ballistic small arms and a couple of bursts of full automatic fire that sounded louder. It quickly became obvious it was coming closer.

"What's happening?" she called up the hatch.

A face appeared above her, a female sublieutenant she didn't recognise. "Stay there!" she was ordered. "Stay off the deck!" Then the face was gone.

More firing. She could hear the captain up top giving terse commands. *Fine*, she thought, *I don't have to be up there to find out what's happening.* She walked to the station where she'd seen Petrov operate the lights and exterior cameras and examined the controls briefly. Her cybernetics teacher had always said that the more sophisticated a system was and the better designed it was, the simpler it seemed to be. "All the functionality, none of the knobs and dials," recited Katya under her breath. Whoever had designed this console had known their trade well. In a few seconds she was using the *Novgorod*'s cameras as easily as she once operated the *Baby*'s.

Captain Zagadko had deployed his marines and armed crew behind any available cover facing into the tunnels; crates, raised hatches, even the boat's exposed hull all sheltered waiting crew as the shooting in the tunnels got closer. There was little time for tension to build further before Lieutenant Tokarov and his team came into sight, the ones at the front pausing to provide covering fire for those at the rear as they moved to the front and returned the favour, the tactical leapfrogging that Katya had only ever seen in screen dramas about the war or crime thrillers. As soon as the angle of the tunnel gave them enough cover from their pursuers, they just ran for the *Novgorod*.

They'd barely made it when their foes surged out after them. Katya thought there must have been about fifteen or twenty of them, mainly men but she spotted a couple of women. There was no pattern or consistency in their clothing or armament; they looked like a mass escape from an FMA holding facility that had bolted through a weapons museum.

So this was what real pirates looked like.

Unlike the ordered retreat of Tokarov's team, they ran headlong into the cavern and stopped in a shocked rabble when they saw the mass of the FMA boat beached there. She snorted derisively – how did that bunch of morons think the Feds had got into the mining complex in the first place? That they'd swum there? All of a sudden, the smart and wily pirates of fiction looked like a grand exaggeration of the truth.

"This is Captain Alexander Zagadko of the FMA boat, the *Novgorod*!" roared the captain's voice from above. It was perfectly audible through the open hatch and Katya quickly wound down the volume on the hull sensor relays before the speakers blew. "By the authority vested in me by the Federal Maritime Authority and by the Russalkin legislature, you're all under arrest! Drop your weapons immediately! Surrender or die!"

The pirates, to their credit, had a third alternative. As one, they ran back down the tunnel before the captain could give the order to fire.

Zagadko swore a pithy but venomous oath of the kind that comes easily to sailors. "Tokarov! Report!"

"We just ran into them in the corridors, sir. They looked more surprised to see us than we were to see them. We'd already found signs this place was occupied."

"Any idea where their boat is?"

"We saw signage about another dock on the other side of the mountain. They must be moored there."

"Kane's people," growled Zagadko. "No wonder he knew so much about it. Well, perhaps he's done us a favour. Do you think you could reach this other dock quickly, lieutenant?"

Tokarov considered the question quickly. "Yes, sir. If that's where they're headed, we'll be on their heels the whole way."

"Take the marines. I want their boat. It's our way out of here. What are you waiting for? Jump to it, man!"

Tokarov was off and running to the captain of the marines in a moment.

Katya didn't like it. The crew were trained in combat, but wouldn't have the sharp edge of the marines. She could see the captain's reasoning, but she really didn't like the thought of the boat's defences being cut like this. It made her feel vulnerable and she'd heard too many ugly stories about what pirates did with prisoners to want to take risks.

There was something else she didn't like either. Something about the pirates she'd seen on the cameras. She sat down and watched the screens as Tokarov and the marines headed off into the tunnels in pursuit and tried to put her finger on what was bothering her. There was an imbalance somewhere, an inequality. On the one hand there were those pirate clowns and on the other, there were... There was...

"Kane!" she said, her eyes widening in horror. "Oh no! Oh no, no, no, no!"

She skittered up the ladder, her feet on the rungs clattering like gunfire. Once on deck, she ran to where Zagadko was giving orders to the same sublieutenant who'd ordered her to stay below.

"Captain!" blurted Katya. "Please, I've got an awful feeling– "

"Not now, Ms Kuriakova," said Zagadko. "I'm busy." He continued telling the officer his orders to set up defensive positions along the dock.

"It can't wait!" Katya was in a fury of indecision. Was it really worth antagonising the captain over? It was just a gut feeling she had really. Was it enough?

"Didn't I order you to stay below?" said the sublieutenant.

"Yes, but this is important!" Every second Tokarov and the marines were getting further from the moon pool. Every second the danger was increasing. If she was right.

Zagadko sighed. "Carry on," he told the sublieutenant who left to carry out his orders with a backward narrow-eyed glance at Katya. He turned to Katya and looked down at her, crossing his arms. "Very well, Ms Kuriakova. What is so important?"

Now she had his attention, she didn't know where to start. "Those pirates, didn't they bother you?"

"I've encountered worse. What do you know about it, anyway? You were below decks during the attack, such as it was."

"I was watching on the hull cameras." She saw the

captain's eyebrows rise and pushed on before he got into a lecture about illicit use of FMA equipment. "They were a joke. I can't imagine that bunch getting dressed without help. Can you?"

Zagadko laughed. "No, not really. Who'd have thought Kane would…" Then his slightly patronising smile abruptly faded. "Oh, gods," he said hoarsely. Then in a full throated roar, "Petrov! Recall Tokarov! *Now!*"

Petrov whirled to face his captain, saw this wasn't a time to ask for clarification and jerked the radio from his belt. "Tokarov!" he said into the handset. "Pull back to the boat! Captain's orders, most urgent!" For answer he only got the dead tone of a clear digital channel. Petrov shook his head. "I'm sorry, captain. These damn tunnels soak up signals like sponge."

"Take two men. Catch up with them and get them back here immediately. Go!"

Petrov had barely taken three steps before the surface of the moon pool exploded off to the starboard of the *Novgorod*.

"Down!" shouted Zagadko, grabbing Katya fiercely by the arm and almost throwing her at the open hatch. She sprawled on the metal as the wave smashed into the *Novgorod*'s side, making the boat roll ten or fifteen degrees, her hull groaning hideously under the strain. It swept over the deck, blinding Katya for a moment as she covered her head for protection. Zagadko's legs were swept out from beneath him and he fell heavily before being carried back and almost dumped off the port side.

The huge wave hitting the docks caught the *Novgorod*'s crew by total surprise. Katya cleared her face of seawater in time to see the sublieutenant who'd ordered her around previously caught in the backwash as the tonnes of water rolled back into the pool. It looked as if the wave had first smashed her against the wall; Katya couldn't tell if she was dead or only unconscious. Katya jumped to her feet to run to her aid, but the captain's voice stopped her in her tracks.

"No, Ms Kuriakova! Below! Get below!" He was crawling forward, his sidearm maser – a monster of a gun and definitely not FMA standard issue – drawn and aiming out into the moon pool. Katya stole a sideways look and almost froze. Another submarine was in the pool – leaner and smaller than the *Novgorod* but just as deadly. Its hydroplanes were up and Katya realised the massive wave had been deliberate. Hatches were already clanging open on her deck and atop her rakish conning tower, and people – pirates – were streaming out. She watched in horror as a forward hatch opened and a great pintle-mounted weapon rose on a cargo lift, two pirates already manning it. Katya had heard enough war stories from her Uncle Lukyan to know a "deck-sweeper" when she saw it; a great brute of a machine gun engineered so that no two bullets would travel quite the same path. Accuracy wasn't its strength, just massive firepower delivered in broad strokes.

Behind her, she heard the distinctive half *krak*, half *hisssss* of a maser and realised the captain had opened fire. Part of her was watching all this as if it was happening to somebody else. *I don't want to see anyone die,* she thought, the sick feeling of fear beginning to grow in her gut.

One of the pirates at the machine gun stepped back as if they'd just remembered something important and then collapsed. Katya knew he was dead. Then she saw the machine gun come to bear on her and its barrels started to spin with a high electrical whine. She dived headlong down the hatch as the first large-calibre rounds hailed heavily against the *Novgorod*'s hull, stripping off matte-black anechoic tiling and blowing it into the air in a shower of lightless fragments.

She got tangled with the rungs of the gangway ladder and hit the bridge deck heavily, sprawling on her back. Hurt and stunned, she listened to the scream of the machine gun for a few seconds, realising that the captain was very probably dead by now. They'd been fooled, conned by the pirates with their display of comical incompetence into underestimating them. All the while, the pirate vessel had been making its way around the mountain to attack them from behind. And now the captain was probably dead, Tokarov and the marines had probably been ambushed and were dead, Petrov had probably run into the ambushing force and was dead, even that tight-lipped sublieutenant who'd been so off-hand with Katya was probably dead. There was only one thing left to do.

She found the arms locker easily enough. It was still unlocked; after the urgent arming to repel boarders, they'd obviously been in too much of a hurry to secure it. Besides which it was empty, stripped bare.

Almost bare. In one corner there were some small drawers containing spare parts, cleaning kits and manuals. In the lowermost, she found a box that held what she needed.

Havilland Kane was lying on the bunk in the brig when Katya opened the door. He looked at her out of the corner of his eye and then went back to considering the ceiling.

"Noisy outside," he commented. "I gather my Brethren

of the Deep, to coin a phrase, are making life difficult for the good captain?"

"The captain's dead."

"I'm sorry to hear that. Truly I am. My colleagues can be a little heavy-handed at times."

"You planned all this." Katya's hand closed around the little maser pistol concealed in her pocket. Lukyan had never balked at showing her how to maintain, activate and operate weapons. The very fact that she didn't like guns had encouraged him. If she'd been fascinated by them, he'd once told her, he would have taught her about hydroponics gardens instead.

"Planned? No, that's a very strong term for what I've done. I've extemporised. Made it up as I went along. I certainly didn't plan for your uncle's craft to be attacked or this one, for that matter. I just took advantage of opportunities as they've presented themselves. I'm sorry about the violence, though. Without my calming influence, my crew can get... excitable."

His self-control and the knowledge that he'd been stringing them along all the way were almost more than she could bear. "You dirty Grubber," she snarled.

Nothing seemed to bother him. "You know, I've never liked that term. It says more about some vague Russalkin sense of inadequacy than anything bad about Earth. Landgrubbers..." He snorted. "What do most Russalkin know about it? You've never had real ground under your feet, just blasted rock or deck sections. You've never lain on your back in a field and reached up," he raised his arm towards the ceiling, "feeling you can almost touch the clouds. Fluffy white clouds against a cobalt blue sky this is, not those filthy dark clouds that Russalka gets all the time. You think I want to be on your foul little planet? If I could leave, I would have left ten years ago."

"Get up."

"No." He lowered his hand, but still didn't look at her. "I'm quite happy here, thank you."

"Get up!"

"Or what?" He sounded bored or perhaps just tired. "You'll shoot me?" He finally turned his head to look at her. She had the gun drawn and levelled at him. His eyebrows raised. "Oh. Perhaps that was an ill-considered thing to say."

She stood with feet apart and both hands gripping the pistol. "I'm not joking. Get up or I *will* shoot you."

He turned away from her to look at the ceiling again. "You won't shoot. You're too well-mannered to shoot anybody, never mind an unarmed man."

The pistol made a surprisingly loud *krak!-hisss!* in the small room. Katya did a better job of hiding her startled reaction to the sound than Kane. Then again, a maser bolt hadn't just gone past the tip of Katya's nose to fry and bubble the paint on the wall by her head.

"You don't know anything about me," said Katya, "and I'm not that well-mannered."

Kane swung his feet onto the floor and looked at her, trying not to appear worried. "Okay, so I'm up. Now what?"

The shooting had died down by the time Kane emerged on deck, Katya standing close behind him with the barrel of the maser pushed hard into the small of his back. Kane's boat sat at an angle across the moon pool, her guns trained on the surviving members of the *Novgorod*'s crew lining up on the dock side with their hands behind their heads. There were some unmoving bodies on the stone floor and a couple floating face down in the pool itself. Katya found she accepted this without a qualm, and the ease of that acceptance nauseated her far more than the sight of death itself.

Armed pirates were moving onto their boat's deck to back up the remaining machine-gunner, sweeping their muzzles to cover the area. They were looking in every direction except hers and, for a crazy moment, Katya considered sneaking back below. Then one looked over at the *Novgorod*. Instantly, she had six or seven long arms trained on her. More specifically, they were trained on Kane, behind whom she was hiding. For a less crazy and more fearful moment, she wondered if they'd recognise him from sixty metres away and, even if they did, who was to say his captaincy hadn't been usurped in his absence? Perhaps even the pirates wanted him dead.

But they didn't fire, neither before or after one of them cried out, "It's the captain!"

"Are you all right, captain?" shouted another.

"Fine, thank you," called Kane, as casually as if they were meeting in a corridor. "Well, apart from the maser being stuck in my back by this young lady."

The pirates' weapons, which had been lowered when they recognised him, snapped back into aiming positions.

"I think I can get her," Katya heard one say, the sound floating across the water with great clarity.

"You are to do no such thing," said Kane, in a cold, hard voice that carried at least as much threat and authority as Zagadko's roar. "I don't want any more shooting. The time for violence has passed."

"But you agree that violence was necessary?" said a new voice.

A figure stepped aside from the rest of the pirates, a woman somewhere in her late twenties or early thirties, with short black hair that barely reached her collar and an angular face that hinted at determination. She was wearing the distinctive body-armour of an FMA marine from the war, but without the helmet. The black ceramic armour panels had been recoloured, however, in dark reds and oranges to create a striped effect that Katya knew were called "tiger stripes" after some animal the Grubbers had driven into extinction.

"Hello, Tasya," called Kane. He waved at the churned surface of the *Novgorod*'s hull. "Was the deck-sweeper really necessary?"

"Yes," she replied brusquely. "We've lost Ovinko doing this. I think it was necessary."

"Well, you were the one on the spot. I'll leave it to your discretion. I'm back now, though, and I don't want the girl shot if it can be avoided."

"Who is she?"

"A waif and a stray. Katya Kuriakova. She's the surviving crew of the boat the Feds commandeered to take me to the Deeps. She's not FMA. It's just lousy luck that has brought her here."

"Hey!" hissed Katya, jamming the gun more firmly into his back. "Stop it! I've got the gun here. You don't talk unless I say so."

"What was the name?" called the woman Kane had called Tasya. "Did you say Kuriakova?"

Kane raised his hands. "Sorry. She's armed and a bit nervous. I should shut up."

There was activity aboard the pirate vessel. Some crew members disappeared below. "What are they doing?" Katya demanded of Kane.

"I don't know. How should I know?"

Her curiosity only had to wait a couple of minutes to be sated. The pirates returned and this time they had company, a huge and distinctive figure.

"Uncle Lukyan!" cried Katya as he was forced to his knees on the pirate vessel's deck. A moment later, the equally bedraggled figure of Suhkalev joined him.

Kane laughed out loud. "You were shadowing us the whole time?"

Katya hardly heard him. She stared at Lukyan, a miracle in the flesh. Part of her wanted everyone to just vanish so she could hug her uncle so hard that he would never, ever die, that she would never have to feel grief and loss like that again. This part of her would have flung the gun down right away, filled as she was with a joyous, childish belief that everyone would smile at her happiness and would not stand in her way.

But the greater part of her could still smell the blood and the tang of air ionised by maser bolts. She could feel the deck beneath her feet, the gun in her hand, and Kane's spine beneath the muzzle as she dug it into his back. She'd been taught from when she was old enough to reach an airlock control that curiosity could kill, that panic could kill, that impatience could kill. For the first time, she realised that even joy can kill you on Russalka.

With an effort, she forced herself to be cold and rational, to think through what had happened and what was likely to happen.

Step by step, she worked it out. Kane's boat had been in the sonar dead zone behind them – their baffles – as soon as they'd left the locks. It had tracked them with the intention of scooping up the *Baby* in its great salvage maw when they were halfway through the trip and boats responding to a distress signal would have taken too long to reach their location to do any good.

"We lost you in the Weft. Then we heard all sorts of noise on the hydrophones. We got there to find that little sub going down and we grabbed it." Tasya crossed her arms. "Typically, you'd already left. Never where you're meant to be, are you, captain?"

"I got bored of waiting for you," replied Kane nonchalantly.

Tasya stood over the kneeling prisoners and drew her gun. "Drop your weapon and surrender, girl, or your uncle dies."

"I'd do it," said Kane quietly to Katya. "She's more than capable of squeezing that trigger."

Katya looked at all the forces ranged against her and suddenly the maser in her hand seemed a pathetic sort of thing to have put her hopes in. If she surrendered, what then? The pirates didn't need her, didn't need Lukyan. They knew that the pirates used the old mining site as a hideout, too. Surely they'd be murdered? But if she didn't surrender, what could she hope to accomplish? She didn't stand a chance of hitting anything on the pirate boat at this range, all she could do was shoot Kane and then they'd shoot her anyway.

"You know who Tasya is, don't you?" murmured Kane, interrupting her train of thought. "She's the Chertovka. You know that name, surely?"

The Chertovka. The She-Devil.

"She's a war criminal," said Katya, an awful sense of dread welling in her. A war criminal, and worse. "You sail with a... a... a monster like her?"

"She's no angel," admitted Kane, "but you should be a lot more suspicious about what the Feds put on criminal records. Don't underestimate her, though. She doesn't do threats, just warnings."

"I'm getting bored," called Tasya. "Maybe you don't think I'll do it." She jammed the gun against the back of Suhkalev's head. "He's expendable. Here's your demonstration, girl." Katya could hear Suhkalev's whimpers turn to panicked hyperventilating, a sob of fear on every outward breath.

She's going to kill him, thought Katya, she really is. She thought of her experiences with the arrogant young Federal officer and how all this was his fault. If he'd just bothered somebody else with his stupid little problems, Lukyan, Sergei and she could have done the round trip and been home celebrating by now. Stupid, stupid Fed.

Just for a second, one tiny fleeting second, she thought, *Go ahead. Kill him* and she was ashamed.

She dropped the gun and stepped away from Kane. "You win. Leave him alone." The Chertovka – Katya couldn't think of her in any other way now – stood over the sobbing man for a moment longer, apparently disappointed. She stepped back and sent Suhkalev sprawling on his face with a kick in his back.

Kane picked up Katya's gun. He looked at her grimly, but made no move to point it at her. "Very wise, Ms Kuriakova. I'm glad that's over. Now, if you've finished waving guns around and otherwise demonstrating what you're not very good at, we can concentrate on the real problem."

"Real problem? I... I don't understand?"

Kane sighed. "Nothing like a bit of a firefight to distract people from the big picture, is there?" He shook his head and walked towards the *Novgorod*'s prow and the dockside, not even making Katya go first or ensuring she was following. She stood for a moment, wondering what he meant. Realisation was cold and fearful.

The Leviathan.

SEVEN

SCUTTLING CODE

Katya was having trouble breathing.

Uncle Lukyan was showing no sign of releasing her from the bear hug he'd flung around her the first chance he had. "I thought you were dead, Katinka," he kept saying, more than a suspicion of a sob in his voice. "I thought you were dead." He rarely used the familiar form of her name, preferring Katya. It took a lot to make him use Katinka.

When he finally let her go, she said, "I thought the same of you, uncle." She could feel the tears running down her cheeks and was aware some of the pirates were watching their reunion and not being subtle about it. She really didn't care. "Yet here you are. Here we are. Here we are." She couldn't speak anymore and hugged him close, her eyes clenched shut.

"I tried to save you, Katinka. But the damned LoxPak wouldn't go on and by the time I had it secure, you'd vanished. I saw that the top hatch had been blown and hoped… prayed for you to have got clear. The next thing I know, that filthy pirate scow had swallowed the *Baby* whole. As soon as they'd drained the salvage maw, they were waving guns in our faces and demanding to know where Kane was. That Federal cur, Suhkalev, he'd have sold them his own grandmother he was so scared."

Katya let Lukyan go, and wiped her eyes on her sleeve. She looked over where Suhkalev sat on the rock floor of the dock, separate from the *Novgorod*'s crew. They'd treated him with contempt ever since the pirates had concentrated all their prisoners into one group under the unnerving gaze of the deck-sweeper guns aboard the pirate boat. The Fed had his knees drawn up, his chin resting on them, a look of abject misery on his face. He knew he'd disgraced himself and his uniform. Katya thought he looked like he wanted to die. She hoped he wouldn't do anything stupid.

"We really didn't know what had happened, though. The acting captain, Tasya something – the one they call the Chertovka – she's a clever one. She put the boat on silent running and we just hung at neutral buoyancy for what seemed like hours while they listened for whatever had attacked us. They heard something in the distance, but couldn't get a decent lock until it hit the surface. She went up on one-third ahead to investigate but there was nothing there. The *Baby*'s distress beacon cut out at the same time and she guessed it had been picked up."

"It had. Kane and I were hanging onto it when the *Novgorod* picked it up," said Katya.

Lukyan nodded. "So they brought us here while they figured out what to do next. Next thing we know the pirates are running around because they thought the mining site was under attack by the Feds." He sighed. "She played the FMA people for fools and they fell for it. What happened to bring you here in such a great hurry, Katya?" Katya noticed he'd dropped the familiar form of her name. He must be calming down.

Slowly, putting in as much detail as she could remember, she told Lukyan about how they'd been attacked again by the same thing that had attacked the *Baby*, the thing Kane called Leviathan. He listened quietly, asking only a few questions to clarify her story and iron out ambiguities.

"Leviathan," he said when she'd finished. "That's an old Earth name for a sea monster. Is...?"

"He's from Earth," she confirmed. "He didn't even try to deny it when I confronted him with it. He seems proud of it."

"He would be. He should be. A man who has no pride for his birthplace is a hollow man. I don't begrudge him that much. Still..." his expression darkened, "...Earth."

It was no secret that there were still Grubbers on Russalka even ten years after they'd lost the war. Stranded away from their units, trapped when the Terran ships ignited their drives and ran back to Earth with their tails between their legs. Abominated and loathed by the Russalkin, it was hardly surprising that most ended up in the world of crime. She'd seen lots in action dramas: pirates, terrorists and insane killers. They'd always seemed so ineffectual, though. Perhaps, she thought, it was time to stop watching everything that came out of the drama studios of the Department of Public Enlightenment quite so uncritically.

"What about the Chertovka?" she asked. "She seems Russalkin."

"She is," growled Lukyan, "to our shame. She was a collaborator during the war. She worked for the Grubbers against her own kind. If the FMA ever capture her, there's nothing waiting for her but a maser bolt through the brain in a quiet corner somewhere."

"And Secor?"

He looked at her suspiciously. "What about Secor?"

"The captain of the *Novgorod*, Captain Zagadko, he was going to hand Kane over to Secor."

Lukyan frowned. "Well, I don't suppose it's any less than he deserves," he muttered, but Katya doubted he really meant it. He looked past her and his frown deepened. "Speak of the devil..."

Kane and Tasya were approaching, with a couple of pirates acting as bodyguards. Tasya looked like she could look after herself pretty well and wouldn't need guards, but Kane seemed tired and ill.

"Captain Pushkin, Ms Kuriakova," said Tasya, nodding politely at each.

"Hello again, Katya," said Kane. His voice sounded strained, the pleasantries forced. "We meet again, Captain Pushkin. I'm very happy you made it."

Lukyan said nothing but glared at them both.

"The *Novgorod*'s captain," said Tasya, "Zagadko. Where is he?"

"We're telling you nothing," spat Lukyan.

"He's dead," said Katya. She caught her uncle's furious glance. "So what if I tell them, uncle? None of us are ever leaving this place."

Tasya laughed, a pleasantly throaty sound. "This sea monster Havilland has been telling me about?" It took Katya a moment to remember that was Kane's first name. "We travelled from the north docks right around the mountain and came into the moon pool at speed, making plenty of noise. We weren't attacked. Whatever it is, it's long gone."

Kane shook his head slowly like an old man. Katya could-n't believe the change that had come over him so quickly. It was as if he was dying before her eyes. "Oh, Tasya, no. Whatever it is, it's outside. It has cunning, you see."

Tasya gave him an exasperated look and, Katya realised, one with some underlying affection. "So why didn't it attack, hmmm? Tell me that."

Kane opened his mouth, but it was Katya who answered. "Now it only has to watch one docking tunnel. It's got both boats trapped in the same moon pool. You won't get out as easily as you got in."

"She's right," said Kane. His voice was so weak that even Tasya, who'd seemed blind to his rapid deterioration, noticed.

"You ought to go aboard," she whispered urgently, moving closer to Kane in an attempt to make the conversation private.

"I will," replied Kane in a croak that wouldn't have seemed out of place coming from a man in his last minutes. "Don't fuss so, Tasya. I'll be fine."

"Captain!" the shout floated across from the pirates who were securing the *Novgorod*.

"Damn," said Kane. "Now what?"

Kane had insisted on coming aboard the *Novgorod* to see what the problem was, overriding Tasya's increasingly forceful demands that he go back to the pirate boat. They'd been gone for a few minutes when the pirate who'd called across came back up on deck and shouted to Katya that Captain Kane wanted her present. With a few calming words to her uncle, she climbed up the gangway that had been placed up against the prow, walked down the tilted deck and climbed back down the hatch into the bridge.

It was very different from the last time she'd seen it. The lights were out, illumination now provided by work lanterns and torches the pirates had brought. A cluster of pirates was grouped around the captain's chair, speaking quietly. They moved aside to allow Kane through.

"Something you should see, Katya." He looked back as if internally debating something. "Though you won't thank me for it." He stepped back and parted a way for her. She took a step forward and stopped, horrified.

Lit obliquely by the harsh white lights of the work lanterns, Captain Zagadko sat in his command chair quite at peace. He seemed so serene, almost happy, with a faint smile on his lips, that the realisation that he was dead was a long time coming. "Oh, captain," said Katya in a tiny whisper. "Oh, Captain Zagadko."

"It looks like he was hit by a round from the machine gun," said Kane. Out of the circle of light, Katya realised that the captain's uniform was glistening slightly, soaked. She took an unconscious step back and was appalled when her boot stuck to the floor for a moment. "Yes," Kane spoke again. "I'm afraid it's blood. The floor's thick with it. At a guess, the femoral artery in his leg was nicked. He bled out quite quickly."

"Why," said Katya, her voice shuddering with revulsion, "are you showing me this?"

For his answer, Kane shone his torch on the dead man's left hand. It lay on a panel of the captain's status board; a security plate over the panel had been unlocked and lifted.

"You recognise a handprint scanner of course. This one's special. Between needing a key to access it, requiring the handprint of a senior officer and then the inputting of a code, it's very secure. Not the sort of thing you can do by accident."

"A code…" Katya knew what the captain had done and realised why all the lights were out.

"The scuttle code. The captain crawled back in here after being blown off the deck with half his leg dangling off by a thread – don't look, it really isn't a pretty sight. He must have come in by one of the rear locks. I can't even imagine swimming while that badly injured. Then he crawled forward, straight past the sickbay where he might, just conceivably, have managed to save his own life by getting into the automedic. Of course, that would have drugged him into a dreamless sleep where we'd have found him. He knew that and that's why he kept crawling. All the way back to the bridge and into his chair, to open that panel and issue the scuttling code, killing his beloved ship rather than let her fall into our hands. Then he sat back and fell asleep." Kane drew strength from somewhere and straightened up. "In a fairer universe, captain, they'd sing songs about you. I salute you." He snapped a salute of a type she'd seen in the same stupid dramas that said the Grubbers had no honour, that showed them spitting on the corpses of their enemies. He held it for a long moment and then finished it, and seemed to age even more as he did so. "Organise the funerals for tomorrow morning, please, Tasya. Ours and theirs. I want a full turn out."

He started walking slowly, almost shambling towards the hatch. "Why did you show me this?" asked Katya again.

"Duty, Katya Kuriakova. He knew his duty, as I know mine." He paused to look back at her. "Do you know yours, Katya Kuriakova?" He turned to continue walking but paused instead, touching his brow with his fingers. "Oh dear," he said to himself, and collapsed.

The crew of the *Novgorod* and the *Baby* were moved off the waterside and put into a large, low room that appeared to have been an open plan office at some point in the past. It only had two exits and the pirates welded one of them shut, putting a chain and lock on the other. Petrov and the other surviving commissioned officers gathered around and listened grim-faced as Katya told them what had happened aboard the crippled war-boat. They showed little reaction, but the way Zagadko had chosen to die seemed to give them some satisfaction. Petrov nodded when she told them the *Novgorod* was dead at her captain's hand and another officer muttered "good man" under his breath. They seemed uninterested in Kane's health beyond hoping that, whatever was wrong with him, it was terminal. In this they were to be disappointed.

A couple of hours later, the door was unchained and Lieutenant Tokarov and the marines were escorted in at gunpoint. Once they were clear of the door, Kane entered, with Tasya the Chertovka close behind, flanked by guards. "As you're doubtless aware," said Kane, "your captain is dead." His voice was strong again and he carried himself with authority. "I regret that. I had a little time to know him and, well, I regret his death. You also know that he issued the *Novgorod*'s scuttling code. Your boat is dead. It will take months to strip out all the systems permanently damaged by the code and replace them." A ragged cheer went up from the *Novgorod* crew. Kane waited until they'd quietened down again. "He did the right thing, as far as he knew. We, however, know the bigger picture. Beyond these stone walls is the Russalka ocean and somewhere in that, very close at hand, is the Leviathan. It sank their boat," he pointed at where Katya and Lukyan sat, "it crippled yours. Now it has our boat, the *Vodyanoi*, stoppered up too. Before long, it will realise that we haven't run to a settlement after all and there will be no more boats coming and going. When it realises that, it will go on and search for settlements. Lemuria's closest; it will probably be the first. Before the Leviathan leaves here, though, it will make damn sure we're all dead. Novgorods, Vodyanois, it really doesn't care."

"How does he know so much about it?" murmured Tokarov to Petrov, who only nodded slightly in agreement.

"With the *Novgorod* operational and reparable, we might have been able to bluff it. Now we've got just one boat. We'll be working on a plan to try and get past it, to get us all past it. In the meantime, it would be appreciated if you would curtail any attempts to escape. We really don't need the distraction. If you, however, feel obliged to try, be warned that all your guards have been ordered to fire first and not bother asking questions afterwards. I'm not in the mood for FMA heroics; you either stay in line or you die. Just remember, we're trying to save your lives too." They left to a chorus of catcalls and swearing.

"You know what I don't like?" said Lukyan. "What I really don't like is the way he kept calling whatever's out there 'it'. You saw it on camera, didn't you, Katya? You said it looked like a submarine?"

She nodded. "Yes, but I've never seen a boat so featureless. And its size..." She shook her head in disbelief. "Colossal."

"That's what I don't like. Kane may be a Grubber by birth but he's a submariner by adoption. He would never call a boat 'it'. A boat is always a lady. All the way through that little speech, though, he kept saying 'it's this' and 'it's that'. Never once 'she's this', 'she's that'. Perhaps it is a monster after all."

Lieutenant Petrov was listening. "It's a sub. We all saw it. Besides, it launched torpedoes."

"That's as may be," replied Uncle Lukyan, his frown heavy and dark, "but even a submarine can be a monster."

Katya looked closely at him, wondering why he'd become so abstruse all of a sudden. Then she understood, and coldness curled around her guts; he was frightened. Nothing frightened Uncle Lukyan. At least, nothing had. What, she thought, do you do when the man who has always been there, always met every emergency, always been the anchor of your life... what do you do when he is afraid? Except grow afraid yourself?

"He knows what it is," said Tokarov.

"What?" blurted Katya, startled by the intrusion into her own thoughts.

"Kane. He knows what that thing is. How, I don't know." He pursed his lips. "Hold on, he's a Grubber, isn't he?"

"My own suspicion exactly," agreed Petrov, cutting straight to the conclusion. "This Leviathan is some sort of Terran weapon. It must have malfunctioned during the war so it was never used against us."

"Thank God," said Lukyan.

"Yes. It's highly formidable. Perhaps it lost the ability to tell friend from foe and was deactivated. That would explain Kane's comment about us all being at risk."

"And it's been sitting there at the bottom of the Weft

ever since," finished Tokarov excitedly. He paused. "I wonder what reactivated it."

"It came under fire," said Katya wearily. It all made a sort of sense now and the worst of it was that they were indirectly responsible.

The others were looking at her. Lukyan's widening eyes showed he was reaching the same conclusion. "What do you mean, it came under fire?" asked Petrov.

"We detected it on the seabed and thought it was a metal deposit. We were probably the first boat to have gone through there since the war. Nobody's stupid enough to go through the Weft unless some dimwit Fed orders them. We detected what looked like enough high quality metal ore for us all to retire on, even me."

"We fired a probe at it," said Lukyan in a ghastly voice, disbelief at their staggeringly bad luck etched in every syllable.

It all made horrible but perfectly logical sense, Katya found, as she reran the events through her mind. The Leviathan had probably heard them coming – they'd made no attempt to be stealthy – and gone to a low level of alert. Then they'd pinged it hard with sonar and as good as told it that they were looking right at it, taking it to still higher states of alert. The probe torpedo was the last straw, the moment when it believed it had been located and attacked by hostile forces, and its old wartime programs took over.

"There was never anything wrong with the *Baby*'s sensors," said Lukyan. "That thing must have some sort of stealth gear well beyond anything we have. Even active sonar didn't show it up."

"It came for us," said Katya. "It launched torpedoes.

That was the cavitation I heard, wasn't it, uncle? The sound of the launch tubes opening."

"Torpedoes," Lukyan echoed. "Strangest damn torpedoes I've ever come across. No motor sound, no active sonar pulses, and no explosion."

"It was the same with the *Novgorod*," agreed Petrov. "Just holes punched through. What kind of warhead could do that?"

Katya was thinking back to something she had heard earlier. "Kane said the *Novgorod* was deliberately damaged just enough to force her back to port."

"Rubbish," scoffed Lukyan. "No torpedo is that accurate."

"Yes," agreed Petrov quietly. "No torpedo is that accurate. So what exactly was used against our boats, Captain Pushkin?"

The men fell silent, unable to make anything but vague guesses.

Katya couldn't guess what form these mysterious weapons might take, but, then, she didn't need to guess, not when Kane definitely knew.

"I need to talk to Havilland Kane," she said standing.

"Kane certainly has some answers," agreed Petrov, "but why would he talk to you?"

To be honest, Katya wasn't entirely sure, but she knew he would. "I think he feels obligated somehow, responsible for dragging me into this. He won't talk to any of you; you're the enemy. You were taking him to be delivered to Secor. He'll talk to me."

"He'll talk to *us*," said Lukyan, joining her. "I'm not letting you wander off in the company of a bunch of pirates."

Katya didn't argue. It would be pointless, and, anyway, she would be very glad of his company.

They walked to the door and opened it as far as the chain would allow. The pirate on the other side stepped away and raised his gun. "You should pay attention, girl. The captain's orders are to kill anybody who even looks like they're thinking about escaping."

"I'm not escaping," she said, trying to look waif-like and unthreatening with her face framed between the door and jamb. She was glad that Lukyan was out of sight behind the door. It would be hard to stir sympathy with his glowering face visible above hers. "We need to talk to Captain Kane."

"Yeah, of course you do," said the pirate in a bored tone. "Now get back in there before I give you a maser burn."

"I'm serious. Tell him Katya Kuriakova wants to talk to him urgently."

"And I'm serious. Get your head back in there before I kill you! I'm not joking, girl."

"Please…"

The pirate made a show of releasing his gun's safety catch and levelling it at her face. Katya decided that she'd rather back down than be shot down and moved away. Lukyan's expression indicated that he might be about to attempt punching through the door and strangling the guard, which probably would not work out well for him or any of the prisoners. As soon as the pirate closed the door, she shot her uncle a "don't you dare" face. He shrugged and stepped away from it with surly grace.

They turned to the corner where Petrov and Tokarov waited and Katya shook her head. Her uncle walked back to them, but she paused and looked at the door. Perhaps if she left it a couple of hours and tried again, there might be a more sympathetic guard on duty? It was worth a go. She started walking back to the corner to suggest a second attempt later, and had perhaps taken five paces when the thin steel wall between their makeshift prison and the corridor exploded behind her.

Katya was thrown headlong and finished sprawled untidily on the floor. The lights flickered frantically before going out altogether except for some red emergency lights out in the corridor. She looked aghast at the damage. It seemed as if a great claw had torn an untidy rent across the metal wall, six metres long. The door was about two-thirds of the way along the cut and had lost its upper hinges as well as half its height. Katya blinked in disbelief; the edges of the tear were glowing in the dim light. The wall hadn't been torn or blasted. It had been *melted*. It seemed that the Leviathan had finally run out of patience.

Out in the corridor from the direction of the moon pool, the sound of shooting started.

EIGHT
DEVIL DRIVEN

"Orders, sir?"

Katya rolled over and found Petrov crouching nearby the engineer who'd asked the question. Of course, she thought; with Captain Zagadko dead then Petrov was the new commanding officer. In any military hierarchy, the chain of command is never broken.

"We're leaving," said Petrov bluntly. "I think the *Vodyanoi*'s crew have their hands full and don't sound as if they're having an easy time of it. If we stay here, whatever is killing them will exterminate us like fish in a blender." He stood up. "Everybody! We're leaving here and heading for the second dock. This place is still well signposted, Lieutenant Tokarov? Good. Make your own way there and don't be afraid to take circuitous routes. Getting there quickly isn't important, only getting there alive matters. Don't bunch up and don't get killed. Go!"

He was the first to the door and, after a fast look to check that the pirates really were too involved in combat to notice them, led the way. Katya felt her uncle take her hand in his but didn't look up at him. "Is he doing the right thing, uncle?" she asked.

"It's crazy to go out there. It's suicide to stay. Yes, it's the right thing to do. Let some more Feds go and then we'll take our chance." They waited in the shadows as the room thinned out by ones and twos. Katya had assumed some crewmembers were behind them so it was a shock when they found that they were the last ones. They crept closer to the destroyed wall and listened but could only hear the occasional crack of maser fire, now sporadic and reflexive. Lukyan squeezed her hand and they stepped out into the corridor.

Tasya the Chertovka, the She-Devil, was waiting for them, her gun levelled and ready. "Kane sent me to let you out. Said you deserved a chance. And here I find you scurrying into the shadows like vermin." Her lips thinned and she raised the gun to aim at the ceiling. "Very wise."

"What's attacked?" demanded Katya. "How can the Leviathan reach us in here? It's too big, it can't possibly have got up that tunnel."

"It didn't need to. Come on, we have to get moving unless you want to end up like that." She gestured casually at the floor. Katya looked down and found the pirate who'd threatened her at the door - or half of him at least. From the navel upwards he'd been vaporised. He'd been right on the other side when whatever had hit the wall had struck. He had never stood a chance. Strangely, the sight was less horrifying than she would have thought; grotesque rather than nauseating. The stench of burnt human flesh was something else altogether, though, and she covered her mouth and nostrils with her hand until the half-corpse was behind them. Katya and Lukyan followed Tasya into the warren of tunnels at a trot.

The emergency lighting was patchy; whole stretches of

corridor were in darkness and they had to stumble along holding hands. "We can't slow down," hissed Tasya at one point, "it can see in the dark."

"What is it?" asked Lukyan, full of frustration, but the She-Devil didn't answer. *Perhaps she just wants to get us out of the way and then abandon us,* thought Katya. *Or perhaps shoot us and report back to Kane that she couldn't find us.* This was the woman who'd led Terran troops through the maintenance tunnels beneath the Dory industrial complex to launch an attack on half-built warboats as they sat in their dry docks, the woman who'd murdered the yard's supervisor in front of the workers because he wouldn't open the hatches to the munitions stores. She was a war-criminal, a cold-blooded killer, a traitor to the Russalkin people and she was holding Katya's hand right that minute. Katya tried to concentrate on not tripping over anything rather than the possibility that the last thing she'd ever know would be the Chertovka's gun barrel being clapped to her temple. It wasn't easy.

Then the darkness started to thin with red light leaking around the angle of the corridor ahead and Katya could see a little again. What she couldn't see was Lukyan.

"Where's your uncle?" asked Tasya suspiciously.

"He was holding your hand," Katya snapped back. "What have you done?"

"My hand? He was holding your hand." She looked back into the gloom from which they were emerging. "He'll have to make his own way. Come on."

"No!" Katya shook herself free from the Chertovka's grip. "I'm going back for him!"

"Suit yourself." The Chertovka started on ahead. "But

you'll never find him. We've passed the heads of a dozen corridors in the dark. He could have wandered down any of them. You've more chance of running into..." She paused and looked back. "Come on, girl. You don't know what's back there. I wouldn't leave my worst enemy to that thing."

"What about my uncle?"

"He's a survivor. I know his type – clever and cautious. He won't take any chances. You've got a rendezvous point, haven't you?" Katya reluctantly nodded. "Then he'll be there. You should be concentrating on reaching it too. He'll be worried if you're not there to meet him." Katya knew she was right, but pride made her hesitate for a moment before following.

They walked in silence for a few minutes before Katya asked, "What attacked you?"

Tasya chuckled dryly. "You've been bursting to ask me that ever since we met in that corridor, haven't you?" She sobered. "Some sort of robotic drone. It came out of the moon pool and opened fire before we knew it was there."

"It carries a laser, doesn't it?"

The Chertovka paused in her walking and looked at Katya with an eyebrow raised as if examining an interesting specimen. She started walking again. "Havilland has quite a high opinion of you, Katya Kuriakova. I can see why. What makes you say it has a laser?"

"I saw what it did to the wall of the room we were being held in. A maser wouldn't do that. I've read about lasers but I've never seen one in operation." She frowned. "None of this makes sense."

"Why not?" Katya noticed that Tasya had slowed her walk, the better to look at her. She didn't know whether being of such interest to a woman like the Chertovka was a desirable situation.

"Look, masers are common sidearms because they're great for killing people, but not so good for punching through metal and plastic, right?" Tasya nodded. *Of course,* Katya thought, *she* would *know all about weapons.* "Lasers and bullets penetrate; that makes them bad choices. A gunfight that lets the ocean in doesn't leave any winners."

"Then we should be careful because, believe me, that drone carries a big laser."

Katya shook her head. "But that's not the point. Why is it carrying a laser at all? We went through all this in tech classes. High energy lasers are expensive to build, and they'd make pathetic weapons underwater anyway. Even with an X-ray laser, water refracts the beams. That's apart from the water boiling and then turning into plasma in front of the beam, giving you even worse scattering. The effective range of a laser with a range of hundreds of kilometres in air will be a few metres at most underwater."

"That's all they needed. I've looked at your uncle's minisub. One of those drones sunk it with a laser bolt; same with the hole in the *Novgorod*'s salvage maw. They can get close enough, that's a given."

"But why? Why go to all the trouble when a normal torpedo with a simple explosive warhead could do the same with none of the cost and trouble? It makes no sense. The Leviathan's drones have only shown what they're really capable of when one has got out of the water."

"And that's your conclusion?"

Katya hadn't been deliberately working towards a conclusion, but suddenly realised that this answered the questions that had been bothering her all along. "It was never designed for submarine combat. Its drones can do the job, but its real function is to fight in the dry." She imagined what would happen if it reached Lemuria, standing off while its drones patrolled the corridors, cutting down all resistance with their terrible laser cannon, not caring if they brought the ocean crashing through ruptured walls. "We can't let it reach Lemuria," she breathed, shaken by the terrible vision.

"Very much what Havilland said," replied Tasya, "but he was short on details as to how to manage it too. One drone killed five or six of the Vodyanois before they had a chance to draw their guns. Even when we returned fire, we did nothing to it. Maser bolts barely register, and bullets bounce off. If you've got any bright ideas on how we can stop it, I'd be fascinated to hear them." Katya was silent. "Thought as much. In that case, we'll just carry on running."

Two hundred metres further down the corridor, Tasya abruptly pulled Katya to one side, putting her hand over her mouth, and Katya thought she'd finally lost her patience and was going to kill her. Instead, she signalled Katya to be silent and left her crouching in the shadows while she moved ahead in utter silence, her gun drawn. She braced against the edge of an alcove where some equipment must once have stood before the base was stripped, focussed, and spun around the edge as she brought the maser pistol to bear. Katya thought she heard a gasp of surprise and terror. The Chertovka growled with exasperation and reached into the alcove with her free hand.

"Get out of there, you worm," she hissed, and dragged Suhkalev out into the open. He was whimpering so pathetically that Katya couldn't help but feel at least a little sorry for him.

"You're a poor excuse for a Federal agent, aren't you?" Tasya said as he sprawled on the plastic decking plates. "If they were all like you, life would be a lot easier for the likes of me. Stop that blubbering before I stop it for you."

"Leave him alone," Katya found herself saying. "He's been through a lot."

Tasya looked at her with surprise. "No more than you, Katya Kuriakova, and you're bearing up well."

Katya knew it was true but wasn't going to agree. She didn't know why she hadn't come apart at the seams yet; she found it hard to believe it had anything to do with bravery. She didn't feel brave and surely you felt it when you were brave? She felt scared most of the time. The only thing that seemed to keep her going was the pragmatic streak that used to drive her friends mad whenever they wanted to just be crazy and have some fun once in a while. "I'm scared," she said to Suhkalev, "I'm scared too. But we have to keep moving."

"We're all scared," growled Tasya, exasperated. She was looking back down the corridor as if she expected the Leviathan's drone to appear at any moment.

She probably did. It possibly might.

"Show me a man without fear and I'll show you someone with a death wish. They make poor brothers in arms, believe me."

"I didn't…" Suhkalev spoke in a careful voice, terror threatening to flood over every syllable, "I didn't want this… I don't like it. I don't like it." He sounded like a frightened child.

Please don't say his mind has broken, thought Katya. *If he can't function, how can we save him as well as ourselves?*

Tasya, apparently a disciple of applied practical psychiatry, simply backhanded Suhkalev hard. He was sent sprawling on the floor. In a second he was back on his feet and charging at her in a fury. Getting the muzzle of her maser pistol, a big ugly gun that made Zagadko's look quite civilised, placed neatly between his eyes slowed him to a stony halt.

"Better," said Tasya. "You do have some fight in you after all." She reached around to the small of her back, drew a gun and lobbed it at him. He caught it and stood there uncomprehendingly. "It won't do you much good against what's after us, but it may come in handy."

It certainly did. He snapped it up to a firing pose and barked, "You're under arrest! Drop your weapon!"

"Yes, yes. Plenty of time for that later. Come along." She carried on up the corridor. Suhkalev followed a few paces behind, assuring her that, really, she was under arrest. He meant it. He did. Katya sighed and followed him.

He continued to inform Tasya she was under arrest for the next fifteen minutes and Tasya ignored him for every second of it. Katya tried telling him he was wasting his time, but he just looked at her with an expression of faint embarrassment and carried on. Eventually, Katya started to wonder if the whole pantomime to appear competent and capable was being put on for her behalf.

Tasya put up with being arrested three to four times a minute very well for quite a while until even her patience finally gave out as they were entering a T–junction. "Look. I'm pleased you're not blubbing like a baby anymore. I'm pleased we have somebody else along who's had arms training. I'm pleased you're so motivated now. On the other hand, if you offer to put me in FMA custody once more, I'm going to forget all about how pleased I am and burn your head into a smoking stump just to make you shut up. Do you get a faint feeling for how irritated you're making me? Hmm?"

For his answer, he pushed her to one side and opened fire down the corridor. Tasya braced herself and looked, brought her gun up and fired a couple of shots before shouting, "It's useless! Run!"

Before they hared back down the corridor they'd just walked up, Katya risked a quick peek around the corner at what was pursuing them.

When Tasya had spoken of a "robotic drone", Katya had formed a mental picture of something like a mining drone: a fat little body, tracks, stubby arms with tools or, in this case, weapons at the ends. The reality was entirely different. The drone looked like nothing so much as a torpedo three metres in length and half a metre in diameter. It hung effortlessly a metre from the floor and glided soundlessly, but with infinite menace, towards her. The end facing her was fronted with a reflective port like the lensed casing of a searchlight. That seemed likely to contain its sensors, she thought. Belatedly, it also struck her that this would be the focussing element for the drone's devastating laser. She threw herself sideways barely in time. The corridor bloomed with brilliant light and the corridor junction was suddenly full of smoke and flying droplets of molten rock. One pattered to the floor right in front of her face where she lay prone. The drone could reduce cold stone to lava in less than a blink of an eye. This is what had sunk the *Baby* and crippled the *Novgorod*. How could they possibly beat it? Katya got her feet back underneath her and ran madly in pursuit of Tasya and Suhkalev.

Suhkalev had slowed to flag her down a side corridor,

Tasya was nowhere to be seen but the rhythmic pounding of her combat boots as she sprinted in the half-darkness could still be heard. "Where's the Chertovka gone?" demanded Katya.

"She said she was scouting ahead," replied Suhkalev. "I wish it wasn't quite so far ahead." He smiled unexpectedly and then ran down the corridor too, Katya close on his heels.

They almost ploughed into Tasya coming back. "Dead… end…" she said between trying to get her breath back. "Old… mine workings. We have to… get back to the main corridor before it cuts us off."

It was too late. The silent cigar shape of the drone was already turning the corner ahead of them. They pulled back and dog-trotted in as near silence as they could manage down a side gallery. Soon, the corridors became more and more roughly-fashioned until they were moving through mine workings. The floor had been smoothed for equipment to track more easily across, but all manner of tools and debris littered the tunnels – a strange mix of mechanically excavated shafts and plasma-melted passages – making it almost impossible to move quickly and quietly. "This is hopeless," muttered Katya, "a blind man could find us with all the noise we're making."

"What's that?" Up ahead a dark shape lurked in the patchy illumination of work lights that might well have been running for the last five years. Tasya pulled a torch from her belt and revealed the shape to be some great hulking piece of mining equipment. "Well," she said sourly, "I suppose we could hide behind that for the few milliseconds it takes the drone to vaporise it."

"It's a plasma cutter," said Suhkalev slowly.

"How would you know?"

"Mining family," he replied. "You see some of the work-related injuries miners get, and joining the Federal services looks pretty good. What I'm saying is, it's a plasma cutter. Why's it still here?" He walked up to it and started pressing buttons.

"Suhkalev!" gasped Katya. "What do you think you're doing?"

He didn't look up, but spoke as he worked. "These things cost a fortune. My father spent ages scraping together enough money to buy one with my uncle and aunts. If it had come down to a choice between leaving a cutter behind or a family member, they'd have had to think hard about it. These don't just get dumped. If I can get this running…"

"We might be able to do to the drone what it was planning on doing to us. Best plan we've got. Only plan we've got." The Chertovka kicked among some of the junk on the floor and picked up a handheld plasma cutter, a tiny cousin of the mining machine. "I don't think it'll let us get close enough to use something like this on it." She moved to the bend in the tunnel and peered cautiously around it. "Quick as you like, Fed. It'll be here soon."

Katya stood beside Suhkalev as he punched buttons with increasing irritation while watching a small display screen set in the cutter's side. There seemed to be a lot of red print appearing. "How bad is it?"

"It's a crock," he said as he read the diagnostic report. He winced. "It might be reparable, but not in the time we have. The fusion generator's working and the coolant system is running. It's sucking and liquefying nitrogen out of the atmosphere right now. Stupid of me; even if the plasma torch had been working, the safety cut-outs would have prevented ignition until the coolant tanks were full. I guess we're sunk."

"How long to fill those tanks?" asked Tasya.

"They hold twenty litres full. They're up to about eight litres now."

"Eight, in the couple of minutes it's been running? That's impressive." She looked at the machine, her eyes narrowing with concentration. "Is that thing mobile?"

"Too cheap a model to have a contragravitic system," he reported as he bent to look underneath. "Just tracks."

"Okay," she nodded. "Anybody want to hear my stupid plan that's going to get us all killed?"

Ninety seconds later, the drone turned the corner. Silent and implacable, it scanned the area with infrared sensors and detected human heat signatures coming from behind a piece of machinery. The focussing elements in its single eye clicked and shifted as it prepared to fire, moving a little way into the chamber to achieve maximum destructive effect.

Behind the plasma cutter, Katya, Suhkalev, and Tasya crouched, their backs braced against the machine's metal hull. Katya hardly dared breathe, and she could see that Suhkalev was pale with terror. Only Tasya was calm, watching the drone's advance reflected in the surface of an old metal box she had found and placed as a mirror. Katya watched her nervously, waiting for the signal. Tasya's coolness was almost as inhuman as the thing hunting them, she thought. That they might all be dead in a few seconds did not seem to disturb or distract her in the slightest. She simply watched and waited for her moment.

Tasya gave a sudden nod and started pushing backwards, heaving the maimed plasma cutter forward on its tracks. Taken by surprise, it was a second before Katya and Suhkalev joined her, pushing as hard as they could.

The drone halted and watched this new development for the moment it took for it to decide upon a response. What that response would be was never in doubt. The lens elements clicked and rotated once more, and then the drone's eye emitted ten megawatts of laser energy directly at the plasma cutter.

The drone was only as intelligent as it needed to be, and so it was no surprise that at no stage of its programming had anyone ever bothered to include what happens when a laser bolt ruptures a liquid nitrogen tank.

Katya was surprised into crying out by a sharp bang from beyond the cutter, and the battered hulk of the cutter jumped back at them as if surprised itself. Tasya was already moving, though. She'd pulled the small plasma torch she'd found from her belt and was already running from cover. Suhkalev watched her go and then shot a look of horrified astonishment at Katya, as if to say, "She's insane!" For her part, Katya leaned out the other way and peeked past the bulk of the mining cutter to see what was happening.

The liquid nitrogen tank had exploded, spewing first nitrogen superheated by the blast and then the liquefied gas, hundreds of degrees cooler. Katya could barely make the shape of the drone out in the billowing clouds of vapour, but she caught a momentary glimpse of the drone's eye covered with ice where the liquid nitrogen had splashed onto it and frozen the moisture out of the air onto the smooth casing.

The drone was blinded and, judging by the tortured clicking and ratcheting sound coming from its eye, was unable to do much about it. It was running through its protocols, but this situation was beyond it. Until it could restore its sensors, it knew no other options.

It certainly had no instructions for what to do if a human with a plasma cutter were to leap astride it and, swearing fluently, cut open a small ragged hole in the drone's hull and fire a maser bolt inside. The drone started to bob and sway erratically as a general systems failure occurred.

Katya and Suhkalev spent the first few seconds after the drone fired getting away from the damaged cutter and the pool of liquid nitrogen that was forming around it. They both knew that, if it touched them, it might not kill them but it would freeze blood solid in a second and give them an agonising case of frostbite that would take flesh cloning and surgical transplanting to repair. Having fingers or toes fall off would not be advantageous in their current situation. They got to a safe position at about the same moment the drone crashed to the floor. Tasya stood over it, panting heavily, with a maniacal grin on her face, her maser pistol in one hand, the hand-held cutter in the other sparking evilly and under lighting her. Katya could easily see where the Chertovka label had come from.

"There now," said Tasya, thumbing her cutter's power off and sticking it into her equipment belt, "that wasn't so difficult."

"We just need an infinite supply of large machines with liquid nitrogen tanks," said Suhkalev as Katya helped him to his feet.

"How many more of those do you think we need to worry about?" said Katya.

Tasya shrugged. "Don't know. But I know a man who might. Let's find Havilland and ask him, shall we?"

NINE
FRIENDLY FOE

Uncle Lukyan had often spoken of the comradeship of combat. It was a universal truth, he said, that when men and women are in the thick of the fighting, it is not love of their country, their political beliefs or even of their families that drives them on. "Nothing makes a better cement to hold together a fighting force than looking out for your comrades. Shoulder to shoulder or back to back. You keep them alive, they keep you alive. That is what welds an army together and makes soldiers commit great acts of bravery – fear of letting your unit down. Ah, my little Katya, you look at me as if I'm sullying some great romantic ideal, but it is true. Perhaps one day, although I pray not, you will have reason to understand what I say."

Now she did have cause to understand him and he'd been right. He'd also been right to pray that it wouldn't happen. But, here she was, running through tunnels trusting her life to, and willing to risk her life for, an arrogant Fed and a war criminal. It was, as her grandfather Vanya would tell anybody who stopped near his chair for more than a few seconds, a funny life.

They were passing signs for the secondary docking area more frequently now and Katya was relieved that they had seen no sign of any further drones. It was impossible that something as large as the Leviathan only carried the one. It was more of a mystery why the corridors weren't full of hovering cigar-shapes eager to evaporate any human that crossed their laser sights. The Leviathan was being very careful with its resources it seemed, but why? She knew they were relying on Kane having the answers. Tasya seemed confident that his knowledge was available simply for the asking, but Katya had her doubts; he'd been very cagey about everything up until now. Sometimes he behaved as if the Leviathan would simply go back to sleep if nobody spoke about it. Katya, on the other hand, knew perfectly well that ignorance was not safety.

They arrived at the docking area to find it apparently deserted. "Get up!" barked Tasya at the old crates lying around the staging area. "Do we look like a combat drone?"

There was no reply, and then Lukyan stood up from behind a tarpaulin covered stack of cargo pallets. His face lit up when he saw Katya and he rushed over and gave her the second painful bear hug of the day. As she wriggled her way loose, other faces were appearing from behind cover.

"Where's Kane?" demanded Tasya.

"Behind you." They spun around to find Kane standing there with a metal cylinder in his hand. "I've been behind you for a while, in fact."

"You've been following us?" said Katya.

"In effect, but I wasn't shadowing you, I was trying to catch up. Previous to that, I *had* been shadowing, but that was when I was following the drone. I'm sorry I wasn't there to see you kill it. Very good work, incidentally."

"Don't patronise me, Kane," said Tasya. She pointed at the cylinder. "What's that?"

"What is it? It's ant pheromone... a password... our golden key to the kingdom of wonders. This is why it took me so long to catch up with you. Fancy killing something like that drone and not taking a trophy. I stayed a minute to get this little beauty."

"Did a rock fall on your head when you were in the mine workings?" asked Katya, losing patience.

Kane looked at her, disappointment on his face. "Oh, Katya. I thought you had a poetic heart. Very well, if you want to reduce everything to the bare bones, it's the drone's IFF unit."

Katya thought she had a vague memory of the letters from her uncle's war stories. "Identify Friend or Foe?" she hazarded on the faint recollection.

"Exactly. This is the best bit of luck we've had since that monstrosity woke up."

It bothered Katya when he spoke like that. She wanted some definite information. Apparently Tasya felt the same. "For God's sake, Havilland, what exactly is the Leviathan? You talk about it as if it's a machine one minute and a living creature the next. Which is it?"

Kane's expression sobered. "From one minute to the next, I'm not sure."

The docks on this side of the complex were more conventional docking bays then the extravagant moon pool on the far side. Tasya led the way to the one they'd used to dock the *Vodyanoi* and opened it. Inside the otherwise empty bay sat a small forlorn form.

"The *Baby*!" cried Katya, almost as pleased to see the

redoubtable vessel as she'd been to see her own uncle. Lieutenant Petrov went over to inspect the damage while Tokarov crossed his arms and looked at the little sub with a jaundiced eye.

"This plan is insane. The Leviathan will sink you the instant it sees you."

"Not so," replied Kane, patting the IFF cylinder. "It will send an interrogation signal, this splendid device will reply with the correct response, and the Leviathan will welcome home its drone with open docking hatches."

"Even if we do get inside," said Petrov, "what do we hope to accomplish? We do not know what the vessel, if it is a vessel in any conventional sense, contains. How can we formulate a plan when we are entering entirely into the unknown?"

"Or you could just tell us what to expect, Captain Kane," said Katya. Kane looked sharply at her. "You've been hinting and dancing around the point ever since you saw that thing on the *Novgorod*'s screens. All our lives are in danger now and I'm getting sick of it. Just tell us what you know, and we might stand a chance of getting out of here alive."

There was a short, awkward pause. Her uncle was having trouble repressing a smile at Kane's evident discomfort, while Petrov merely raised an eyebrow. Unexpectedly, it was Tasya who nodded slightly at Katya, her approval for Katya's outspokenness evident.

"It's not that easy," said Kane.

"Yes, it is! You just say what it is, and how we can sink it or cripple it or just put it off the idea that sinking boats is fun. It *is* that easy! It *is* that simple!"

Kane's eyes were flicking back and forth as he looked around him at the surviving members of the *Novgorod* and

Vodyanoi crews. He suddenly looked very uneasy. "Very well," he said finally. "You want to know what the Leviathan really is?" He walked to the *Baby* and sat on her starboard ballast tank housing. The crews silently formed a semi-circle around him. He sighed, and said, "It's a warship. It's a Terran warship. It was sent here as a last resort during your war of independence. If all else failed, the Leviathan was to engage and destroy the entire Russalkin fleet. It could do it, too."

"Why wasn't it used then?" rumbled Lukyan. "Why did the Terrans die in battle when they had this thing all along?"

"Because this particular devil needs a bargain made with it before it will do its worst. That bargain was never made."

"No riddles," snapped Tokarov, "just tell us the damned truth!"

"This is the truth, and it's more damned than you'll ever know. It needs a sacrifice to be made to it. The sacrifice was too great–"

"What does that mean? What sacrifice?" butted in Petrov.

"–foul machine, it should never have been built. You don't know what it's like on Earth, you don't know what they're capable of–"

"How could it be worse than what it's already doing?" demanded Lukyan.

"–a generation of collapse, three generations of barbarism, one of totalitarianism, people don't count for anything–"

"You said it would destroy settlements," said Tasya.

"–neither a machine or a synthetic intelligence, they made their monster and then they wanted to give it a soul–"

"What sacrifice?" persisted Petrov.

"–silicon-woven synapses, quantum neurones, not better or worse than a human brain, just different, very different–"

"The sacrifice?" Tokarov asked.

"–a new biology, a new life form, unknowable, a *tabula rasa*–"

"The sacrifice, Kane," said Katya. He stopped suddenly, his eyes on her. He seemed very old suddenly, an echo of fear in his eyes.

"Yes," he said almost in a whisper, "the sacrifice. Kane. Me. I was the sacrifice." He took a deep breath and looked at them slowly in turn. "The Leviathan is currently nothing more than a very clever robot ship. It was intended to be an extension of a human will, a Terran will. It was built to… use… a human to fire its mind, to become a living creature." The others had grown very quiet. "A human who would become bound to it, become the Leviathan, even as the Leviathan became that human."

In the silence, Katya asked, "But, if you didn't want to do it, if you didn't want to become this *thing*, why would they choose you? You'd be a thousand times more dangerous. They'd choose somebody they could trust, somebody who wanted to merge with it."

"Perhaps I did want that once, Katya Kuriakova," he said darkly. "Perhaps I wanted that more than anything else. To burn and destroy all Russalkin resistance, to sink your boats and drown your cities. Perhaps I dreamed of that every night." In his eyes, Katya saw he meant every word and she unconsciously took a step back.

"But you didn't," said Petrov, in cool tones that verged on cold. "Why not?"

"Things change," said Kane vaguely. "When I left my home, I wanted to burn Russalka so thoroughly it would appear as a new star in Earth's sky. By the time I arrived, I wasn't so sure. Then I saw our troops go in, wave after battering wave. They came back, patched themselves up, and dived straight back in again. Again and again and again until they were all dead or deserted. And then there was just me."

"They didn't all die, they went home," said Petrov.

Kane looked at him as if Petrov had laughed at a funeral. "Yes, that must be it," he said bitterly, "they all went home." He lowered his face. "So it was just me in the Leviathan. The power to kill you all right there in my hands. And I thought," he looked up, "'Stuff it. I declare this war over. No more deaths.' I should be in the history books, really. The only man to decide to stop a war unilaterally just like that. So I escaped from the Leviathan and took up the happy life of a rollicking pirate. And look where it's got me. Telling fairy stories to a bunch of people I wanted to kill ten years ago who now think I'm mad."

"Good enough for me," said Petrov. "We'll carry out this mission, Kane, and disable the Leviathan. You're coming."

Kane blinked with mild astonishment. "I was under the impression it was my idea in the first place."

"What internal defences does it have?"

Kane frowned at him. "How would I know? I was on good terms with it."

"You must have seen schematics?"

Kane laughed humourlessly. "You really don't get it, do you, lieutenant? I wasn't along as a trained and trusted executive officer or something. I was along as potting mulch for the Leviathan to plant its intellect in."

Now it was Petrov's turn to frown. "I don't know what that means."

"It means, lieutenant, that it was a suicide mission. I'd be a god, if only of war, for a few months and then I was to destroy the Leviathan and myself, not that there'd be much difference between us by that time. Nobody knew what the effects of being bound to a synthetic intelligence for very long would do. As I said, using the *Leviathan* was supposed to be a last resort."

Tasya was looking at Kane oddly. "Let's get that minisub repaired and seaworthy," she said in a strange, uninflected voice. Petrov looked at her, then at Kane and nodded.

Kane walked away without looking left or right. Katya followed him to a crate by the far wall where he sat and watched the technicians from both crews examine the *Baby*.

"I have a feeling I know what you're going to ask me, Katya," he said, watching them work.

"I doubt it." Inexplicably, she felt herself growing angry. She couldn't understand it; here was a man who *hadn't* unleashed certain death on Russalka and yet she somehow found herself resenting him. "You said you knew your duty."

"I did. I do."

"Then why didn't you... merge or interface or whatever it was you were supposed to do with that thing out there?"

He looked at her, raising his eyebrows warily. "If I had, you'd probably be dead now."

"Not the point. Your duty was to Earth; to Terra and all the Grubbers. You were supposed to mop us up so they could have our world. But you didn't."

"I couldn't."

"You betrayed your own people and then turned pirate here."

"Looks like I've got quite a death wish."

"So why didn't you fulfil it in the war like you were supposed to? Do you like letting people down?"

Anger flickered across his face in a spasm. Katya was surprised to see it shadowed by sorrow. It gave her a small thrill of pleasure and that made her ashamed. She was getting to him.

"You don't know what I wanted then or what I want now."

"Why didn't you just go home? Come up with some story about the Leviathan malfunctioning and then just go home? Why did you stay here?"

"And why would I want to do that?"

"I don't know. To be with your Grubber friends, with your family."

His face whitened and for a second she thought he was going to hit her. "You think I should stay with my family?" he said in a tight whisper that sounded nothing like his normal voice.

Katya was very aware that she'd travelled into dangerous waters. "I just thought…"

"I'm with my family, okay? I'm with them." He stood up and walked quickly away, through the open air lock and into the complex. Katya watched him go with a sinking feeling that she'd just said the most stupid thing she had ever said in her life, though she didn't know why.

She turned and almost walked into Tasya. "What did you say to him?" she demanded.

"Nothing," Katya replied, confused. "Well, nothing much. I just asked… if he's a Grubber… a Terran, I mean, why didn't he go home?"

"What makes you think this isn't his home now?"

"He doesn't have family here, does he? They'll be–"

Tasya interrupted her.

"Tell me you didn't ask him that."

Katya found that if she didn't tell Tasya that, she had nothing to say at all. Her mouth opened and closed a couple of times.

"Stupid little girl," said Tasya and ran after Kane.

Katya watched her go. She felt wretched. She couldn't even manage to be resentful. Tasya was right; she was just a stupid little girl. She had no idea what she was doing. She walked over to where they were already patching the *Baby*. Uncle Lukyan looked over at her and frowned.

"Are you all right, Katya?"

"Yeah," she replied, not feeling anywhere near right at all. "I'm fine."

The work progressed rapidly. The laser-cut holes in the *Baby*'s hull were neat and hadn't gone through any vital systems. Her electronics were sealed against water anyway, so the flooding of the compartment was of little consequence. After an hour and a half, Lukyan was sitting in the pilot's seat and running a diagnostic test. Katya watched the Judas box light mostly green apart from a few ambers further down the board.

One of the pirates had pointed out that, as their vessel had recovered the *Baby* it was technically theirs by salvage right. Lukyan had told the pirate he was wrong on two counts. Firstly, Lukyan had never abandoned the vessel but had still been aboard when it was picked up. It was therefore never legally salvage. Secondly, and more telling to most of those listening, Lukyan had offered to tear the ribcage out of anybody laying claim to his boat. The pirates collectively agreed that these were good arguments and renounced their claim.

"Will she swim, Mr Pushkin?" asked Petrov from the aft hatch.

"She will, lieutenant," replied Lukyan. "She's quite well considering what she's been through. Is that IFF device wired in properly? Then let's try it." He reached over and flicked a switch that started feeding power to the cannibalised drone component. Nothing obvious happened. "Hmm," grunted Lukyan, "if this thing only works when the Leviathan sends an interrogation signal, how do we know it's working properly beforehand?"

"We don't," answered Petrov. "If it isn't working, we'll find out soon enough."

Lukyan looked up at the patch over one of the laser holes. "That's comforting."

"Glad to be able to put your mind at rest."

"So, who's going on this fool's errand with me?"

Petrov didn't argue with Lukyan volunteering himself. "As few as possible. You'll pilot, we'll need Kane for his special knowledge and one or two FMA personnel along to keep him honest."

"With respect, Lieutenant Petrov," said Tokarov, "you shouldn't go."

"Oh?" said Petrov, who clearly had been planning on doing just that.

"You're acting captain here. You can't just hand off command because you're curious to see inside that thing."

Petrov pursed his lips; he knew very well Tokarov was right but that didn't mean he had to like it.

"Besides," added Tokarov, "my specialisation is engineering. I'd probably be more use."

"All right, all right," said Petrov wearily, "you've made your point. You're going."

"I'm going too," said Katya. Both lieutenants looked at her with surprise and Lukyan started to open his mouth. "I'm still the *Baby*'s navigator. She needs a co-pilot and, short of Sergei just wandering in, I'm the only other person here with hours logged on her."

She neglected to mention that the vast majority of those hours were simulator time, and she was grateful that Lukyan didn't point that out. Instead he said, "She's right. She's crew."

"It's dangerous," Petrov said directly to her. "The chances are that this plan won't work. I'd give it a forty per cent chance of success at most. Nobody would think any less of you if you don't go."

"I'm going. I'm crew."

Petrov heaved a sigh of exasperation. "Breed them awkward in your family, don't you?"

"Oh, yes," smiled Lukyan.

The waiting was by far the worst part. Between the excellent training of the Novgorods and the ingenious jury-rigging of the Vodyanois, the last of the repairs proceeded far more quickly than would have seemed reasonable, but time still crawled by for Katya. She passed back and forth, itching either to be seaborne or to back out of her insistence that she go. She knew Petrov was right; nobody, not even her uncle, would blame her if she dropped out. It wasn't as if the short trip around the mountainside even needed a navigator. "The pride of the Kuriakovs" her grandmother had called it, speaking of it half as if it were something glorious and half as if it were a curse. Right then, it felt very much like a curse; Katya had the uneasy feeling her pride was about to get her killed.

And then, with the abruptness of a shot, the work was done and the *Baby* was being rolled into one of the smaller locks.

Kane had come back with Tasya. He looked drawn and upset still, and wouldn't look at Katya. That was fine by her; she felt she should be apologising for something but she wasn't sure what it was. Whatever the problem, she couldn't quite bring herself to look him in the eye.

She took her position, Lukyan his, then Tokarov sat behind him and Kane behind her, just as he had – it was hard to believe – only just over twelve hours before. The main lock door closed behind them and the chamber started to flood. "Here's where we find out if the welds will hold," said Tokarov with an attempt at gallows humour. He found no response and settled into the same silence as the others.

The water boiled and frothed on the other side of the main port as the level rose, the crew and passengers watching it without comment, past the level of their eyes and over the top of the plasteel port. Kane looked up and watched the small dorsal port grow dark as the water rolled over it.

"Sonar to passive," said Lukyan. After a moment he repeated it.

"Eh? Oh!" Katya reached for her control board. "Check."

"Wayfinder… offline, I think."

"Check."

They went through the same sequence they had a few hours before, when life was a great deal simpler. They worked down the list until Lukyan came to, "IFF transponder."

"Ah," said Katya uncertainly. "It's powered up and that's about all I can say for it. I don't know if it's actually working."

"Good enough, I suppose," said Lukyan.

"Yes? In that case, check."

"Check list complete." He toggled open the radio link to the FMA ensign who was at the dock controls. "We're set, I think. Open the lock doors, please, son."

"Opening external lock doors," replied the ensign in the crisp tones they taught at the academy for making voice transmissions clear. It always sounded a bit theatrical to Katya, as if the speaker was on stage declaiming Chekov or something. "You're clear to depart, *Pushkin's Baby*." A moment later he broke protocol by adding, "Good luck."

Lukyan smiled wanly. "Thanks, control. Going to radio silence. RRS 15743 Kilo over and out." He closed the link as the *Baby* lifted from its landing skis and nosed her way out into the open sea. They were on their own now.

TEN

MEDUSA SPHERE

The *Baby* travelled around the mass of the mountain keeping the vertiginous slopes to the right. It was very quiet aboard; after a couple of attempts at humour, even Tokarov had shut up. Now there was just the hum of the boat's impellers running through the hull and the quiet whirr of the ventilators.

"Uncle?" said Katya, suddenly spotting a flaw in the plan.

"Hmm?"

"How are we supposed to find the Leviathan? It's virtually invisible when it wants to be. We could swim backwards and forwards all day two hundred metres from it in this murk and never see it."

"Ah, well," said Lukyan in a voice that indicated that he hadn't considered this either, but wasn't about to admit it.

Kane saved him by saying, "It will find us. It will interrogate the IFF unit with a coded signal, detect the correct reply – if we've made a mess putting in the IFF then that will be about the point where this pleasure cruise finishes – and try to bring us in on remote control, or command the drone's artificial intelligence to bring itself in. When neither works, it will assume there's been damage, and recover us for repairs."

"How violent is this recovery likely to be?" asked Tokarov.

"Not violent at all. You'll see."

"You said the drone had artificial intelligence?" said Katya.

"Yes. They have to have some autonomy. Those tunnels block communications so the drone was given its orders and left to complete them."

"But the Leviathan itself has a synthetic intelligence?"

"Yes."

"So what's the difference?"

"Is this relevant?" Tokarov interrupted.

"No," said Kane, "but it's better than listening to your weak puns. An artificial intelligence, Ms Kuriakova," Katya noticed the formal use of her name, "only looks like intelligence. A machine is taught a lot of responses to assorted situations and uses them if such a situation arises. The more contingencies are covered, the more intelligent the AI seems. The best have heuristic routines programmed in; that means they observe how well what they've been taught works and how other approaches work. If something else is better, then they'll start using that in future instead. They're 'learning', for want of a better word. Artificial intelligences can get very good, even passing the Turing test."

"What's...?"

"It's a rule of thumb test for intelligence. If you can talk to an AI for a few hours and never realise that you were talking to a machine all along, then it's passed the Turing test. That's artificial intelligences; they're artificial because they're not real minds, just good impersonations.

A synthetic intelligence is something else again. The Leviathan carries a massive silicon analogue of a brain. At the moment nothing much more sophisticated than a good artificial intelligence programme is in it. The idea was for it to interface with a human…"

"You," said Tokarov, fascinated.

"…me, and the human intelligence would act as a catalyst to spark the same sort of cascading sapient effect in the synthetic brain. The result would be a single intellect, the will and experiences of the human combined with the massive knowledge resources and capabilities of the Leviathan.

"It's not just a theory either. They've done it on Earth. Nothing quite like the Leviathan, though."

"What's different?"

"The interface had to be more… I'm not sure how to describe it. Thorough, perhaps. Intimate."

Tokarov laughed. "You make it sound like a marriage."

Kane didn't laugh along with the joke. He only said, "Till death do us part."

Katya's right-hand multi-function display started showing a flashing box and bleeped urgently. "The IFF unit has been hailed," she said quietly. A faint sense of fear was growing in her. She'd secretly hoped the Leviathan had moved on, but the indicator on the MFD showed that to be a vain hope. How many times did she think she could encounter that monstrosity and live? She was starting to hate the stupid pride that had made her volunteer for the mission.

"I'd cut the engines, if I were you," suggested Kane to Lukyan. "There's less chance of an accident if we're not moving when it takes us."

Katya didn't like the sound of being taken at all. It made them sound like prey. But Lukyan cut the engines and now they had only the sound of the life-support fans and their breathing as they waited and listened for the Leviathan to make its move.

The seconds turned into a minute and then minutes. Katya was wondering whether to suggest sending an active sonar pulse to try and provoke the Leviathan into doing something (she wasn't wondering it very hard, though, since it didn't seem to respond well to having sound waves blasted at it) when something touched the hull. A whispering light scraping as something travelled cautiously across the *Baby*'s skin.

"Here we go," whispered Kane.

Suddenly the boat lurched and then started to move swiftly and smoothly upwards.

"What's happening?" growled Lukyan. "Have we been grappled?" He looked to Kane for a reply, and the pirate nodded.

Grappled. Somehow the Leviathan had managed to attach lines to the *Baby* with barely any warning at all. Katya had read and seen stories of historical grappling actions and having harpoons banged through your hull was usually a very obvious process. This was something else again. The hiss of water travelling quickly over the hull modulated into a gruff roar for a moment and then, suddenly, they were bathed in harsh, white light.

Out of the ports, they could see the *Baby* was being dragged through a great hatch in the floor of a white circular chamber, perhaps twenty metres in diameter. Through the top porthole, they could see cables as thick as a man's wrist running from a cluster in the roof and down to where they encircled the minisub. They flexed and moved like the arms of a russquid, Katya thought, even though they were obviously made from metal. She'd never seen anything like them before. Beneath the *Baby*, a great iris valve slid shut, sealing them off from the sea. They were trapped in the belly of the beast now.

The tentacle-cables – or cable-tentacles, Katya didn't know which – gently lowered the *Baby* to the floor of the chamber and then slid back into the ceiling above. As they watched the metallic hemisphere in the ceiling into which the cables had retracted, they saw its image distort with ripples and realised the chamber was being pumped out. The water level dropped rapidly, much faster than the dock had flooded back in the mining site. Within a very few minutes, the minisub was sitting on its landing skids in the middle of the white chamber, dripping dry as the last dregs of water were efficiently sucked away from the floor.

They sat in silence for a few seconds, everybody waiting for somebody else to make the first move.

Tokarov was the first to find his voice. "Now what?"

Kane unbuckled his seat restraints. "The aft hatch, please." Uncle Lukyan flicked a switch, and the aft hatch unsealed and swung open. Kane walked back and stopped just before stepping out. "You might as well follow," he said. "There's no getting the sub back out of this chamber without the Leviathan permitting it, so there's not much point in staying behind." The others released their restraint buckles and climbed out after him.

Katya stood by the *Baby* and looked around in wonderment at the chamber. It was so harshly white in here, with no obvious source of light as though the walls themselves were glowing. Everything was white except for the unpainted and untarnished dome in the ceiling, pocked with the large regular holes in its surface that were home to the tentacles, and the iris valve they were standing on. She couldn't see any way of getting into the rest of the Leviathan from here.

Lukyan obviously thought the same thing.

"Kane, is this place connected to the rest of the boat?"

"Anything's possible," replied Kane vaguely. He crossed his arms and said "Open internal access." Nothing happened. He cleared his throat and tried again. Still nothing happened.

"Great. Now what do we do?" asked Katya.

Kane looked uncomfortable. "It's been years since it's heard my voice. Maybe it's changed more than I thought." He tried again. "Open internal access." Nothing. As an afterthought, he tried adding "Please."

One side of the circular chamber started to draw back, the flat white plates sliding to expose a broad armoured door five metres across by three high. "Manners maketh the man," Katya heard Kane say to himself. Tokarov made a step towards the door but Kane stopped him. "Me first, lieutenant. It might be nervous around strangers."

"*It's* nervous?" said Tokarov.

"It's alive in a way," said Kane. "It has its foibles, a little like a small child."

"Oh? It might throw a tantrum?"

"Yes, it might. And its tantrums come with a body count. Follow me."

The layout of the Leviathan was nothing like any vessel Katya had ever seen or been taught about at school. There was no sense of space being at a premium, of every cubic centimetre of ship being functional. Instead, it felt like being inside an iceberg. Everything was white and there was no feeling that, beyond the bland walls and ceilings, there was anything she could have looked at and recognised as part of a boat. Even the word "boat" – traditionally applied to even the largest submarines – failed to express the alien nature of the Leviathan.

"How big is this thing?" she asked.

Kane looked back at her and she was relieved that he no longer seemed as angry and distant as he had been back at the mining site. "Big enough. Just short of seven million cubic metres, I believe."

Lukyan stopped so abruptly that Tokarov walked into him. "Seven *million*?" he echoed in disbelief.

"Not quite. I was rounding up." Kane said, not even slowing his walk.

"Strangest boat I've ever been on," said Tokarov. "Strangest one I've even heard of. Where are the stations? The berths?"

Kane stopped by a hatch set into the wall. "This is the only berth aboard. It used to be mine. You have to get it into your head, lieutenant, it isn't a ship or a boat or any kind of vessel of any type that you're familiar with. It's a weapon. A really big, intelligent weapon that happens to have a small living space aboard for a pet human."

"A pet?" said Lukyan. "That's not a good comparison, is it? It wouldn't have let a pet go."

"Maybe it had no use for me," said Kane.

"I thought the whole point of it having you along was…"

But Kane was walking away and the question was never asked.

The corridor ended abruptly with another hatch much like the one that had led to Kane's old quarters. He stopped and stood before it as if steeling his nerve. His nervousness communicated itself to Katya.

"Is that the bridge?" she asked.

"No," he answered in a strange, distracted voice. "There's no bridge." He reached out and touched the door very gently, barely brushing it with his fingertips. Immediately, they heard the hiss of seals being released, the door swung smoothly inwards and to one side. Kane took a deep breath and stepped through the opened portal. After a moment, they followed him.

The chamber they had entered was similar in form and proportions to the bay where they'd left the *Baby*. If anything, however, it was almost more spartan. Here there was no iris valve taking up much of the floor and metal dome on the ceiling housing cable tentacles. There was only one thing of note here, but a thing so extraordinary, it drew their gaze irresistibly.

Mounted exactly in the middle of the room was a chair. No, *chair* was too small a word. Mounted exactly in the middle of the room was a throne. An ugly, brutal thing made from dark metals and dark imaginations. It sat... it *crouched* in front of them, grey metal spires rising from its back and its feet merging into a circle of the same materials that seemed almost like a plug thrust into the floor.

Katya allowed a gaping expression of utter disbelief onto her face. The chair was as out of place as it was possible to imagine. "What," she said, "is that?"

"It's a chair," said Kane, accurately but unhelpfully. Lukyan made a step towards it but Kane grabbed his arm. "No!" he said, both fretful and fearful. "Don't go near that. It's the single most dangerous thing the Leviathan possesses."

Lukyan looked at him as if he were mad; they were aboard a synthetically intelligent killing machine armed with attack drones that were so far ahead of anything Russalka had that they were bordering on magical. It seemed absurd to suggest that these were somehow less dangerous than furniture.

"It's the interface. It's where the Leviathan and a human..." he looked for a term they might understand, something that explain the horror he felt inside towards the throne. He could think of nothing. "...interface," he finished, weakly.

"And what's that?" asked Katya, pointing upwards.

In the centre of the gently vaulted ceiling, a circular aperture had appeared so silently and so neatly that none of them had even noticed it open. From the deep darkness within the aperture, a sphere was slowly descending. A metre in diameter, utterly black, the sphere came down upon a thin supporting rod as elegantly as a drop of oil rolling down a metal surface. When it had descended perhaps three metres, it stopped abruptly and without a tremor.

"What is it?" demanded Tokarov quietly. The sphere was so perfect and so utterly inscrutable, it was easy to imagine terrifying levels of violence lurking within.

"It's a Medusa sphere," said Kane. "Nobody make any sudden moves."

"A Medusa sphere?"

"You asked whether the Leviathan had any internal security measures," replied Kane, "I can now assure you that it has. The sphere will..." He stopped as a ghostly violet dot appeared on his chest. Slowly it moved upwards until it was lying between his eyes.

Katya looked back to Lukyan to point it out but found him rooted to the spot by an identical dot. Tokarov was the same. Katya's hackles raised and her stomach tightened. "Uncle," she asked, sounding far more in control of her emotions than she felt, "Have I got a purple dot of light on my forehead?" Lukyan looked at her sideways without turning his face from the sphere and nodded slightly.

"I don't want to be overly dramatic at this point," said Kane, "but we have all been targeted by the sphere with lasers. If the Leviathan decides it doesn't like us being here, these beams will intensify inside perhaps a thousandth of a second and the results will be painless, but terminal. Therefore, please don't do anything to antagonise the Leviathan."

Katya knew very little about the legends of Earth, but she knew what a Medusa was, and the sphere's name was well chosen. In the stories, the Medusa was a woman so hideous that to look upon her face turned the hapless observer to stone. Here, the four of them stood there terrified to move, to do anything that the Leviathan might consider aggressive. They might not have been literally turned to stone, but they were still petrified.

"What are you going to do, Kane?" said Tokarov, trying not to move his lips.

"I have no idea," Kane replied in a tone of resignation.

"No idea," echoed Lukyan, with hollow disgust.

"No idea at all. I wasn't expecting garlands and flowers when I came back, but I was hoping for a little tolerance at least. Perhaps I should have come by myself."

Nobody answered, but nobody argued. Suddenly more beams sparked out of the sphere, bright reds and blues, the dots travelling across the walls clearly visible against the slightly reflective whiteness. They swept and whirled and then quickly drew together on Kane. They travelled quickly across him like scurrying beetles. The only one that didn't move was the dull violet dot in the middle of his forehead.

"You are identified."

Katya had no idea where the voice came from; it seemed to be in the air all around. Deep and sonorous, like the dying tones of metal striking metal in a large cavern, the voice was full of incorrect inflexions and emphasis. It was clearly not the product of a human throat.

Kane looked upwards, uncertain how to respond. Finally, he tried. "Hullo."

"You were rejected. You have no function here."

"Yes, I know. I was…" he shrugged, rolled his eyes looking for inspiration, "…just passing. Thought I'd drop in."

"Where is drone six? The object in the retrieval bay is not drone six."

Lukyan winced to hear his beloved *Baby* called an "object".

"I'm afraid it – drone six, that is – I'm afraid it met with a bit of an accident." Kane waited for an immediate reply, but none was forthcoming. "Sorry for your loss." Still no answer. "So, I took its IFF unit so I could visit you."

"You were rejected," repeated the voice of the Leviathan. Katya wondered what it meant by that. Kane had simply left, not been rejected. At least, that's the way *he* said it had happened. "You have no function here."

"I think I do have a function here. It's your current activities; they are not within your operational parameters."

"Operations are within acceptable parameters."

"No," replied Kane in a chiding voice, "they are not. I'm very familiar with them and you are operating outside

them." He crossed his arms – slowly, so as not to antagonise the Medusa sphere – and started to lecture the
Leviathan. "You are pursuing a seek-and-destroy strategy.
You know full well you're not supposed to do anything
that is actively aggressive without a human in that seat
over there. Self-defence is all very well, but you saw off
the vessel that first reactivated you. That should be that.
You should have stood down afterwards, because that's
what your standing orders tell you to do." Kane stopped
and waited with his chin thrust forward as if expecting an
apology.

"You are incorrect," said the Leviathan.

Kane couldn't have looked more surprised if he'd been
told he been spelling his name wrong for the last year.

"What do you mean, *incorrect*?"

"Parameters state that when discovered, strategies of
covert offence are to be employed. These strategies are
being employed."

"That's not right," said Kane under his breath. Then,
speaking up, "What are your targeting priorities?"

"Category one combatants comprise the following." The
Leviathan started to list possible targets in the most
abstract ways. Katya could follow them at first, but after
a while even Tokarov started to look confused. Then Kane
interrupted the list.

"Hold on, hold on. I need some clarification here. Which
target category are we in now? Three? Four?"

"One."

The colour leeched out of Kane's face. "But you were
listing civilian categories. Non-combatants. You were listing babies and the sick."

"Category one targets."

Kane spoke as if he didn't want to hear the answers. "What is in category two?"

"Category two contains no definitions."

"Category three. What's in category three?"

"Category three contains no definitions."

"What is in category blue?"

Katya looked sharply at him. During school, they'd seen historical simulations of important battles of the War of Independence. Category blue was the generic name for allies.

The Leviathan replied immediately.

"Category blue contains no definitions."

Something was terribly, terribly wrong. The Leviathan was prepared to attack and destroy even vessels from Earth. There was only one possible conclusion; the great warship was insane.

Lukyan, Tokarov, and Katya stood in silence as Kane tried to find what had gone wrong. The Leviathan answered each question fully and, as far as they knew, accurately, but none of it helped. Artificial intelligences are complex, but they are predictable at least as far as their motivations and goals, for these are the very things programmed deep into their fibres. An AI simply couldn't go mad and decide to kill everybody because it felt like it. Nor could a simple malfunction suddenly turn it from a precision weapon into a threat to all sides. The only other possibility was that the vessel had somehow been reprogrammed. Kane was trying to find out by whom in the hope that this might reveal the reasons behind such an irrational act.

"Those were *not* the operational parameters you left Earth with," Kane said, his irritation starting to show. He barely seemed aware of the Medusa's sighting and sensor dots on him anymore. "They were not the ones you had when I left, either. You have been reprogrammed. Identify any and all personnel who have accessed your command levels since arriving at Russalka."

"Kane, Havilland."

"Yes, but when and for what purpose?"

The Leviathan gave a date ten years before and added, "Maintenance and examination protocols were enacted."

"What changes were made?"

"None."

"Fine. That's good. I didn't break anything by accident. Now, list all subsequent accesses."

"None."

"None?" Kane shook his head angrily as if somebody was telling him black was white and expecting him to believe it. "What do you mean, none?"

"No subsequent access demands were made to command levels subsequent to arrival at Russalka."

"Kane," whispered Lukyan, very conscious of the laser dot on him, "perhaps the Terrans programmed this in before you left."

"What?" said Kane. He snorted with derision. "They told it to regard them as deadly enemies? Does that seem likely to you? Besides, even if they were crazy enough to enter such a program it would still have been registered as a command access."

"Not if it was programmed not to–"

"No," interrupted Kane firmly, "it does not make sense. They had no way of knowing I wouldn't end up in that chair, no way of predicting this little scene. Therefore, why spend a lot of time and effort covering up a trail they never expected anybody to even have the chance of finding? It can't be so."

"Kane," said Tokarov, "something's bothering me about all this."

"Only one thing? You're ahead of the rest of us then."

"Seriously, if it considers us all enemies, why are we still alive?"

Kane started to open his mouth to reply, but stopped. He frowned. His gaze wandered back and forth across the floor as he worked through possible reasons and discarded them one by one. "You know, lieutenant," he said finally, worry evident in his face, "I have no idea." He looked back at the exit. "I'm not even sure how we're going to get out of here."

"Go?" said Katya. "We can't go. We came here to..."

A warning glance from Kane made her reconsider her words. She'd been about to say "...destroy this thing." Saying out loud that they were a threat to the Leviathan while it was pointing high-energy lasers at each of them might have been a fatal mistake. Instead, she said, "...deal with the situation."

"I think," said Kane, choosing his words just as carefully, "that *the situation* is very much in control of the situation. If we were to attempt to deal with *the situation*, I fear *the situation* would deal with us first."

"We've proved that we can get in," said Lukyan, "and that's enough to be getting on with. It will have to be enough. I suggest we leave and reconsider what to do next."

Kane nodded. "I agree. Lieutenant?" Tokarov also nodded. "Well, we're all agreed, then."

"I agree too," said Katya.

The three men had the grace to at least look embarrassed. "All agreed," said Kane quickly. They turned to leave. "Would you open the hatch, please?"

"Which is the replacement?" said the Leviathan.

Kane stopped and looked back, his mouth working soundlessly. "What?" he managed.

"Which is the replacement?"

"Clarify your statement," said Kane, but Katya could see he already knew full well what the Leviathan meant, just as she knew.

"Which of these three humans is to replace you as the biological component in my intelligence?"

"What makes you believe any of them are?"

For its answer, shimmering multi-coloured beams spat from the surface of the Medusa sphere. Suddenly, there were two Kanes. The new one was faintly translucent and Katya realised it was a projected, animated hologram, a technology unavailable on Russalka since the war destroyed the few facilities that contained it. The new Kane was nothing like the one she'd first met back in the launch locks. He seemed younger and was wearing a Terran uniform. With a small shock, she realised that this was Kane as he'd been ten years ago. He was pacing up and down in front of the door, his eyes and hair wild. He looked like a man at the edge of a breakdown.

"Why do you wish to leave?" boomed the Leviathan.

"I... I just," the holographic Kane ran his fingers through his hair and clamped his palms to the sides of his head in frustration and fury. "I just need to go, that's all."

"You have your function."

"I cannot fulfil it, you *know* that."

"Then you are without function."

"In that case, I might as well go." The younger Kane looked optimistically at the door, but it remained sealed.

"You may still have utility for the mission. You will be retained."

"No!" barked Kane. "No! I will not… You… This mission is over!"

"You do not have the authority to declare the mission aborted. You will be retained."

"And what if I never have 'utility' again?" Katya could see the fear in the recorded Kane's face. The real Kane looked away. Katya couldn't read the expression on his face. It may have been sickened, or it may have been humiliated.

"You will be retained."

"I could die here! I could get old and die in this… this cybernetic mausoleum. With just you! You for company." There was a sob in his voice. "I'm in Hell."

"You are aboard the Terran attack cruiser *Leviathan*."

The recorded Kane laughed a horrible bitter laugh that quickly subsided into sobs again. He hammered at the closed hatch with his fists. "Let me go," he begged, "please let me go."

"You will be retained," said the Leviathan, its intonation exactly the same every time it repeated the damning phrase.

Then Kane stopped his sobbing and looked back into the chamber with an air of cunning on his face. "I have utility," he said.

"Specify your utility."

"You require a person to interface with, to attain full operational status, yes?"

"That is correct."

The recording of Kane stepped closer to the throne and pointed to it. "I'll find you somebody who can sit there for you. I'll find you somebody to merge with."

"There are parameters to be observed."

"I know, I know. I know all about all that. I can find you somebody."

"Your mission is to locate and retrieve a suitable candidate." Katya could tell that the Leviathan was not thinking it over with those words; it was telling Kane what to do. In the gap between two sentences, Kane had gone from the Leviathan's prisoner to its agent. The door, the holographic door, slid open, leaving the real one still in place. "Proceed to the launch area. The escape pod is being readied."

"Yes!" cried the holographic Kane exultantly. "Yes!" He ran through the shadowed door.

The coruscating, brightly coloured beams faded and the laser-fed echoes from ten years before vanished.

"You have fulfilled your function," said the Leviathan. Lukyan, Tokarov and Katya all looked at Kane with horror.

"Which is the replacement?" demanded the Leviathan.

ELEVEN
MYTHICAL CREATURES

"You did this deliberately!" roared Lukyan.

"No!" Kane looked in as much shock as the others. His eyes wavered around even as he tried to explain himself, as if he were trying to deal with the present and the future simultaneously.

"Dirty Grubber…" Lukyan wanted to say something so vicious that it exceeded even his vocabulary. Instead he reached for the sidearm he'd strapped on before they'd left the mining station.

"Hold on," snapped Tokarov, grabbing his wrist. Lukyan glared at him as if to say he could be next if he liked, but Tokarov's steady eye-contact gave him pause. "If you draw that gun, the Leviathan will kill you before you've even got the safety off. Calm down. It's the only way we're going to get through this."

Lukyan slowly subsided, but the looks he gave Kane were still venomous.

"I'm sorry," said Kane hopelessly to nobody in particular, "I'm so sorry. I forgot that I ever said such a thing. I was desperate, I had to get out. I'd have said anything. I *did* say anything."

"Leviathan," rumbled Lukyan, his fury suppressed but evident, "this man here, Kane, you said he was rejected. Why?"

The reply was curt, factual and unhelpful. "Interface misphasing."

"What does that mean?"

Kane shook his head. "You're wasting your time. It doesn't understand language in the same way you do. It was never programmed to act like a thesaurus."

Lukyan turned on him. "Fine. *You* tell me then. What the blazes is 'interface misphasing'?"

"I don't think this is the time or the—"

"It's exactly the time and the place," said Lukyan, darks threats in his voice.

"It's not like we can walk out of here," said Katya. "Please, Kane. If you were rejected, we need to know why. Maybe we can make it reject all of us."

Kane heaved an exasperated sigh. "Simply put," he said with a sideways glance at Lukyan, "it means the Leviathan couldn't interface with my nervous system. It's supposed to attach itself to nerve endings and the grey and white matter of the spine and brain for full interface. For some reason my nervous system rejected it, or it rejected my nervous system. I don't know which. All I know was that the attempt was very painful." He shuddered at the memory.

Tokarov looked cynical. "You don't know why it happened?"

"No. I don't know why it happened."

"It just strikes me as strange that the Terrans should choose you to go with this extraordinary vessel…"

"I volunteered."

"Were you the only volunteer?"

Kane's lips narrowed. "No."

"Well then, *chose* you from a pool of volunteers to be part of a vital mission and entrusted this astonishing craft, the Leviathan, to you. They did all this, gave you such a responsibility and *never* tested you for compatibility with it?"

"They tested me." Kane seemed to be growing, in his own way, as angry as Lukyan under this inquisition. "I was fully compatible."

"So what went wrong when it came time to do it for real?"

Kane's voice was tight and Katya half expected him to refuse to answer or even to strike Tokarov. "If I could tell you," he hissed through clenched teeth, "I would tell you."

She was getting a little angry herself. All this bunch of so-called "adults" was doing was making enemies of one another when what they really needed to be concentrating on was how to get out alive.

"Leviathan!" Her voice sounded less impressive echoing around the chamber than she'd hoped, but it still stopped the men bickering. They looked at her in bewilderment. "When one of us is selected, what will become of the rest?"

"They will be without function. They will be stored until a function arises."

"Clarify *stored* in this context." Katya had spoken to enough artificial intelligences to know the terms it was easiest to communicate in. At the moment, the Leviathan was clever in military AI terms, but nowhere near as intelligent as it would be when it got its human... component? Victim? At the moment, it could be fooled easily enough if you were careful and clever.

"Confined to living quarters."

"Those were designed for one person," groaned Kane behind her. She ignored him.

"What if we had a function to fulfil for you? Would we be allowed to leave then?"

"That would be dependent on the priority of the utilisation."

"We will attempt to recover drone six for you," said Katya. "You cannot build new drones, each one you lose must be a serious drain on your resources. We can try and get it back."

She heard Tokarov make a pleased little "Heh!" sound and Lukyan said, "That's my niece."

"That is of utility," said the Leviathan.

"Then we can go? And try and get it for you, that is?"

The Leviathan didn't hesitate. "No."

"What?" She thought she heard herself echoed by at least two of the others. "Why not?"

"Recovery of drone six is of a lower priority than locating a replacement for Kane, Havilland. A human is required for maximum efficiency. This is the higher priority."

Katya wasn't beaten yet. "Kane, when you sat in that seat, when the interface with the Leviathan failed, were you forced into it?"

"I had no choice."

"But that Medusa sphere up there was a surprise to you just now. It didn't force you into the seat at gunpoint, so why did you sit down?"

"Because I had no choice. I couldn't leave and there was nothing else to do except grow old in here. It kept demanding I took the seat, but I was never forced to. I just…" he closed his eyes and hung his head, "…wanted to get it over with."

"Fine. Thanks." She turned to face them all. "I'll stay."

"Katya…?" said her uncle, appalled.

Kane's eyes had snapped open and he stared fiercely at her. "You must not. The process is irreversible."

Katya shook her head, they just didn't get it. "I'm *not* going to sit down in that ugly great heap of a chair. I'm just going to stay here for a while – like you did, Kane."

Tokarov was looking at her curiously. "For how long?"

They *really* didn't get it. "Until you figure out a way to rescue me, of course. I'll be fine. I'm patient."

Nobody seemed very impressed. "That's not a very good idea," said Kane, "you don't know what you're letting yourself in for."

"If you've got a brighter idea, let's hear it," she countered.

"I'll stay," said Lukyan.

"Uncle!"

"No, Katinka. You are young. I've already lived, seen a lot. Perhaps too much. I'll stay."

"What rank were you, Captain Pushkin?" asked Tokarov. "You're a veteran, aren't you?"

"I am," replied Lukyan, but he did not swell with pride the way Katya had seen in the past. His great patriotic war was starting to look like it had only been paused, not won. If the Russalkin had won, it was only through default. "I made chief petty officer."

"And you're in the reserve?"

Lukyan nodded.

"Then, by the powers vested in me by the Federal Maritime Authority, I recall you to duty, Chief Petty Officer Lukyan Pushkin."

Lukyan looked confused. "But, why?"

Tokarov smiled wearily. "Because now you're under military discipline. And I outrank you. You're not staying, Pushkin. You're leaving with Kane and Katya. That's an order."

"I…" The desperate need to find some flaw in what Lieutenant Tokarov had done was clear in Lukyan's expression just as the failure to find that flaw was evident a few moments later. "Yes. Yes, sir," he said numbly.

"Oh, no," said Katya firmly. "This was my stupid idea. I'm the one who should do it."

"As you said yourself, Ms Kuriakova, all I have to do is sit around and wait to be rescued. As long as I don't sit in *that* chair." He smiled again as he jerked his thumb at the interface chair.

Once it had its volunteer, the Leviathan released the others to return to the *Baby* so they could locate, repair and return the damaged combat drone. Even succeeding in this deceit and escaping did little to lighten their mood. Even Kane whined like an old woman about the state the craft's internal corridors were in since he had left a decade before. He had found some dirt by the door leading back into the docking bay and had carried on as if it mattered, as if the Leviathan should have spent some time spring-cleaning before deciding to kill everybody on the planet. Katya had been very glad when they'd finally managed to get him through the door and back inside the *Baby*.

Katya finished strapping herself in and, while she waited for the others to finish, looked over her shoulder at Tokarov's empty seat. "He's a brave man."

"He's paid to be brave," said Lukyan gruffly. "It's his job to be brave." He still seemed to be smarting over the way

Tokarov had outmanoeuvred him.

"I hope he realises how brave." Kane secured his restraint buckle and leaned back in his seat with an air of infinite weariness. "I'm not sure he does."

Lukyan snorted and started going through the checklist. "All he has to do is confine himself to the crew quarters and wait. He'll be fed. There are amusements there?"

Kane nodded. "Texts. Dramas. Thousands of them."

"Then he won't get bored. This is not bravery. He is in no danger."

Katya couldn't believe her ears. "Uncle? Are you serious? We have no guarantee that will ever find a way to get him out of there. He could die an old man in there. Just because nobody's shooting at him doesn't make it any less courageous. He's let himself be locked up in a prison that might never release him."

Lukyan grunted dismissively, but he couldn't meet her eyes.

The Leviathan released them from the docking bay with no ceremony, threats or reminders. It was as mundane and banal as any recorded voice in a navigational simulation. Except, Katya reminded herself as the *Baby* hummed quietly away from the immense bulk of the warship, simulations weren't likely to kill you in an instant if you got anything wrong. When they were several thousand metres away and there was no indication that they were being followed ("Not that we'd stand any chance of detecting it if we were," Kane noted with mock cheerfulness), Katya laid in a course for the moon pool entrance of the mining complex. The *Baby*'s inertial locator indicated that the Leviathan had been moving away from the site in a neutral direction the whole time they'd been aboard. Apparently it had lost interest in the *Novgorod*, the *Vodyanoi* and their crews.

Katya knew appearances could be deceptive and that a machine-mind like the Leviathan's would not abandon its attack simply because it had grown bored with it. Everything was organised in priorities, complex relationships of function against requirements. If it had left, it was because there was something more pressing that it was going to apply itself to. She wondered what that might be, with a sense of dread.

Unexpectedly, the communications channel crackled into life making them all jump. "*Vodyanoi* to minisub *Pushkin's Baby*. Do you read me? Come in, please."

Lukyan toggled open a channel. "Pushkin here. Who is this?"

Katya reached across and patched her own headset into the link. "Katya here, Lieutenant Petrov. Good to hear your voice again."

Abruptly she had her headset pulled off. She started to protest but then saw the anger in Kane's face as he put it on. "Kane here, Petrov. Making yourself comfortable aboard my boat, are you?"

"Quite comfortable, Captain Kane. She's an interesting vessel."

"Let me speak to Tasya this instant!"

There was a moment's pause, then, "Calm down, Havilland."

"Tasya?"

"Yes." Her calming voice filled the cabin. "It's all right. We have an agreement. When it looked like the Leviathan was going to leave us alone, we went back to the moon pool. It hadn't touched the *Vodyanoi*, so we piled in and got out while we still could."

"But Petrov—"

"Relax. We don't have enough people left to man the boat at battle stations, not after those damn drones cut half of them down. Between our attack on them and some of their people running into the drone in the tunnels, there're not a lot of the Feds left either. We think there must have been more than one drone; maybe as many as three or four. The upshot is that neither we nor the Feds have got enough people left to properly crew a boat by themselves. Working together, we can do it."

"And this agreement?"

"They don't try and take control or try to arrest us, any nonsense like that. We don't kill them and dump them in deep waters. When this is over, we drop them somewhere safe and sound. The enemy is the Leviathan. I think we can all agree about that."

Kane frowned, but only as an expression of his reluctance to accept the reasonable. "Well, where are you then?"

"About a hundred metres behind you. We've been shadowing you for the last couple of minutes."

"What? What for?"

"Just to make sure the Leviathan was keeping its distance before we hailed you. Are you ready to be taken aboard?"

Lukyan didn't seem any happier than Kane about the way things had moved on in their absence, but neither could he deny the practicality of it. He spoke with a coldness verging on ill-grace. "Slowing to five knots. Level and steady."

They waited in taut silence for almost a minute before the *Baby* started to be buffeted by the turbulence of the *Vodyanoi*'s open salvage maw. It became worse as they were slowly overtaken and engulfed by the gaping mouth and then, abruptly, it became very calm. Lukyan cut the engines without comment and sat with his arms folded as the maw closed around them.

Petrov's first words when they reached the *Vodyanoi*'s bridge were, "Where's Tokarov?" While Lukyan explained, with the occasional clarification from Kane, Katya looked around the boat's bridge with interest.

It was very alien to anything she'd ever seen before. The whole philosophy of design was different from FMA or civil boats, all of which, of course, came from the same yards. Where a federal boat like – the poor *Novgorod*, for example – had all the crew stations ranged around the main screen, the *Vodyanoi* contained niches for most of the bridge officers, each with their own small screens. Only the captain's position – a much more imposing seat with armrests imbedded with repeater displays and communications controls – the weapons officer, and the helm faced a modestly sized but high definition main viewer. It was so unlike anything in her experience, there was only one thing it could be.

"This is a Grubber boat, isn't it?" she asked Kane.

"Hmm?" He turned from listening to Lukyan's conversation with Petrov. "A what?"

"This is from Earth, isn't it? It's a Terran vessel?"

He raised his eyebrows in mild surprise, as if he'd thought they'd been talking about kelp all along and had only just realised his mistake. "The *Vodyanoi*? Why, yes. She was built on Earth and transported here." He smiled. "She's not very big, at least by Earth standards – about equivalent to a frigate if that means anything to you – but you'll appreciate the problems of transporting anything of any size over the best part of fifty light years. She was originally the *Raleigh*, but it seemed altogether too noble a name for a... well, you know."

Katya had no idea who Raleigh was, but she guessed he wouldn't have been happy to have a pirate ship named after him.

"So I renamed her the *Vodyanoi*. It seemed appropriate."

"Did it?" said Katya. She had no idea who "Vodyanoi" was either.

"Yes." He looked at her closely. "You don't know what a vodyanoi is, do you?"

"Why should I?"

"Because your ancestors were Russian."

"I've heard that. I don't know what it means." She saw the shock on Kane's face and added spitefully, "And I don't care either. Russians are Grubbers. We're Russalkin now."

Kane looked at her seriously, then walked over to an unoccupied crew position and gestured to her to sit by him. Reluctantly she complied.

"Don't throw away your past, Katya." He spoke with quiet emphasis. "As a race, we're built from memories. There's an old saying: those who don't learn from the mistakes of history are doomed to repeat them. You're too intelligent to do that."

"You don't know anything about me."

"More than you know about me, I assure you. These Russians, whose memory you so lightly cast aside, they came here on a trip that took years, putting all their hopes and fears into one great gamble, that they could make a home here on this world. Things were starting to deteriorate on Earth, they could see that. You're a product of their fondest wishes."

"So?" She was sounding like a little girl again, Katya thought.

"So, they brought Earth with them. Don't you know why this world is called Russalka? The Russalki were water nymphs from Russian folklore, beautiful and clever. Your ancestors didn't miraculously become Russalkin as soon as they'd shaken the dust of Terra from their feet, you know. They saw this planet in the view screens as they approached and they saw a new home, but they could never forget their old one. Don't you honour them enough to at least understand that?"

Katya felt awkward and confused. Two halves of her were at war: one side that knew full well that her great grandparents had come from Earth, that they had been good people and she quite literally owed them everything for their bravery in making such a long and dangerous journey; the other that could see the history files of the atrocities that the Grubbers had heaped upon Russalka when they had invaded, and knew that Earth was a festering heap of evil – rapacious and violent – that took what it wanted and didn't mind how many died to get it. She wanted to hate the Terrans. That would be easiest. Why did Kane insist on making everything so difficult?

"I renamed this boat the *Vodyanoi* for a couple of reasons," he was saying. "I think both of them are good. In Russian mythology, the vodyanoi were the husbands of the Russalki. It seemed, I don't know, *poetic* to me. Things are difficult here; even before the war they were difficult. I thought a little poetry wouldn't go amiss. The other reason is because of what the vodyanoi looked like. They could change their form. A handsome young man one second, a

hideous ogre the next. They travelled in the water, sometimes above it. They were neither one thing nor the other.
This boat is a little like that. Once it was a legal warboat of
one world. Now it's a very illegal pirate vessel on another.
Few vessels can claim to have a history like that. Quite the
sea change." He laughed a little but quickly sobered. "I don't
suppose you know any Shakespeare either?" He took her
blank expression for agreement. "No poetry here. None at
all."

Tasya had walked in close to the beginning of Kane's
explanations and had been listening intently with Petrov.
"You say that as if it's a surprise to you, Kane," she said and
then, as if to prove her point, said to Petrov, "what are your
thoughts about the Leviathan, lieutenant?"

"Tokarov's in danger every minute he's aboard that…
vessel. We have to think of some way to get him out safely.
How we do that, I have no idea. I'll have to think on it."
He turned towards Kane. "One thing that interests me,
though, is why that thing rejected you. You must have
been hand-picked. It doesn't make sense that you were
incompatible."

Kane shrugged and looked away, but Katya saw the
same hunted expression she'd noticed in him aboard the
Leviathan. He looked like a cornered animal, and she
didn't believe him when he said, "I don't know. The selection process was governmentally organised. Stupid
mistakes are virtually guaranteed." Petrov narrowed his
eyes, making her think that he didn't believe Kane either.

Tasya didn't seem to care. She was already mulling over
rescue plans. "Sensors," she demanded crisply. "Where is
the Leviathan now?"

The *Vodyanoi*'s own sensor officer must have died in the

mining base as the position was taken by the *Novgorod*'s. If he resented taking orders from a pirate, he showed no sign of it. "Whatever its stealth capability, it's not using it. Between passive sonar and the amount of noise it's making manoeuvring, I'm having no trouble tracking it."

Something Kane had said suddenly came back to Katya. If it had been impractical to transport submarines much larger that the *Vodyanoi* or the *Raleigh* or whatever you wanted to call it, how could the Leviathan then be explained? It dwarfed the *Vodyanoi*, but it had been brought the huge distance from Earth. How large a transporter starship would that have required? It boggled the imagination. She made up her mind to ask him the next chance she got. After Petrov's pointed comments, Kane seemed in no mood to answer any more questions for the moment.

Tasya had taken the captain's seat with no argument from Kane. He had claimed to be captain, but Katya thought it looked more like they took turns at being captain and first officer. "What course is it on?" Tasya asked.

"Nothing you can really call a course, ma'am. It was running slow but steadily north while the *Baby* minisub was aboard, but now..." he quickly punched a few keys and the main display echoed his own station's display. A blip labelled Leviathan was tracing out lazy loops and zigzags in the ocean. "Now it's lost all direction. It just seems to be wandering about."

There was some puzzled mutterings from the other crew positions. Tasya cut across it. "Is it searching for something?"

"That's no search pattern I've ever seen. It really does seem to be dawdling about. It's as if it doesn't know what to do next."

"It's a machine," snapped Kane, his tiredness flashing into irritation. "It doesn't 'dawdle.' If it's got nothing to do, it does nothing." He watched the blip draw a lazy "S" on the screen. "I do not like this. There's no reason for this behaviour." Suddenly remembering something, he reached inside his jacket and produced a grimy handkerchief. He looked at it closely for a few seconds, said, "If you'll all excuse me, I'll be in my cabin," and left the bridge.

Tasya barely gave him a sideways glance as he left. "He has these little episodes," she said to nobody in particular. Turning her attention back to the display, her eyes narrowed. "We should consider what to do next. I doubt it will wander around like this for much longer."

"You could try attacking it," said Lukyan.

Katya sat up, astonished he could say such a thing. "Lieutenant Tokarov's still aboard, uncle!"

Her uncle looked at her grimly and she read something she didn't like in his expression. Looking at Tasya and Petrov, they too had it. "You think he's already as good as dead, don't you?" she said, accusation in her voice.

"From what your uncle's told me," said Tasya, "that *thing* won't release him unless he gets a better candidate and perhaps not even then. I'd love to go in there with guns blazing and get him out, but we'd all be dead before we even got close. If the opportunity to rescue him arises, that's well and good. Otherwise, we count him among the dead."

Petrov's lips thinned but didn't argue with her. Katya couldn't believe this; after what he'd done to save them, they were just going to abandon him?

"Katya," said Lukyan, "try to understand. He knew perfectly well he wasn't going to be getting out. What he did, it was like fighting a rearguard action. He got us and the information we gathered out of there. If we try and rescue him, the Leviathan will kill us all and then there will nobody to stand in its way and he will *still* be trapped."

Tasya was looking thoughtful. "The IFF box would get us in again," said Tasya, reluctantly. "There's a good chance of it, anyway. We didn't do anything to antagonise it last time, so it won't have learned not to trust that way of approaching it. It would be a risk, but I think we could get away with it once more. If we do try it, then, it had better be with a plan because there won't be a third visit."

Katya felt torn. Of course she wanted to get Tokarov out if it was at all possible, but the memory of that black featureless eye of the Medusa made her cold with dread. "Once we're in, we're bound to upset it, though," she said, "and that Medusa sphere will punch us full of holes. You didn't see it, it never stops tracking you."

Tasya gave her a complacent look. "Then the plan had better cover that too, hadn't it? Believe me, girl, I have no desire to enter that monstrosity without a fighting chance of getting out again. If we can't find a plan to beat the Leviathan's security system, we have no plan at all."

Lukyan hushed them both by pointing at the main screen. "Look at this."

The passive track of the Leviathan had been replaced by a slowly spinning computer model. "Is that the Leviathan?" breathed Tasya. Katya belatedly remembered that none of the *Vodyanoi*'s crew had actually seen the Leviathan; that dubious pleasure had belonged only to the *Novgorod*'s, as it had swept past them before attacking.

"Yes, ma'am," replied the sensor operator from his position. "The amount of passive sound energy out there is just about giving us enough information to get an idea what the whole thing looks like. I'm running the data through the sonar imaging suite and making a few guesses to help it come up with something that's fairly accurate. At least, I think it's more accurate. What do you think?"

Submarines, by their very nature, don't tend to look very interesting to the eye and the larger they get, the more streamlined and featureless they become. The *Baby* was a minisub and its hull was busy with waldo arms and lighting mounts, all finished in a yellow and black livery. The Leviathan, by stark contrast, was so smooth it seemed organic. Long gentle curves that rolled like titanium surf across the machine-monster's hull before being lost in tapering aft surfaces. It seemed wrong that it didn't have a tail or fins. It reminded Katya of the tiny amorphous creatures that the manta whales fed upon, filtering them from the seas of Russalka. As if a tiny protozoan had been frozen in a single languidly elegant form and then made colossal.

"Where are its drive ports?" asked Petrov stepping closer to the display to peer at the details.

"That's a mystery, sir. I can't find anything that might be drive systems. No drive ports, impeller tubes or even an old fashioned sea screw. I'm not even picking up engine noise; what ambient sound it's creating is all being caused simply by the water travelling over the hull at speed. Microcavitation effects. That's why the image has so much guesswork in it. It's just not making the amount of noise something that big should be."

A possible explanation jumped into Katya's head, but she didn't consider voicing it until it had become plausible. By the time it had reached that point, however, it was suggesting some other possibilities about the Leviathan. These corollaries bothered her for a moment and she mentally went to swat them away. Then she stopped herself. Suddenly, she could see the explanation for some other little details that had been bothering her.

"Are you all right?" said Lukyan. "You look terrible, like you'd seen a ghost."

She almost laughed, but she knew it would have sounded hysterical. She wished she *had* seen a ghost. What she had just deduced was much, much worse.

"I... I'm fine, Uncle Lukyan. I... May I be excused?" She left without waiting for anybody to say yes or no. She walked aft looking for the officers' cabins. Only Kane could tell her if she was right. But, a small voice inside her asked, if it *is* true, then this is something he has deliberately concealed. Why? And what will he do when he knows you know his secret?

TWELVE
SIN BOTTLE

She didn't even have to ask her way; the doors were labelled. In less time than she would have liked, she was standing in front of one of the *Vodyanoi*'s executive officers' staterooms, the door simply labelled *KANE*. She stood indecisively for a long moment, wondering whether it would be better to suggest her idea to the others back on the bridge. It would be so much easier to put the problem into somebody else's hands. But... she looked at the name plate again. Kane knew it all. If she came here from the bridge leading a mob, he'd shut up and claim ignorance.

There was something going on within him, some aspect of all this that was torturing him. He'd believed the Leviathan was gone and arranged his life accordingly. Now it was back and it thought the war was still on. He wanted to stop the Leviathan, she was sure of it, but the damage was already done. People knew too much about him for his own security and comfort. Even if they stopped the Leviathan, what would he do next?

The Leviathan, she scolded herself. It will cause untold misery and death. You need to know what Kane knows and you need to know it now. She knocked, waited a second, and entered.

Perhaps she should have waited until he'd asked her to come in. She found him in a frenzy of concealment, throwing an awkward handful of things into an open desk drawer and slamming it shut. Something stopped the drawer closing completely and he slammed it twice more in frustration before pushing the obstruction down inside and finally getting the drawer shut. He turned to Katya and spoke with false calmness.

"How can I help you, Ms Kuriakova?"

Katya pointed at the closed drawer. "What was that?"

"None of your concern. Now, what…"

"It was a syringe, a pressure syringe."

He looked at the drawer and then back at her. "You're mistaken."

"I had to train to use those things for the paramedic certification on my officer's card. Don't treat me like some idiot off the corridors, Kane. I know a pressure syringe when I see one."

"I don't care what… Wait!"

Katya, anger growing in her, had stepped the two short steps needed to take her across the small stateroom to the desk and jerked it open. It was a syringe all right, and nestling against it was a slim loading-bottle of an inky black fluid. It had no label. It didn't need one. She snatched up the syringe. The dose chamber was empty, but there were still the faint traces of black fluid there. She turned on Kane, her anger becoming fury. "You!" She almost screamed it. They'd trusted so much to him and all the time… this. "You're a waster!" She flung the syringe at him. It bounced off his chest and fell into his lap.

He looked at it sadly, as if somebody had just flung a gift back in his face. He picked it up and put it back into the drawer, slowly and carefully this time. He slid the drawer shut and looked at her. "Ms Kuriakova. Katya... this isn't what you think."

Not what she thought? Ever since she'd been born, a loathing of wasters had been drilled into her. It was inconceivable to her why anybody should want to corrupt their bodies with drugs just for a brief... what? A release from reality? Why? Reality was all there was. Russalka society tolerated alcohol, but it was controlled to levels that would have appalled their ancestors. Russalka was as unforgiving as the hard vacuum of space. Being drunk could kill you. Being tired could kill you. Hell's teeth, even being momentarily distracted could kill you. Not just you, either. With such a small overall population, everybody had a weight to carry for everybody else. Every Russalkin shouldered responsibility, and they shouldered it young. Deliberately using drugs was a dereliction of that responsibility and that could not, *would* not be countenanced. She'd heard tales of men from the early days of the colony, bad men, who'd tried to make themselves rich by supplying drugs, creating wasters and so creating their own little herd of criminals who needed the next little bottle of stolen or illegally synthesised narcotics more than they needed their pride. These bad men, so the stories went, ended up inside airlocks without breathing gear while grim-faced citizens on the other side of the door cycled open the outer lock and let in Russalka's implacable ocean. After a very short while, there were no bad men left.

Kane seemed to know pathetic it would sound but he said it anyway. "It's not what you think. It's medicinal."

"In an unmarked bottle? How stupid do you think I am?" His weakness earlier, his collapse aboard the *Novgorod*, it all made sense to her now. He must have been unable to use his "medicine" since the FMA captured him. With the trouble in the mining site, unable to get back to this stateroom and the bottle it held, every minute must have stretched on unbearably with his addiction gnawing away at him. Finally, the withdrawal symptoms had become too much and he'd passed out, reducing him to a doddering wreck first.

"There are different types of medicine. You think I'm a waster. Technically, I suppose you're right, but there's more to it than that."

Katya waved his explanations away. "I don't want to hear it," she said, moving towards the door.

"Where are you going?"

"Where do you think I'm going? I'm going to tell my uncle and Lieutenant Petrov that maybe everything you've told us is garbage. For all we know, it was the filth in that bottle talking."

"I've told you the truth." He was quiet, firm, as if convincing her was the only thing that mattered.

She laughed bitterly. "The whole truth?"

"I've told you the truth," he insisted. "You want more of it? Then listen."

They looked at each other in silence for a minute. Then Katya drew the chair out from under the chair and sat down, facing Kane as he sat on his bunk. "Okay," she said, exuding cynicism. "I'm listening."

Kane suddenly seemed uncertain what he was going to say. Making up his mind, he opened the drawer and took out the loading-bottle. The thick black liquid sloshed lazily inside.

"I'm going to have to fill in a few details first. You need to know exactly what this stuff is to understand. To understand why I have to use it. You don't know much about Earth, do you? That blasted war closed the door on your roots for you and your contemporaries. If you're anything to go by, the Russalkin don't much care for their old world."

"Why should we? You invaded us! You wanted to bring your dirty, wasteful ways here and, when we wouldn't just let you stroll in to take what you wanted, you invaded!"

"Did we? Somebody once said that history belongs to the victor. As I think I've already told you, that war was never won one way or the other. Earth just decided it was too expensive. The Leviathan was their last shot. When it was lost, they just gave the whole thing up as a bad job. You didn't win a war; you just won a battle at most. Earth hasn't finished with Russalka yet. The failure of the Leviathan to exterminate the lot of you has given you some breathing time, which – incidentally – you can thank me for."

Katya looked at him with disgust. "I should thank you for being a reject? I was there, remember? I heard what the Leviathan said about you. You were as useless to the Leviathan as you are to us now. I'm not sure thanks would be enough. Maybe we should throw you a big state banquet or something for services to redundancy."

"Such sarcasm in one so young," Kane said wryly. "Yes, the Leviathan rejected me. Yes, that saved your world, at least it has for the last ten years. But Petrov was right. I was extensively tested. I was compatible." He held up the bottle again, rolling it slightly to make the viscous fluid lap against the glass walls. "This stuff is called Sin. There's a complicated literary reason for calling it that; I won't bore you with it. Just some biochemist with pretensions of grandeur coming up with a smart-arse name. It *is* a narcotic in the strict dictionary definition. It *is* incredibly addictive; one dose normally causes full dependency. As a way of having a good time, it rates slightly lower than having your eyes burnt out with red-hot wire loops. The first dose you have will make you a little light-headed, probably nauseous too. After that, you feel nothing at all when you take it. You might as well be giving yourself a shot of sterile saline."

Katya was wondering how good her understanding of the wasters' vice was. "I thought the idea was it made you feel good?"

"Not Sin. It's the ultimate progression of what drug dealers want in a drug. Total dependency. Sin doesn't make you feel good; it addicts you, and then, if you don't get regular doses, it kills you." He looked at the bottle with a strange expression somewhere between loathing and longing. "Sin was never created to give wasters some pathetic escape from reality. It was created to enslave. The Terran government, when Earth finally got one after the collapse, commissioned this stuff. One injection and you've got a slave for life. It doesn't affect the performance of their duties, but if they don't get another dose when the last one starts to wear off, they descend into Hell, one ring at a time. It's indescribable, foul. Nobody willingly takes this stuff, Katya."

She looked at him, her mouth open in shock. Her anger of only a few minutes ago had quite gone, replaced by pity and disbelief that people could do such a thing to another human being. "Before you came, they used it on you? To make you obey orders?"

He was surprised. "Heavens, no. This stuff was banned

sixty years ago." He smiled wanly at her obvious confusion. "I managed to secure a copy of the formula and synthesised it before I left Earth. Katya, I used it on myself." He put the bottle away before continuing. "It was my insurance policy. When I left Earth, I had visions of what Russalka would be like. A colony world fallen into barbarism, people capable of the most brutal, merciless things. That's what I believed when I offered myself to the Leviathan programme. As the day came closer, I started having doubts. I wasn't sure if I'd want to be a part of such a devastating attack if it turned out the situation wasn't right. I wasn't a soldier, you see. My motives… it wasn't patriotism. So, I made Sin and smuggled it aboard." He frowned as he thought back. "Russalka wasn't anything like I'd expected. I just found a hardy race of survivors trying to hang on. This should never have come to a war. There should have been negotiations, we should have sent diplomats, tried to salvage something from the mess. Instead we sent ships and troops and certain death in the form of the Leviathan. If I let it interface with me, I had no idea what it would do to me. My personality might have been destroyed, my doubts about the war lost. I had to escape."

Katya nodded slowly. She was beginning to understand. "And the only way you could get away was to be rejected. So you used the Sin, knowing it would interfere with the interfacing process."

Kane leaned back against the bulkhead and crossed his arms. "You *are* clever. Everybody says so."

"But, the addiction..?"

"Permanent."

"There must have been some other way," she protested, "some other drug?"

He shook his head. "No. Believe me. I researched it very thoroughly. If anything else could have done the trick reliably, I'd have used it. It had to be that stuff, though. You can imagine how I felt when I finished the database search and only *that*…" he nodded at the drawer, "…would do. I was going to be sacrificed one way or the other. The only question was would I be sacrificed to Sin or the Leviathan?" He paused. "That sounds very biblical, doesn't it?"

"So, you really did stop the Leviathan?"

"Without undue modesty, yes, I did. I wish I could have done it by just pulling out a fuse or by pissing through a transformer cover but, as you saw, the Leviathan is very touchy about letting people near its vitals." He stopped, thoughtful. Then he reached into his jacket pocket. "Which brings me onto *this*."

Before he could show Katya what he had, the communicator mounted on the wall clicked into life. "Kane?" It was Tasya's voice, sounding distracted and puzzled. "Come to the bridge immediately." She'd broken the connection before Kane had a chance to reply and he glared at the communicator with frustration.

"It's always something, isn't it?" he said peevishly to Katya and his theatrical irritation made her smile. "Come on, you're as much a part of all this as anyone."

As she followed him out of the cabin, she noticed on a bookshelf by the door the small maser pistol she'd used to hold Kane at gunpoint aboard the *Novgorod*. It felt strange and unexpected to see it abandoned like that and, acting on an impulse she barely understood, she picked it up and slipped it in her pocket.

● ● ● ●

On the bridge, Tasya was in the captain's chair. She made no effort to relinquish it when Kane entered, but neither did he make any move towards it, instead perching on the edge of an inactive console. "Well, what's so fascinating?"

Tasya nodded at the main screen. "Our large lumbering friend has developed a sense of direction again."

Katya was already looking at the screen as Tasya spoke. The Leviathan had, indeed, pulled itself out of the doldrums and was travelling with a definite sense of purpose. But, she noticed, it wasn't heading north towards Lemuria. Instead, it was heading roughly easterly, perhaps eighty degrees. "Where's it going?"

"Not sure yet, Ms," said the sensors operator. "Working on it."

Katya looked around and saw the navigator's position was empty. She knew the *Novgorod*'s navigator had died in the pirate attack. It seemed that the pirates had lost their own to the combat drone. Without asking permission, she sat at the post and pulled on the headset. Behind her Tasya shot a glance at Kane, who just smiled slightly and shrugged.

Katya took a few moments to familiarise herself with the layout of the position's interface and a few moments more to reorganise it to her liking. The Terran-designed interface wasn't hugely different from its Russalkin counterpart, but that was hardly surprising. There had to be a point where the interface couldn't be improved much further and all versions would tend towards that. The only thing she could think of that might move it on would be interfacing directly with the computer. An image of the Leviathan's interface throne loomed in her mind and she pushed it away, nauseated. No, she'd stick with the sort of interface you could walk away from afterwards.

She requested the sensor data via her console and fed it to the navigational systems. It was simple stuff; she'd done far more complicated plots to get her card. When she was satisfied she'd got it right, she issued the data to the main screen. A relief map of Russalka sprang up upon the screen. Marked in exaggerated size was the *Vodyanoi* and, not nearly so exaggerated, the Leviathan, the pair hanging between the submerged mountain ranges like airships traversing a valley. Katya tapped in a command and a red line sprang out of the Leviathan's prow, streaking away until it was lost off the edge of the screen. Katya pulled back the viewpoint, further and further until some objects appeared, the red line of the Leviathan's projected path running neatly through the tight cluster. Katya selected them and zoomed rapidly in.

Kane slowly stood, his face grim. "That would make a lot of sense."

Tasya stood too, but her expression was in stark contrast to Kane's. Where he seemed sanguine, she was horrified. "The Yagizba Enclaves!"

Katya could see Kane's point, but she couldn't move herself to feel empathy with Tasya. The Yagizba Enclaves were a confederation of floating towns. The fact they spent most of their time on Russalka's angry surface was strange enough when they could withdraw easily to the serene depths, but the Yagizban also bore reputations of arrogance and vile eccentricities. They were, however, also the production powerhouses for the whole planet. In their robot factories were built almost all the machines that the submarine communities depended upon. Yes, there were other production facilities elsewhere, but Yagizban technology was of a consistently high quality and reasonably priced. When the war against Earth had opened, their floating cities had been obvious targets, especially since the Enclaves were the only serious users of aircraft and had floating airstrips dotted around the seas. The first Terran attacks had sunk every one of the airstrips and two of the smaller towns before the others had managed to flood their ballast tanks and sink to a safe depth of their own volition and choosing.

The Yagizban had been the backbone of the resistance, supplying boats and war materiel wherever it was needed. Towards the end, however, even their resources had drawn thin. It was just as well, Katya reflected, that the Terrans' had drawn even thinner.

The Enclaves had remained aloof from the victory celebrations when the embattled Russalkin finally realised that the Terrans had given up. They had pulled together what floating towns they had left and moved off to rebuild. Now they held their distance from the rest of the planet's settlements, supplying technology as they had always done and being paid in resources but never going any further towards integrating themselves. Uncle Lukyan called them a strange people. Katya had heard others call them much worse.

She zoomed in still further until the mapping image resolved into a cluster of five main domes and perhaps eight smaller ones. The red line ran unerringly right through the middle of the group. "It means to destroy our main means of production."

"It would seem so." Despite his words, Kane seemed unconvinced. "Lemuria can breathe easy, at least for the moment." He rubbed his chin and stared at the screen, deep in thought.

"If it attacks them, we've lost before we start," said Tasya. Her face was taut with some emotion. Concern? Indecision? Fear? Katya couldn't identify it, but she would never have expected it on the Chertovka's face, whatever it was. Even from their brief acquaintance, Tasya had only ever seemed to run from grim determination to grim humour. "We have to warn them."

"We can't, Tasya," said Kane gently. "You know we can't."

"Why not?" said Katya.

Kane turned and spoke abruptly, angered at her breaking into his conversation. "Because we don't carry a long wave array. Who would we want to talk to? And if we use a narrow-beam submarine transmission, it will go straight past the Leviathan who will certainly intercept it and probably jam it. If we're lucky, that's all it would do."

Katya decided not to ask what might happen if they were unlucky. Instead, she turned back to her console, trying to hide the fact that her cheeks had turned red. Kane had been right to bark at her, she knew; butting in like that had just made her look like a big-mouthed kid.

She busied herself with the navigational data, trying to take her mind off what an idiot she was. She concentrated on plotting and replotting the Leviathan's course, on the small chance that she had made some sort of childish mistake in her earlier plots, but no. Every time she went through the stages, the red line still struck neatly through the middle of the Enclaves. It was a sharp piece of navigating on the part of the Leviathan, she thought. Considering that the Yagizba Enclaves weren't even permanently anchored...

A horrible thought occurred to her. *The Yagizba Enclaves weren't permanently anchored.* Ten years ago, they'd been in an entirely different part of the Russalkin ocean.

"Hail the Leviathan." Kane's sudden order cut across her train of thought and she looked up at him in confusion.

"What?" Lukyan roused himself from where he'd been leaning against the wall looking over the sensor officer's shoulder. "Are you mad? You've said yourself that monstrosity is trigger-happy. If an active sonar ping is enough to put it on the warpath, what will it make of a tight-beam transmission right up its baffles?"

Kane looked seriously at him. "I am very much afraid, *very* much afraid that the situation has changed, and not for the better. Communications, hail the Leviathan."

The communications officer looked at him uncertainly and looked back at Tasya for confirmation. She seemed worried herself, not the confident and commanding personality Katya was used to at all. Finally she nodded quickly, as if wanting the act over and done with.

With obvious misgivings, the communications officer opened a channel. "Leviathan from *Vodyanoi*, Leviathan from *Vodyanoi*. Come in, please."

"Put it on the speakers," ordered Kane. Immediately the bridge was filled with the gentle hiss of an empty communications channel, rising and falling slowly. They listened in silence for almost a minute before Kane ordered another hail.

No happier than last time, the communications officer complied. "Leviathan from *Vodyanoi*, Leviathan from *Vodyanoi*. Are you receiving, please?"

Silence was the only reply. Kane waited impatiently. After a minute there was still no response. "Sensors, any change in the Leviathan's speed and heading?" The sensors officer shook his head without looking away from his instruments. On Katya's console, the red line never wavered.

Kane grunted with frustration. "Hail it again."

The communications officer looked beseechingly at Tasya, but she only nodded curtly. For the third time, he sent a hail.

This time, Leviathan spoke.

"This is... is Leviath..." The rest of the sentence seemed to fade away. They waited for a moment, but nothing more came.

"Hail it again," said Kane slowly, brooking no argument.

"Leviathan from *Vodyanoi*, Leviathan from..."

"This... is... Lev... i... a..." Every syllable seemed to be a gargantuan effort. Katya listened to it with a mixture of trepidation and hope. Perhaps Tokarov had somehow managed to sabotage it. Even its voice, so controlled and sterile before, seemed shot through now with uncertainty and, what was that? Fear? Fear; now she realised it had been fear on Tasya's face. How odd. But not as odd as a machine showing fear. That was so...

"Oh no," she said out loud. "Oh no!"

The voice of the Leviathan continued, still halting, but becoming stronger now. "This is... Leviath... This... This... is... *I*... I *am*..."

Katya couldn't speak anymore. Her hands were over her mouth in revulsion and terror and in pity. Kane's eyes were shut as he awaited the inevitable.

"I..." the machine's voice was strong now, certain, "... am..." and it contained tones and undertones that had never been programmed into it.

"Tokarov," said Kane. "You fool."

And the machine that was now more than a machine

and the human who was now less than a human spoke as one, filling the bridge with their unified voice.

"I AM LEVIATHAN!"

THIRTEEN

VODYANOI

Through nameless waters, the *Vodyanoi* pursued the Leviathan. Near her maximum speed, although still comfortably short of what they knew the Leviathan was capable, the *Vodyanoi* struggled to maintain sensor contact. If it had wanted to, the Leviathan could have shaken them off in a minute either through accelerating or by performing its feat of near invisible stealth and vanishing from the passive sonar screens. Yet it did neither, as if contemptuous of anything the little *Vodyanoi* could throw against it.

Kane had called an immediate council of war with Tasya, Petrov, and even Uncle Lukyan. Katya, however, had been excluded. She felt she should have been insulted, but instead felt oddly relieved. She had hardly had a moment to herself since the *Baby* had left the locks. And how long ago had that been? She was losing track of time. Two days ago? Three? Brief moments of sleep had broken the time into awkward irregular lumps of recollection, and she longed to simply put her head down and sleep eight hours at a stretch so she could start counting days once more. She'd never thought that something as simple as a handful of hours sleep could mean so much to her.

Now she had a little while to collect her thoughts and stop pretending to have all the answers. On the one hand she was flattered that intelligent men like Kane and Petrov thought she, too, was intelligent. On the other, she just wanted to be divorced from responsibility for a little while. Just for a few minutes, she wanted to be fifteen-almost-sixteen again.

She found the senior officers' mess, or what would have been the senior officer's mess if the *Vodyanoi* still had any senior officers after the carnage at the mining complex. She thought it was empty at first and stepped in. By the time she realised her mistake it was too late to back out. Suhkalev was sitting in the corner at the far end of the bench at the table.

She hadn't seen him at all since they'd arrived at the mine's northern docking area and, she realised with a small shock, hadn't thought of him at all since then either. Despite their successful sally against the Leviathan's combat drone, he'd fallen completely off her list of things and people to worry about. She felt slightly ashamed for that and sat down on the opposing bench at the end nearest the door. She might spend a little time with him, but that didn't mean it had to be spent very close to him.

He managed a wan smile as she sat. "I hear you've been having adventures. Been aboard the Leviathan." He shook his head. "What's happening there? Something to do with Lieutenant Tokarov. Nobody will give me a straight answer."

Katya sighed. This was going to be difficult. Slowly, as much to explain recent events to herself as him, she went through the recent developments, the nature of the Leviathan's artificial intelligence, its capability for synthetic intelligence and the fact that this capability had now been achieved. She didn't explain why Kane had been unsuitable as the seed from which the Leviathan's synthetic intelligence had been intended to grow ten years before. That was Kane's business. She half wished she didn't know about it either.

When she had finished, Suhkalev didn't seem very much the wiser. "So the Leviathan must have absorbed Lieutenant Tokarov against his will?"

"Not according to Kane. The Leviathan was never programmed to expect anybody but a volunteer. The lieutenant would have had to sit in the interface chair himself."

Suhkalev looked at her dubiously. "But the way you tell it, it's suicide. Why would he do it after only a few hours? I can imagine a man doing it if he was trapped in there for months and months..." Like Kane had been, thought Katya. "...but he was only in there for, what? Three hours? Why would he do it?"

Katya shrugged; she had no idea. She wasn't the only one.

The first thing Kane had asked Petrov as soon as the communications channel with the Leviathan was closed was, "Lieutenant Petrov, you know Tokarov best here. In your opinion, is he, *was* he sane?"

Petrov had not hesitated. "He's a good officer, a rock solid man. I've entrusted my life to him on more than one occasion in the past. I would have done so again without any reservations. I cannot explain why he has done this." For once, even Petrov's cool demeanour seemed shaken. "I cannot explain it at all."

All she could offer Suhkalev was, "Maybe we can board the Leviathan again, try and find out what happened."

"You think it will let you?"

"Maybe. We can barely keep up with it at the moment, though, and the *Vodyanoi*'s a fast boat. The *Baby* wouldn't have a chance. Anyway," she said, changing the subject, "how are you? Aren't the Novgorods talking to you still?"

"They're not so bad, now. I think helping to kill that drone and get its IFF unit got me some respect. They're glad a Fed was involved, even if it was just some punk from base security."

"You can't blame them. Secor mainly draws from the bases." She looked at him, trying to work him out. "Why'd you join base security in the first place? You know everybody hates them."

"Fast career track. I wouldn't mind ending up in Secor. You're bright, you must have thought of it."

"Hah!" she laughed sarcastically. "For about half a second!" She could see him flushing with humiliation and made an effort to tone down her contempt. "Oh, c'mon. People are scared of Secor. I don't want to scare people. It doesn't matter how good the job is; they've got reputations out of horror stories. You can't want that."

He didn't answer her or even meet her eyes. Her shoulders sagged with dismay. "That's a selling point with you, is it? Look," she got up to leave, "Suhkalev, there are better ways to get respect. What you did in the mine workings, staying cool getting that machine working with the drone bearing down on us, that was brave. That's got you some respect. Real respect, not that fake stuff that Secor have. That's just fear by another name. If that's all you want, be my guest. I think you're a better man than that."

She left the officers' mess and headed back to the small cabin she'd been given wondering whether her words had made any impact at all.

She managed ninety minutes sleep before her cabin's communicator woke her with a request to go to the bridge. She was too sleepy to be sure, but she thought it sounded like Kane. Why couldn't everybody just leave her alone? She struggled back into the *Novgorod* uniform coverall – which wasn't fitting her any better than when she'd gone to sleep, she was disappointed to note – and headed forward to the bridge while she tried to remember the last time she'd eaten.

On entering the bridge, she was greeted by Kane who'd reclaimed the captain's chair. She was rather more pleased to see the plate of sandwiches from the galley than she was to see him and helped herself with only the briefest of requests and no waiting for an answer.

Kane let her eat in silence for a couple of minutes before speaking. "I thought you might like to know what we've decided to do, Katya Kuriakova. We're breaking off the pursuit of the Leviathan." Katya didn't say anything – her mouth was full of mulched bread and reconstituted turkey analogue – but her expression conveyed a great deal. Kane answered her unspoken criticism. "No, we're not giving up. We're going to break off onto a perpendicular so that we can attempt to send a message to the Yagizba Enclaves without the Leviathan intercepting it. My former experiences with that monstrosity count for nothing now; with the synthetic intelligence finally in command, it's drawing on Tokarov's own knowledge and instincts. It's no longer just a machine. Before, if it had intercepted the message, it would have ignored it, possibly only turning to attack us instead if the conditions were right. Now, we have no idea what it might do. Therefore, we can't allow any chance of interception. We're already heading away to get some clear water between the pair of us."

Katya swallowed, took a drink of water and asked, "What will you tell them?"

"The truth. That an artefact of the War of Independence, an automated Terran battleship, is heading their way and they can't hope to fight it. If they take us seriously, and without FMA codes there's no reason they should, they may try and disperse the cluster or even evacuate there and then. I don't know."

"They'll wait," said Katya. "They'll wait to see if it's a real threat and, by the time they realise it is, it'll be too late."

"Don't underestimate the Yagizban," said Tasya. She'd commandeered the navigation position and had given no indication she was listening. Katya noticed, with some irrational irritation, that the Chertovka had reconfigured the display away from Katya's favoured layout.

Kane caught Katya's eye, nodded shrewdly in Tasya's direction and mouthed *Yagizban*.

Still absorbed by the navigation display, Tasya didn't notice. "They took the heaviest and most sustained attacks at the opening of the war and still managed to keep this world fighting back. They'll realise how serious the situation is in plenty of time, believe you me."

Katya thought she'd believe that when she saw it. The Yagizban might be the technological cutting edge of Russalka, but the Leviathan was an entire magnitude beyond anything that had ever been built in their factories.

The only way to believe the Leviathan was to see it, and then it would be too late for anything.

Once she had been made aware of the plan, there seemed little point in staying on the bridge. Tasya told her that it would be four hours before they were in a safe position to transmit so Katya decided to take the opportunity to catch up on a little more sleep. She stole the remaining sandwiches and headed back to her cabin, where she ate in her bunk, filling it with crumbs, before dousing the light and finally getting some uninterrupted sleep.

Her watch's alarm failed to penetrate the exhaustion that had settled upon her in full force and she slept a further two hours before finally stirring. She dressed quickly and went forward. Neither Kane nor Tasya were on the bridge, only Petrov with a skeleton bridge complement. He looked neat and alert and Katya wondered if he ever needed to sleep or just had his batteries replaced once every week or so.

"Good afternoon, Ms Kuriakova. You slept well?"

"Have we already signalled the Yagizba Enclaves?" she asked.

His eyes flickered up to the chronometer over the main screen. "Just over a hundred minutes ago."

"And?"

He raised an eyebrow. "And... what?"

He could be so vague sometimes, she thought. "And how did they react to being told a synthetic intelligence displacing about seven million tonnes was coming to pay them a visit?"

"Oh, that. They were surprisingly unconcerned. Perhaps they were just being careful what was discussed over an open channel, but I was expecting a slightly more violent reaction to learning about the Leviathan."

"So, what do they plan to do? What do *we* plan to do?"

"They gave us some coordinates and a time to make a rendezvous. I would guess they have a patrol vessel in the area and we're supposed to be meeting up. Anyway, we're supposed to get there, surface, and wait."

"It won't be an FMA vessel?"

Petrov shook his head, frowning slightly. "There are no FMA facilities in the Enclaves. They refuse to have them, regard the Federal administration as an obstruction to their work. Given that they're so important to the planet's defence if and when Earth ever tries again, it was decided to cut them a little slack. That's not something we're inclined to advertise, though," he added with a conspiratorial look.

"How long to the rendezvous?"

Another glance at the chronometer. "Not long. About another ten minutes now." He looked at her again. "You know, Ms Kuriakova, you hold a very privileged position in this company."

She looked at him with blank surprise. "I do?"

He nodded. "You do. Everybody seems to trust you with their confidence. Your uncle, obviously, but also the pirates. The Chertovka is remarkably tolerant of you. You're aware of her reputation?"

Katya felt awkward discussing Tasya behind her back. "She says that reputation isn't deserved."

"Reputations rarely are, whether they're good or bad. As for Kane, he treats you like a daughter. Ms Kuriakova," he leaned towards her and spoke quietly, "I would be very careful of trusting him in any respect. Few people are quite what they appear, but he seems to make a hobby of being utterly unexpected. We just thought he was another lowlife at first, and then he turns out to be Terran and a failed component in a plan to commit genocide against us."

"Genocide?" Katya started to grow angry, but then paused. Only she and probably the Chertovka knew of Kane's sacrifice and his enforced addiction to that filthy Sin stuff. She longed to tell Petrov just how wrong he was, but didn't feel the secret was hers to impart. Perhaps this was why she was trusted with so many confidences; she kept them even when she burned to tell. Unaware of her inner confusion, Petrov was talking.

"He knows so much about the Leviathan. He's obviously only telling us what we need to know from minute to minute, never anything like the whole picture. For all we know, he has the secret of how to destroy it and is keeping it back for some reason. We cannot trust him."

Katya shook her head firmly. "If he could destroy it, it would be in pieces right now." She would have said more, but the bulkhead hatch opened and Tasya came in, graciously ushered through by Kane who followed her.

"About time, isn't it?" said Kane, full of the heartiness and cheer that Katya now knew meant that he'd used Sin recently to stop the sickness of its addiction crushing him. The knowledge made her feel sick herself.

Petrov, pointedly staying in the command chair, nodded. "Another couple of minutes and then we'll start the ascent. I hope we can convince the commander of whatever ship we're meeting with of the urgency of the situation. With every wasted minute, the *Leviathan* is closing on their homes."

"We'll convince them," said Tasya with a certainty that intrigued Katya. She could see Petrov had noticed it too, but – as with so much – he didn't comment, just filed it away in the grey perfection of his memory.

As good as his word, two minutes after Kane and Tasya had entered the bridge, Petrov ordered the ascent by the book so exactly that Kane pronounced it drill perfect and as good as any he'd ever seen aboard a Terran boat. If it was meant as a compliment, it didn't work.

The *Vodyanoi* surged up from the depths and hit the surface exactly on location and on schedule. A visual scan of the open sea only confirmed what their sensors had already told them; there was no boat to greet them.

Petrov settled back into the captain's chair and smiled a little smugly. "So much for Yagizban efficiency."

The Chertovka fumed, and Kane added warningly, "Give them a moment, lieutenant. We don't know what they may have encountered en route."

Suddenly, the pirate sweeping the horizon with the external cameras spoke up. "Visual contact! Bearing twelve degrees absolute!"

The FMA ensign at the sensors console was stunned. "Nothing on sonar, sir," he reported in disbelief. "Nothing on hydrophones. Not a whisper."

Katya saw the frown that passed over Petrov's face and knew he was thinking the same as her. Did the Yagizban have stealth technology like the *Leviathan*'s on their boats? And, if so, why hadn't they shared it with the FMA? Any such conjecture was blown away the very next second by what the ensign had to add.

"Speed estimated at two hundred klicks pee-aitch, altitude..."

Katya was thunderstruck. Altitude?

"...one thousand metres. Decelerating and descending.

Three thousand metres and closing."

She couldn't believe it. The Yagizba Enclaves had sent an anti-gravity car out to meet them? At this range? They must be crazy; the elements would rip it to pieces if it had to fly more than a short distance. Perhaps it had been launched from a Yagizban ship to make the rendezvous in time. It is a poor habit to theorise without data and, when Petrov ordered the images from the camera relayed to the main screen, she saw she had been profoundly wrong in a very unexpected way.

"What," said Petrov in clipped tones that somehow served to make him seem angrier than if he'd jumped to his feet and started swearing, "is *that*?"

It was no little AG car coming towards them. Flying close to the tops of the storm-tossed sea, the always furious sky of Russalka boiling and spitting lightning behind it, came a huge aircraft kept aloft by AG pods but propelled forward by the hideous blue light of quantum drives, as blue as cobalt, yet still flickering on the edge of perception. These were the manoeuvre drives of starships; she'd never dreamt she'd see a craft use them in atmosphere. And it was a *big* craft, at least half as long again as the *Vodyanoi* and noticeably wider.

"Incoming message," reported the signals officer. "Requests we order all stop to engines and batten down."

Petrov was glaring at the image of the closing aircraft as if it were a personal insult. Katya guessed that the Yagizban had been keeping the development of a new air fleet to themselves. She could see why the FMA would not regard this as a pleasant surprise. "Tell them…"

"That we are complying," interrupted Tasya. "All engines stop. Batten down and brace."

Petrov shot her a look but did not countermand her order. They might have reached an agreement to share command, but the *Vodyanoi* was still a pirate vessel and Petrov would never feel he had the last word aboard.

The aircraft was close now, spinning about to approach the last few hundred metres backwards. As it made its final approach, a great seam in its belly opened and the fuselage skin slid back, revealing a great empty cavity within. Katya looked around at the others: Petrov and Lukyan were watching the spectacle grimly; Tasya's expression was content; Kane seemed faintly bored. Was she the only one who was amazed by this? The craft was some sort of extraordinary transporter, but she'd never heard of the like. What other wonders would the Yagizban have back at the Enclaves?

"Brace!" ordered Tasya over the *Vodyanoi*'s public address speakers. Katya found an empty seat and strapped herself in. Barely had she done so when the transporter settled over them. The screen went dark and the boat lurched. Hollow metallic clangs sounded through her hull as grapnels secured her into the transport's cavernous belly. Then the boat pitched back to about thirty degrees. As the realisation that the *Vodyanoi* had been picked up and was airborne hit home, lights flickered on outside and the camera revealed the inside of the transport aircraft around them, its girders and catwalks. They could see a hatch open and people in the distinctive yellow buff uniforms of the Enclaves enter. A minute later, there was a clanging on the metal of the *Vodyanoi*'s squat conning tower. The deck angle had returned more or less to the horizontal so Tasya unstrapped herself and climbed quickly up the ladder into the tower. They heard her open the hatch and a voice ask permission to come aboard. Moments later, the bridge was full of Yagizban troops.

Tasya made a point of introducing Petrov to them first although the leader of the boarding party – a solidly built major called Moltsyn who sported an impressively square jaw – had noticed the presence of FMA uniforms as soon as he'd come aboard. Petrov was cool and formal when he shook Moltsyn's hand, but he made no comment about the nature of the craft that had gathered them up from the waves and was now, presumably, flying them back to the Enclaves. Katya was glad he didn't. She didn't like the way things were going and suspected Petrov was of the same opinion. The pirates and the Yagizban seemed to know each other of old, and it was a very comfortable relationship.

At the major's invitation, the bridge crew went up top. Katya didn't want to miss the opportunity to see what the transporter's cargo bay looked like for herself and climbed up to the top of the conning tower. Standing there, the roof of the hangar-like bay was almost within her touch, still wet from the sea in which it had momentarily rested while grappling the *Vodyanoi*. Below, she could see the other members of the bridge crew on the deck, looking around the bay and chatting to the yellow-clad troops. It all seemed very friendly, but the FMA sailors looked like prisoners the way the Yagizban hedged around them.

"What's going on?" she said quietly to herself.

"What's going on indeed?" Petrov had joined her and was looking down at the scene on the deck grimly. "Look at this, Ms Kuriakova, just look at this. The major tells me that this is an experimental aircraft that just happened to be available. Yet the *Vodyanoi* fits into it like a hand in the glove. Look how closely even the conning tower fits in with just enough clearance. This bay has its grapples in exactly the right places and even the damned gangplank is in exactly the right place to go neatly up against the side hatch on the tower. This aircraft has been custom built to carry this submarine, there's no question about it. As for the major and the Chertovka, they all but embraced when he came aboard. The Yagizban have been consorting with pirates and they're not going to any great pains to hide it." He shook his head in defeat. "They won't allow anybody from the *Novgorod* back to report their complicity. I fear for our safety."

Katya looked at the smiling faces of the Yagizban troops and saw them harden whenever they looked at anybody from the FMA. She suddenly felt afraid. "What will they do to you?"

Petrov looked at her with mild, tired surprise. Seeing him weary just compounded her sense of dismay. "Do to me? Do to *us*, Ms Kuriakova. In case you've forgotten, you're wearing an FMA uniform. I think you may already have been earmarked for disposal just like the rest of us."

FOURTEEN

CUTTING EDGE

It seemed Petrov had a point. When Katya went down on deck, she found herself being treated with the same coolness as the real FMA personnel. She was relieved when Kane took her by the arm and made a point of introducing her to Major Moltsyn. "This is Ms Katya Kuriakova. She was aboard the minisub that the Leviathan first attacked." She was grateful that he didn't mention that they'd also been the ones who had unwittingly reactivated it in the first place. "She has been a great help since."

Moltsyn regarded her with hooded eyes. "And how long have you been in the Federal forces, Ms Kuriakova?"

Kane laughed. "She's not with the FMA, major. She's a civilian. Her clothes were ruined by seawater so she was given these aboard the *Novgorod*."

Katya felt pathetically thankful as the major's slightly threatening expression abruptly lightened, but there was also a spasm of guilt that she was escaping whatever fate the Yagizban had lined up for the FMA people. She felt like she was abandoning Petrov and the rest, and yet she still felt relief. She simmered at her own cowardice. The major didn't help when he said, "Well, we'll have to get you some proper clothes, Ms Kuriakova," as if she was wearing filthy rags.

"No," she said, with a little iron in her voice, "I'm fine with these. I wouldn't want to put you to any trouble."

"Nonsense," laughed Kane, even as he flashed her a *don't be stupid* look. "I'm sure the major can find you something better than an old and, I hope you'll forgive me for saying so, very ill-fitting uniform."

"Yes, we can find you some civilian clothing when we reach the Enclaves."

Katya pricked up her ears. "When will that be?"

The major checked his watch. "In about an hour, Ms Kuriakova." He chuckled. "Can't wait to be in some proper clothes, eh?"

She'd actually wanted to know so she could make a swift calculation as to how quickly the transport was flying – she estimated 600kph, perhaps a little more – but the major's comment was revealing. He seemed to regard the FMA uniform as about as pleasant as a skin disease. She'd never been to the Yagizba Enclaves – very few had – and had never met anybody from there either but, even so, the difference in mindset, mores, and behaviour was surprising. She'd thought all Russalkin were as one; united by the war and unified in their hatred of Earth and trust in the Federal authorities. Yes, everybody grumbled about them, but there was no doubt that Federal leadership had brought the Terran invasion to a standstill and that the authorities did a good job in these difficult times. To meet somebody who regarded the FMA and its sister organisations with utter contempt was outside her experience and expectations.

• • • •

The hour passed slowly. Katya felt uncomfortable around the Yagizban and the pirates, and felt like a traitor to the FMA sailors. The two groups quickly gravitated away from one another, and it pained her to see men and women who'd been working so easily and efficiently together only hours ago starting to regard each other as enemies again. She found her uncle standing on the *Vodyanoi*'s prow, looking down at the closed bay doors below with a thunderous frown.

"You look how I feel, uncle," she said as she joined him.

"If you feel suspicious and uncomfortable, then you're exactly right," he growled, the closest he could usually manage to a whisper. "Always knew the Yags were a weird bunch, never realised how little I understood them. Look at 'em, thick as thieves."

Tasya and the major were still making some small effort to carry on the pretence that they were strangers, but it was cosmetic and everybody knew it.

"That Moltsyn," muttered Lukyan, "he's all pose. An administrator playing at soldiers. Yags... creepy bastards, all of 'em."

The tension in the bay was palpable and Katya was glad when the transporter nosed down and started its descent. The major asked everybody to sit down or otherwise brace themselves for a few shocks during the landing, but the pilot made such a good job of it that there was only the slightest lurch as the landing pylons touched down.

As everybody formed up to leave by the side ramp, Major Moltsyn raised his voice. "The ramp is facing the platform's entrance, so head straight for it. There's a storm blowing outside so expect to get wet, but keep your head down, don't stop to sightsee, and you'll be fine.

Okay," he nodded to the sergeant at the door controls. "Let 'em out."

When Katya reached the head of the queue and walked out of the side of the transport aircraft, she couldn't help but pause for a moment. She'd expected the landing area to be like one of the small pads that some of the submersible settlements had on top of their domes, designed for little more than small AG craft to alight. What she found as she stepped through the doorframe and onto the ramp in the lashing rain was something else again.

The platform was immense, perhaps three hundred metres in radius and a good hundred and fifty metres above the waves. The flat circle was black, marked out with landing stripes and lights, the circumference dotted with meteorological units, sensor cowlings and an observation deck beneath which she could see a cave-like entrance into which those preceding her were scurrying. She could have gawped at it all for another minute at least but an impatient push in her back reminded her of the major's words, and she dogtrotted down the ramp and across the rain-slicked surface of the platform for what seemed like a very long time until she reached the entrance beneath the observation deck. There, she waited with the surviving crews of the *Novgorod* and *Vodyanoi* until they had all made the journey. Then the great doors slid quickly and almost silently shut, clipping the sound of the storm off as neatly as flicking a switch.

The two groups did not have to wait long standing sullenly looking at each other while dripping on the deck plates, before they were joined by a red-headed woman in Yagizban yellow clothing that clearly was not military uniform. "Bureaucrat," murmured Petrov to Katya. "Almost every job has a recognisable uniform. The Enclaves are run like machines and every citizen had better fit."

"Your attention," said the women in a clear, penetrating voice. The chatter died down. "Welcome to station FP-1. I only wish you were here under happier circumstances." Katya could have been wrong, but the comment seemed to be levelled more at the Vodyanois than the FMA people. "Quarters have been prepared for you and you will be taken to them now." She gestured to another two Yagizban who had appeared by the access lifts and stepped smartly back herself.

After a moment's indecision, the crews made their way to the lifts and started to percolate down into the depths of the platform. Katya was heading towards the lifts when the woman stepped out and took her by the arm. "Katya Kuriakova?" She didn't wait for a reply. "You are to come with me." Katya found herself taken at a brisk walk around the corner from the staging area and into a smaller personnel lift. As she was led away, she looked back for Lukyan, but only caught a glimpse of the back of his head as he turned this way and that, apparently trying to find her. Then the lift's door closed and he was gone. She tried to protest, explain that she didn't want to be separated from her uncle, but she might as well have been talking to a robot.

The woman refused to talk beyond polite generalities and Katya spent a frustrating couple of minutes boiling with curiosity as to why she had been separated out as the lift descended deep through the levels. The lift arrived at a floor that surely must have been deep below sea level and Katya was ushered out into a comfortably appointed area of the station. The woman, who finally identified herself as Mila Vetskya, led Katya to a storeroom, tapped out an entrance code on the door's numerical pad and led her in. Inside were racks and stacks of clothing, uniforms as well as more casual wear. Mila cast an apprising eye over Katya and took down a selection of clothes and a pair of boots for her.

"Blues," she said, "they should match your colouring better than those black FMA rags."

Katya bit back a comment about even sea-stained black being a substantial improvement over the unpleasant dull yellow of Yagizban uniforms, and took the clothes with polite thanks. Mila took her to a stateroom and left her with a warning about wandering the corridors, telling her to wait until she was called for. Katya agreed without complaint and smiled pleasantly as Mila left, closing the door behind her.

The instant the door clicked, the smile left Katya's face.

She'd had enough of this, the lies and deceptions. That the Yagizban were apparently working with the pirates was very bad news. If the planet was going to defend itself against a foe like the Leviathan, everyone needed to be on the same side. Somehow, the government needed to know what was happening here and, as she was the only one not under constant supervision, the responsibility fell to her. The Russalkin were bred to shoulder responsibilities from an early age, but the urgency and importance of this one weighed upon Katya almost more than she could bear. It was her or nobody; she had no choice.

She took a few moments to breathe deeply, to calm herself, and to focus on what needed to be done. She had no clear idea how she could communicate with the FMA, but that was the second thing on her list, anyway. She would worry about it once she had completed the first task –

discovering what exactly the Yagizban were up to, and why they were conspiring with the likes of Captain Kane and his Vodyanois.

She quickly changed – the FMA uniform would draw attention like iron filings to a magnet – but she had no intention of staying in her quarters. As she shrugged off the distinctive black coverall, she felt something small but heavy in her pocket. She slowly took it out and sat on the edge of the bed looking at it but not seeing it, thinking fast. The small maser she'd recovered from Kane's cabin. What to do with it? If she was found sneaking around the corridors carrying a gun, she could forget about them treating her like a civilian. Then again, if they found her sneaking around the corridors, they'd think that anyway. In the small bathroom attached to the room, she found a medical kit and took out the stitch-tape dispenser. She turned it down to the bandage level of adhesion – she had no desire to use it at suture level and have to wait for it to metabolise away – and taped the gun to the back of her left calf. She could forget about making rapid draws with it, but at least it wouldn't show up on a casual frisk.

She cast a quick eye over her surroundings as she pulled on the boots and snapped shut the fastenings; the stateroom was large, the sort of place rich prospectors lived in on the dramas. There, the similarities finished. Like everything else she had seen here, there was little embellishment. Space, comfort and functionalism: that was enough for the Yagizban. Katya couldn't bring herself to dislike them for it; they had similar tastes to herself.

The corridor was empty. She'd seen so few people about she assumed that the station was not fully manned yet. Even if they hadn't gone out their way to tell the FMA that they had such a facility, they couldn't have kept it secret for very long. It was likely that it had only gone into operation recently and did not yet have its full complement. In which case, her quarters were probably earmarked for some senior officer or functionary at some point. She grinned to herself; she felt like a rat in a palace cellar.

She walked as quickly as she dared to the clothes store while still trying to appear casual to anybody who might happen upon her. Checking up and down the corridor, she tapped in the code she'd seen Mila use and ducked inside. For the second time in less than five minutes, she quickly changed, this time from the clothes that had been picked out for her into the same sort of bureaucrat's clothes that Mila wore. The Yagizban seemed reliant on administrators and she hoped that by dressing as one, she would be invisible in many of station FP-1's areas. She found a serviceable and efficient-looking carrying-case in the corner that might reasonably be expected to contain record discs, transcriptors, and the other adjuncts she imagined a serious young low-level bureaucrat would carry around. She carefully folded the civilian clothes as tightly as she could and crammed them inside. She might have to dump the disguise at some point and she would prefer to have something to change into rather running around the corridors in her underwear.

She paused in front of the door, straightened her short, blond hair for the third time, tried to think administrative thoughts and went out. She walked to the lift as if she had every right to do so and called it. It arrived after a very long minute and she stepped inside.

This was where her plan became a little vague. The overall scheme was to find out what the Yagizban were up to with their unreported transports and, even this, the first replacement for the aircraft platforms destroyed in the War of Independence, and how the pirates were involved. Where might be a good place to find secrets was not something she had considered in any great detail.

She stood for a moment wracked with indecision. Then, as she had seen Mila do, she pressed a key on the lift's control panel and said in a clear voice, "Command centre." She hoped the system didn't carry out voice identifications as a matter of routine or her little adventure would be stopping very abruptly.

The lift didn't electrocute her, gas her or hold her until security arrived. Instead it just said in a bored mechanical voice, "Destination unrecognised. Please restate."

She tried again and it rejected it again. Perhaps, she wondered, it was a naming issue. In her experience, settlements almost always called their command centres *command centres*, but would the Yagizban? Most of the Enclaves were submersible habitats, capable of moving around the globe if they so desired. In that case, "Bridge."

"Complying," replied the lift and moved off.

The lift rose smoothly for a few seconds and Katya belatedly realised that what she had taken for some sort of ceramic finish to the compartment's wall was actually transparent, the lift shaft beyond so close and so featureless that she had not noticed until now. She was just wondering why a lift would have a transparent wall when it suddenly stopped, paused for a few moments as if ruminating, and then abruptly headed sideways.

Technologically, it was probably no major feat, but it was unexpected enough to catch her off balance and she leaned against the wall bracing herself for another change in direction. The surprise she got, however, had nothing to do with her vector.

The lift compartment suddenly emerged into a transparent tube running high above the floor of a massive internal section. Katya stepped forward, cautiously at first, to see what the floor was used for. Then she was up against the wall, eager not to miss a detail.

The area was a large manufacturing facility. Workers moved steadily around the place as robot arms struck and welded, gripped and lifted. As she had come to expect from the Enclaves, the air was of almost inhuman efficiency, but she had no reason to anticipate what they were actually building, and the realisation made her gasp out loud. Across the shop floor were four cradles in which vessels were being built: submarines. Two were little more than keels, another's hull was forming, but the fourth was nearing completion and its form was very familiar to Katya, from the sleekness of its lines to the rakish slant of the low conning tower. The Yagizban were building a fleet of *Vodyanoi*-class boats. Fast, effective hunter-killers, these new hybrids presumably combined Terran design with Russalka technology. She saw now that the flying transport that had picked them up had not been built specifically to carry the *Vodyanoi*, but any of its sisters too. Being able to deliver a wolf pack of such boats anywhere in the world, over the waves, uninterceptable, undetectable.

The Yagizban were tooling for war; there was no other possibility. And who could the war be against if not the FMA and all the rest of the world's people it represented and protected?

Then the lift compartment finished its travel across the work area and moved back into the bland tunnels. Katya's mind was racing. Who could she tell? Uncle Lukyan? He was a great man in his own way, but what could he do? If she told Petrov, she'd put his life in peril, along with the rest of his crew. She clenched her fists with frustration. This was crazy. The planet was on the brink of civil war and then into the mix comes the Leviathan. Perhaps the Yagizban fleet would be enough to defeat it. But then what? Uncle Lukyan said they'd left Earth in the first place to leave the politics behind. Now it seemed as if they had brought it with them on their boots.

Her train of thought was brought to an abrupt end as the car stopped and opened its doors. Beyond lay the FP-1's bridge. Katya had imagined something like the bridge of the *Vodyanoi* or the *Novgorod* so was unprepared for what she found.

It made sense that the bridge was going to be a little larger than those on board ship, but the scale of it amazed and awed her. It was a great sprawling room, full of military and bureaucratic uniformed personnel striding around with such a sense of purpose that she felt immediately that she was making herself obvious by the very act of standing still. Putting her head down and once again trying to look as if she had as much right to be there as anybody, she walked out of the lift.

It was difficult not to stare: the scale of the bridge was as impressive as the number of people working there. She'd never seen a free-standing holographic display before but this extraordinary place had three of them, the largest and most central being a sphere ten metres across, a colossal representation of Russalka herself in harsh display colours. She could see all the settlements marked, the current locations of the Enclaves, smaller icons that she assumed to be

Yagizban ships, and several markers in the less explored parts of the world. She had an ugly feeling that these were more aircraft stations, undeclared and unknown to the Federal forces. How could they know? The Federal forces were drawn as tight as a falling hawser just monitoring the standard shipping lanes between the main settlements. There was no possibility that they could just search millions of square kilometres of open sea on the off chance that they might find a secret Yagizban platform, even one as large as the FP-1, a small town by itself.

FP-1, she thought bitterly. *How many more FP-some-things are out there?*

She kept walking, imagining herself to be a minor administrative assistant carrying documents for somebody or other in her case. *If you can fool yourself that you're who you're pretending to be*, she told herself, *it makes it easier to fool others*. She was just walking past a console near one of the great curving walls at the edge of the chamber when she stopped in her tracks. Two men wearing headsets were watching a scene on a bank of flat monitors. On each screen was a slightly different view of Kane being debriefed by Yagizban military personnel, military intelligence by the looks of them. Kane was relaxed, almost bored, as he answered their questions. Now and then he would look up at one or other of the cameras and gaze at it steadily for a moment before his attention wandered again. Whatever sound was being relayed could only be heard by the two observers through their headsets.

"This complicates matters," said one of the men. "This was not covered in any of the contingency plans."

"How could it?" replied his colleague. "Nobody expected anything of the sort. This is… outside our experience."

The first man nodded at the screen. Kane's debriefing was apparently over, or at least for the moment. He rose from his chair and sauntered out of the camera's view. "Do we trust him? He's… in theory at least… he should be reliable. But sometimes…"

"Lack of motivation. We understand his limitations and can allow for them. Anyway, he's only confirming what we've already been told. Now we need to formulate a response."

"This complicates matters," repeated the first man. "We're not ready…"

"Oh, we're ready." The second man laughed humourlessly. "If this is all true, we're ready right now."

The first man was about to reply when he half turned and saw Katya hovering around. "What do you want?" he demanded.

Katya's eyes widened. She'd had her lie all prepared, that she was carrying a message from Mila Vetskya for the attention of Major Moltsyn and had been told to find him here. In the heat of the moment, the lie melted.

"I, uh… a message. I have a message for the atten… from Vetskya… Mila Vetskya for… for the attention of…" The major's name vanished entirely from her mind. She could see his face, hear his voice, even remember how his disdain for her borrowed FMA uniform had made her flush with anger, but she could not, *could not*, remember his name. She looked at the men, both of who had turned towards her now, their frowns deepening.

"For the attention of whom?" snapped the second man.

"For… the attention of…" She flailed for the name as it flickered around her memory, grabbed something and blurted it out. "The Chertovka!"

For a horrible moment, they both just looked at her as if she'd opened her mouth and a spline squid had fallen out. Then the first man roared at her, "How *dare* you refer to a superior using that word, girl? *Colonel* Tasya Morevna is a valued officer and a model of loyalty to the Enclaves. She's worth a hundred worms like you, you insubordinate wretch!"

"I'm... I'm sorry..." Katya stumbled. Her mind was racing. *Colonel*? Tasya's a Yagizban *colonel*? "I meant no disrespect. I just..." A new lie presented itself and, sensing saying something weak now was a better strategy than something strong later, she went with it. "It's just... she's a legend among... among the lower grades, sirs... that name... she *scares* them." She didn't explain who "they" were, but she didn't think she'd need to. She was right.

"Developing a little personality cult, is she?" said the second man. He smiled wryly. "We've only ourselves to blame," he said to the first man. "We've made the Federals fear her so much with all this 'she-devil' business, it's hardly surprising that she's becoming something of a heroine to our own people." Then to Katya, "You'll find the colonel in or around the holding facilities on Beta where the FMA people are being held. Go on, deliver you message, but don't call her *Chertovka* to her face!" Both men were laughing as she turned and headed back towards the lifts.

"Don't ask her for her autograph either!" the first man called as she stepped into the car and the doors closed behind her.

Katya stood mute for a moment, then told the lift car to go back to the level her room was on. As it moved off, she leaned against the wall and tried to think it through.

Tasya wasn't really a pirate. Instead she was some sort of, what? An agent provocateur? "She's something of a heroine to our side," the man had said. *Our* side? Katya had been hoping there would an innocent explanation for the new warboats she'd seen. Now she accepted with a sinking heart that there was not. Was it Tasya's job to keep the FMA busy so they couldn't use their limited resources to accidentally stumble upon what the Yagizba Enclaves were up to? That was part of it, she was sure, but was that all? And all the time, the Yagizban had been building secret platforms, new aircraft – she couldn't believe that their air-fleet only contained a single submarine transporter – and those new submarines using the *Vodyanoi* as a template. The resources they had used to build all this must have been enormous and yet they were always starving the other settlements of supplies, citing manufacturing inefficiencies and mining difficulties.

The Yagizban were strong, the FMA was weak. She couldn't see how the rest of the Russalkin could hope to stand against the Yagizban wolf pack. As if to punctuate her thoughts, the lift car emerged once more into the manufacturing facility and she watched with deepening dread the row of partially completed warboats. Every one of them was a mute threat against a peaceful future.

And Kane must have known every detail of this plan. Judging from what she'd overheard on the FP-1's bridge, they might not entirely trust him but he was necessary to them. She wondered why. There were too many secrets around Havilland Kane, she thought; they followed him around like black smoke, obscuring his motivations, hiding the truth. A truth Katya knew she wouldn't like.

This was not to ignore one last minor, trifling,

unimportant little factor, of course. That given half a chance, the Leviathan would kill the lot of them, Federal and Yagizban alike.

The lift compartment came to a halt and she walked out into the accommodation deck. It was as quiet as before and she saw nobody as she walked quickly but without obviously rushing to her door. After a quick look around to make sure she was unobserved, she ducked inside. She could not repress a sigh of relief that she had got away with it and she leaned with her forehead against the cool plating of the door for a moment while she felt the tension drain from her.

"Enjoy your walk?" asked a voice behind her. "I'm not sure that uniform suits you, though." She turned very slowly. Kane was sitting in a chair off to one side of the spacious stateroom. She'd missed him when she'd come in. "Then again, I don't think that shade of yellow really suits anybody."

Trying to look unconcerned, she walked to the bed, opened the case and took out the civilian clothes Mila had given her. As she straightened them out she asked casually, "Are you going to report me?"

"If I do, the chances are they'll execute you. They're very touchy about security at the moment. I'm concerned about what they may have planned for Lieutenant Petrov and his crew."

"You're concerned?" She tried to keep an edge of cynicism out of her voice but only partially succeeded.

If he heard it, he didn't acknowledge it. "Yes, concerned. I'm hoping they'll be declared prisoners of war, but as there's no war actually on at the moment, that might be complicated. The Yagizban are sticklers for the formalities.

The plan was always to declare war against the Federal Maritime Authority just before the first torpedoes struck."

"How noble. To legitimise a sneak attack? To make themselves feel better?"

"The former, obviously. There have been similar events throughout history."

"*Earth* history, you mean." This time Katya made no attempt to take the venom out of her voice.

"Yes, Earth history. You don't have a great deal to draw on yourselves here just yet. Just because it happened light years away and centuries ago doesn't make it less relevant to your situation, Katya Kuriakova. History is about people and the Russalka and the Terrans are the same people. The geography may differ, but what goes on here," he tapped his head, "and here," he placed his hand on his heart, "is just the same."

Katya started to say something, but the effort wasn't worth the thin meanings her words would have carried. Instead she started to change back into the civilian clothes. She shot Kane a look and he swivelled in his chair until his back was to her. She changed quickly, intent on keeping her possession of the maser strapped to her leg secret from him. She was relieved to find the tape holding well.

As she changed, she said, "Not going so well now, though, is it? The whole question of prisoners of war is about to go out of the locks."

"Oh?" Kane was studiously looking at the wall fittings. "And why is that?"

"Am I the only one who remembers that the Leviathan is coming this way? Your Yagizban friends had better get everything that can fly and swim out there right now if they're going to stand any chance against that... that monstrosity."

"That's an interesting… Have you finished yet? I dislike talking to walls."

Katya locked off her belt and sat on the bed to pull on the boots. "Yes, you can turn around now."

Kane turned back to face her. "Where was I? Oh, yes. It's interesting that you seem to be alone in thinking the Enclaves should be scrambling to the defence."

"Yes." Her eyes narrowed. "Why is that?"

"Because the Leviathan that sank your minisub, holed the *Novgorod* and killed so many good people at the mine is gone. Tokarov has been…" Kane suddenly seemed overcome with emotion. He touched his brow and lowered his head and he distinctly paled. "That poor man. He had no idea what it was going to be like, that particular *Siege Perilous*. Poor holy fool."

Katya didn't recognise the allusion and it angered her, although she wasn't sure why. A suspicion was forming and she didn't like the way it was going. "What do you mean? Talk straight for just once in your life, Kane! I'm tired of your stupid games. People are *dying*! You say we're just the same. I don't think so!"

Kane looked at her seriously. "I'm sorry, Katya. Sometimes, sometimes, I think I've grown old before my time, watching things collapse and not being able to do anything about it. Or doing the wrong thing. It's been that way for so long, I'm beginning to think it's my role in the universe, to make sure things go wrong."

Katya's voice was cold. "I don't have time for your self-pity either."

"No. No, of course not. On Earth, there's a very old story about an order of warriors. They used to meet at a round table, so nobody could have the honour of sitting at the head of it. They would all be equal. But there was one place that was never taken. It was called the *Siege Perilous* and it was cursed. Only the most perfect knight in the land could sit there without dying instantly. Nobody ever sat there until one day, a knight turned up who was... unworldly. He knew nothing about the wickedness of life. Good, noble, and so unsullied by the sins of the world that he actually seemed a bit stupid. He sat in the *Siege Perilous* and was not destroyed. He was the perfect knight, utterly pure. The holy fool."

"What has this got to do with Tokarov?" asked Katya.

"I'm sure you already know. Tokarov wasn't forced into the interface throne aboard the Leviathan. He didn't have a sudden nervous breakdown. He made a cool, rational decision to sit there. I had no idea he would. I never dreamt he would." He smiled bleakly. "Perhaps I'm not as good at reading people as I thought."

"Out of nobility," said Katya. Kane nodded. "Out of loyalty?" Another nod. "Kane, Tokarov is... *was*... from the Yagizba Enclaves, wasn't he?"

Kane nodded again. "The Yagizban aren't running around in a panic because they know the Leviathan isn't coming here to attack. It's coming home. Tokarov's coming home."

FIFTEEN
LITTLE GUN

A fait accompli, Kane helpfully told her after dropping it into one of his next comments, meant that the matter was settled before it had even really come to one side's attention. In this case, by the time the FMA even found out that the Yagizba Enclaves had decided that they could do a better job running the planet than the Federals, the Yagizban would already control Russalka's storm-riven skies with their transport and strike aircraft and the seas would belong to the fleet of *Vodyanoi*-class warboats and, of course, the Leviathan.

Katya hugged herself against a chill that existed only in her mind. "Were there ever any pirates? Or was it just you?"

Kane smiled. "Nobody else has ever worked that out. No, we weren't the only ones, but there were never more than five pirate vessels operating at any time. The transports could take us anywhere, drop us off and, as far as the Feds knew, it was another boat operating. You've seen the news reports. They thought there were as many as sixty pirate vessels out there and all the time it was just us, we few, keeping busy. If they'd stopped to think about it logically, they might have realised that there simply wasn't enough trade to support that many pirates. They never did. You know, maybe they *really* don't deserve to govern."

"That's why the *Vodyanoi* was so keen to bust you out. They couldn't afford you talking under interrogation."

"No, that would have been very bad for the Enclaves. I'm fairly feisty... I think I would have held out for a while. The Deeps, though, they have a bad, a *fearsome* bad reputation. Sooner or later, they'd have threatened to break a particularly favourite bone or dislocate some joint that I would rather stay correctly located and I'd have talked. It's more or less impossible to break anybody out of the Deeps, so they always intended to rescue me before reaching the facility. Your little submarine was earmarked for interception as soon as that appalling little man Suhkarov commandeered it in his usual charmless fashion."

"Or they might just have sunk us to stop you talking."

"Yes," replied Kane philosophically. "They might have sunk us. I like Tasya and, in her own faintly psychotic way, I think she likes me. She'd have fired without hesitation if she thought it was the only way, though."

"Perhaps you can tell her, tell them, the Yagizban, that there's no need to hurt the *Novgorod*'s crew. You've already won the war. We can't fight the Leviathan. Enough people have already died."

"I know. I think they do too. That's why Petrov and the rest are being held rather than being unceremoniously shot and dumped overboard. No point in starting the new world order with an unnecessary massacre." He was speaking blithely, but Katya caught a note of bitterness there too.

"You're on the winning side, Kane," she said, "but you don't sound very happy about it."

Kane got up and paced the floor. "I'm happy that the FMA is finally going to be dissolved. It's been a blight on the Russalkin ever since it was founded. It's just a glorified customs and excise service, you know. How it was ever allowed to sprawl into so many other duties and roles I can't imagine. Administrative creep, I suppose. Government by bureaucracy rarely bodes well."

"It did the job."

"It did it very badly. If it's all you've ever seen, it's hard to imagine other forms of government but they exist, I assure you. The Yagizban intend to run the planet as a meritocratic technocracy."

Katya snorted derisively. "And what's *that*?"

Kane stopped pacing and looked at her. "It means if you're a good scientist, you get ahead. You have a good mind, Katya. You should do well."

She ignored the compliment, if that was what it was meant to be. "And that's it? No say in how things go? What if we don't want a meritocratic technocracy? What then?"

"Not really your decision. It isn't a democracy."

"A what?"

"Never mind," Kane checked his wristwatch. "Come on. I was supposed to collect you, not divulge all the Yagizban's nefarious schemes. Don't let on that you already know. Let them have their moment of glory; it's rude to spoil a gloat."

For the second time in less than an hour, Katya went to the FP-1's bridge. This time, however, she was in the company of both Kane and Mila Vetskya who turned up just as they were leaving Katya's room, presumably to see why Kane was taking so long on a simple errand. The lift went up two decks further before moving sideways this time which gave no scenic view of the war fleet under construction. Katya noticed that Mila had entered the destination through the lift's keypad rather than using the voice recognition, and must have programmed in the diversion around the manufacturing area. It appeared that there were a few things the Enclaves weren't ready to gloat about *just* yet.

The bridge was still impressive when they arrived and Katya didn't have to pretend too hard that its scale over-awed her. It would take a few visits yet before she could walk in there and not be shocked by the size of the low-domed command centre. The only real difference was that the main holographic display had been reconfigured to no longer show Russalka in its entirety. Instead one section of ocean was being displayed as a great gently undulating square hung vertically like a banner. Katya watched the undulations and thought, *Is that just for show or do they really know what the wave patterns are from minute to minute? They'd need satellites to do that, wouldn't they?* If the Enclaves had got a surveillance satellite network back into orbit without anybody else knowing about it, then they were years ahead of the Federal settlements in development. She was comforted when Kane leaned towards her and whispered, "Don't fall for the waves on the display. They're just for show. They'll have satellites up soon enough but not just yet."

The display's major points of interest were a large yellow dot labelled *FP-1* in the upper right and an ominous red arrowhead icon marked *Lev.* in the lower left. They never seemed to change position, but the scale ratio in the display's lower right was constantly ticking down as it adjusted to the dot and the arrowhead growing closer together.

Katya nodded at it. "It's not making much effort to hide

itself." *I don't suppose it has to*, she added to herself. *Tokarov's in friendly waters. I wonder if he expects some sort of hero's welcome?* She remembered Kane's horror of the interface process and decided that there was probably precious little of Lieutenant Tokarov left to expect anything.

A senior-ranking Yagizban walked in front of them to reach the operators sitting at the sensors position. "How long until it gets here?" he demanded.

"Two hours, sir."

Satisfied, the senior officer turned to walk away and stopped with shock. He was looking full at Katya and, with an equal shock, she recognised him as one of the two men who'd been monitoring Kane's debriefing.

"Who," growled the officer, "is this?"

Missing all the danger signs, Mila said brightly, "This is Katya Kuriakova, sir. A civilian from the Federal settlements."

"Really? Then perhaps you'd care to explain what she was doing on the bridge less than half an hour ago in administrative fatigues eavesdropping on a confidential conversation."

Mila blanched. "Sir? But, but she's—"

"She's a spy. A Federal spy. Security!" He stepped back from Katya as if she was carrying something contagious and pointed at her. Two troopers ran up. "Take this girl and put her with the rest of the Federal prisoners. Now!"

Katya didn't mind the humiliation of being bundled into the lift in front of the staring bridge crew. What really hurt was that Kane didn't lift a finger to stop them. He just looked at her with disappointment, as if her scout around the station had come as a surprise to him. It had certainly come as a surprise to Mila and Katya felt sorry for her; when it emerged that she hadn't locked Katya into her room, Mila would be in all sorts of trouble.

The holding area on level Beta turned out to be almost as unpleasant as it sounded. It was obvious that the Yagizban had been anticipating taking large numbers of prisoners when they made their move against the Federal authorities and had built extensive holding facilities into the FP-1, and presumably its sister stations, in anticipation of that day. It was equally obvious that "that day" wasn't supposed to be today, as the facilities were not yet completed. The surviving *Novgorod* crew, perhaps twenty strong, had been locked into what seemed to be a building site. Eventually, it would probably be an imposing gaol. At present, it was as extemporised as the disused office that the pirates had locked them in just before the Leviathan had attacked.

Uncle Lukyan loomed up from the floor – there was nowhere else to sit – and came to greet her when she was half-pushed, half-thrown through the door.

"I was hoping you would be spared this," he said, indicating the bare chamber, a couple of hastily placed chemical toilets in one corner its only nod to humanitarian facilities.

"I was, for a while," said Katya. She sat down with him by Lieutenant Petrov and related what had happened to her since she'd been separated from them.

When she had finished, her uncle blustered angrily but Petrov seemed to have been expecting much of it.

"It all makes a sort of sense," he said. "The pirates were obviously hand in glove with the Enclaves, that was clear as soon as we were picked up. I've been sitting here thinking about it and, yes, it had occurred to me that most of our pirate problem might have been nothing but the Enclaves keeping us busy while they worked on all this. I'm disappointed about Tokarov, though. I've read his file, I knew he was born in the Enclaves. It's not common for Yagizban to join the FMA, but it's not rare either. I really thought his loyalty to us was solid. It turns out he was not only a good officer, but a good actor."

"So, what can we do?" asked Katya.

"Do? Nothing. We've already checked the walls and door and, believe me, we're not getting out of here unless they let us. Even if we did, we're trapped on a hostile station thousands of kilometres from the nearest Federal ship. We'd need a cogent plan of action once we're out and we don't have enough information to form one."

They sat glumly for a few minutes. "If only I hadn't got excited about seeing that damned thing on the scope when we were in the Weft, Katya," said Lukyan. "I'd never have accidentally woken it and it could have stayed there for another ten years."

"Not your fault, uncle. Who was to know? Besides, Leviathan or not, the Yagizba Enclaves would have launched their attack on the rest of the settlements and, really, what chance would we have had anyway? They've got the boats, the facilities…"

"They have surprise," agreed Petrov. "They've always been difficult to deal with but we never thought they were intending anything like this. And now they have the Leviathan."

"A fait accompli," said Katya, remembering Kane's words. The Yagizban had effectively owned the planet for months. Only the sudden appearance of the Leviathan had brought forward the surprise party when they'd been

intending to tell this rest of the Russalkin about it. She got
to thinking about other things that Kane had said and as
she did, a faint glimmer of hope appeared. "They might
not have the Leviathan on their side," she said quietly.

Petrov looked up at her sharply. "What do you mean,
Ms Kuriakova?"

"Kane has always talked about the interface process
like it was the worst thing he could imagine. The Yagizban
are acting like Tokarov has become the Leviathan's captain, but that's not the way Kane describes it. He says it's
more like whoever is in the chair is absorbed into the
Leviathan's artificial mind, giving a spark that turns it into
a synthetic intelligence. Capable of imagination, cunning,
lateral thinking, all the sorts of things that artificial intelligences aren't so good at. If Kane is right, Tokarov isn't
really in full control of the Leviathan, he's just a component. He can guide it, but its basic impulses will remain
the same."

"And what are those impulses?" asked Lukyan.

"Destroy the Russalkin resistance, prosecute the war,
take targets important to the Terran invasion," said Petrov,
"exactly as they were ten years ago." He sighed. "You're
thinking that it will attack the Yagizban, aren't you, and
they'd have to fight back, perhaps damage or destroy it?
That might not be the case."

Katya was excited by her idea and his reservations
angered her. "Why not?"

"Because..." he looked at both of them uncertainly.
Then he came to a conclusion and said, "I might as well
tell you. We had evidence – not good evidence, it was
weak, circumstantial stuff – that the Yagizba Enclaves
were collaborating with the Terran invasion."

Lukyan and Katya looked at him as if thunderstruck. "They... collaborated?" Lukyan managed to say after a shocked silence.

Katya shook her head. "That can't be right! The first thing the Terrans did was bombard the Yagizban platforms from orbit. They killed hundreds!"

"The theory goes – and it is only a theory – that the Earth ships attacked before the Yagizban command managed to contact them and offer their services. As for the deaths, they just put them down to the fog of war and forgave the Terrans." He looked at the floor. "It's war. Stupid things happen in war and people die for all the wrong reasons."

"Where's the evidence?" asked Lukyan.

"There was nothing concrete. It's just guesswork based on the question of how the Terran forces trapped on Russalka managed to fade away. We scoured the seas looking for them. The popular theory was that they'd become pirates. The less popular one was that they'd been given safe haven by the Enclaves. Now, it turns out that both theories might be the same thing. Most of the *Vodyanoi*'s crew, I haven't said more than a couple of dozen words to. They could easily be Terran for all we know. I didn't know Kane was until he told us, not for certain. When Captain Zagadko had him arrested as a Terran aboard the *Novgorod*, I wasn't convinced. There are other colony worlds out there, and some of them must use fixed-wing aircraft. Turned out the captain was right, though. Anyway," he concluded, "that's why the Leviathan sticking to its original orders might not help us if it regards the Enclaves as allies."

Then Lukyan laughed and, knowing why he was laughing, Katya laughed too. Petrov looked at them as if they were mad. "I don't see much to laugh about in our present predicament," he snapped.

"I'm sorry," said Lukyan. "You weren't aboard the Leviathan. I hadn't thought about it until now because I'd been thinking like the Yagizban, that Tokarov had total control. If he doesn't... well!" He laughed again.

The usually cool Petrov looked as if he might explode. He turned to Katya. "Your uncle seems to enjoy being obscure, Ms Kuriakova. Perhaps you...?"

Katya fought down her laughter, which she had noticed was becoming a little hysterical and said, "The Leviathan has no allies. Something has gone wrong with it, and it has lost its list of allies. As far as it's concerned, every Russalkin on the planet – Federal or Yagizban – is a target. They might not know it yet, but the Yagizban are as dead as the rest of us."

In the silence that followed that comment, even as her uncle's booming laugh died immediately away, Katya realised that perhaps it wasn't really that funny after all.

"I could have phrased that better," she added quickly. "That's a worst case scenario. That's if Tokarov, or what's left of him, has no control at all, that is," Belatedly, she realised what Petrov already had – that almost every foreseeable scenario was a "worst case".

Any further morale-building was interrupted as the door slid open and a Yagizban trooper stepped in hefting a maser carbine. Letting the weapon's barrel travel across the *Novgorod*'s crew, he checked the datapad in his free hand and said, "Petrov! I'm looking for a Lieutenant Petrov! Step forward!"

"The interrogations begin," muttered Petrov sourly. He climbed to his feet. "Over here."

The trooper turned to face him, putting the pad back into his belt. "You're coming with me."

Petrov crossed his arms and cocked his head. "For what purpose?"

The trooper wasn't in the mood for backchat, and levelled the gun directly at Petrov. "Move!"

Katya saw movement behind the trooper and realised that one of the crew who had been sitting by the door had risen silently and was silently creeping up on him. No, she saw, not one of the crew. Suhkalev.

He almost made it. Perhaps he made a little noise or the trooper saw Katya looking raptly past him or he simply got the feeling that somebody was sneaking up on him, but the trooper wheeled around. Suhkalev threw himself forward, but the trooper was a big man. Suhkalev was too close to give the trooper time to aim, so instead he stopped Suhkalev's charge with the body of the carbine and they struggled for a moment.

Too short a moment for the crew to act upon, though, as the trooper smashed Suhkalev in the face with a vicious head butt. The Federal staggered back clutching his broken nose, blood already streaming down his face, stumbled over his own feet and fell backwards. The trooper didn't hesitate; he raised the carbine and brought it to a firing position aiming at the helpless form of Suhkalev. Everybody in the room heard the click of the weapon's safety catch being released.

"No!" roared Petrov, but the trooper took no notice. There was the crack of a maser discharge, and it was all over.

The trooper lowered his carbine, stood looking at Suhkalev for a moment. Then he fell to his knees. He stayed there for a long, uncomprehending moment, then pitched forward onto his face.

"Oh," said Lukyan gently, "my poor Katinka."

Katya stood, shaking slightly, unable to move voluntarily. The little maser, pieces of surgical tape still dangling from it, shuddered in her two-handed grip.

She couldn't look away from the body of the man she had just killed, couldn't believe that the silly little device that she'd been carrying around with her like a talisman could do that. A twitch of the finger, and a life evaporated.

"He was, he was going to *kill* him. I didn't... he was going to *kill* him." The words stumbled out in a welter of disbelief and horror and guilt.

Lukyan gently took the gun from her. "I know, Katinka. I know. There was no choice. We all saw." He passed the gun to Petrov and shooed him off with a nod.

Katya wanted to speak but the words bubbled without meaning in her throat. She wanted to cry but her eyes burned dry. When Lukyan hugged her, she clung to him, wanting to roll back time, wanting to be a child again, a little girl who wouldn't be in this insane mess.

"Lukyan..." It was Petrov. His crew had formed up and were ready to go. The guard's body had miraculously gone, efficiently and quietly bundled up and hidden in one of the toilet cubicles. Now the only sign he'd been there was his maser carbine in the hands of one of the ratings, regarded as the best shot amongst the survivors. Katya's maser pistol, stripped of the last vestiges of tape, was in Petrov's hand. "Lukyan, they're going to start looking for that guard soon..."

Lukyan nodded curtly and turned back to look sadly at Katya. Innocence is chipped away at slowly, he thought.

To see it torn away like this from his own niece was almost as painful for him as for her. "Katinka, always remember this. You saved a life."

"I *took* a life!"

"If you'd done nothing, that boy would be dead and we'd all still be prisoners."

"I could have warned him, told him to drop the gun–"

"He'd have ignored you, like he ignored Petrov. Or he would have shot you. Did you see the look in his face when he was about to shoot Suhkalev? He was enjoying it. You did the best thing any of us could have done." He took her shoulder in one great hand and gently tilted her chin up with the other until she was looking him in the eye. "You've given us a chance, but we don't have much time. We have to move, Katinka. Can you do it?"

She looked past him at the *Novgorod*'s crew arrayed around the door, some looking at her anxiously, some impatiently, some with pity. Something hardened inside her and she realised with regret that it was her heart.

I will not be pitied, she thought.

She shook herself loose from Lukyan and nodded. "I'm ready."

"You're sure?"

"Positive." She walked to Petrov leaving her uncle looking at her back with an uncertain dismay. "I know where we can get Yagizban uniforms," she told the lieutenant.

They worked the theft in two stages; most of the FMA crew hid in another unfinished room on the next level down while Katya, Petrov and the armed rating, a woman called Olya who seemed indecently happy to have a gun, took a lift car down to the lower levels. The area was as quiet as during Katya's first visit, the code on the clothing store's door hadn't been updated, and they changed into Yagizban worker's uniforms in frantic silence. Once disguised, they loaded up a trolley with more than enough uniforms for everyone else and took it back as if on an errand. If anybody challenged them and proved difficult to satisfy, Petrov had the pistol in his pocket, and the carbine lay under the topmost clothing packet on the trolley, ready for a rapid draw.

They needn't have worried; the few people they did see seemed utterly uninterested in a pile of uniforms being moved around the complex. They reached the rest of the crew still without the alarm being sounded. "So much for the legendary Yagizban efficiency," commented Petrov as he helped hand out the clothes. "They haven't even noticed we're gone yet."

"What's the plan, lieutenant?" Lukyan was trying to find overalls big enough for him and was having little luck.

"Two possibilities. We grab a boat and get out of here, try and warn the FMA. I don't like that one. If the Leviathan is going to be friends with the Enclaves, we're just giving them the chance to cement that."

"It could be hostile," said Katya. "Kane said–"

"Whatever the estimable Kane said, the Leviathan is making its way here with its stealth switched off. That doesn't sound like an attack to me. I think Tokarov is still in control. But, as Kane suggested, that control might be weak. It might not take much to push the artificial part of the synthetic intelligence into the dominant role."

"That's Plan B?"

"Yes, Ms Kuriakova, that's Plan B. The Leviathan is

going to be attacked by the Enclaves. We'll see what happens then."

Lukyan grimaced. "This is too subtle for me. How are you going to make the Yagizban attack their own boat?"

"They're not, uncle," answered Katya. "We are, using FP-1's defensive systems."

Petrov laughed humourlessly. "Plan B in all its glory." His smile vanished. "We're going to take the bridge long enough to launch weapons against the Leviathan. Then we wreck the place and get out of there like our lives depended on it." A shadow of his smile returned. "Actually, now I think about it…"

"What do we use for weapons, sir?" asked Olya.

"My pistol, your carbine, surprise, and animal ferocity. Battles have been won with less."

SIXTEEN
DEEP BLACK

"The lift opens directly onto the command deck. It's big, so don't let that surprise you. There are guards posted on either side of the door as you go in, and there must be at least another four or five scattered around the place."

"Thank you, Ms Kuriakova," said Petrov. They were already in the lift and on their way to the bridge. The cars, although large, could only hold ten people fairly close together and Petrov had said it would be better to take in ten people who had enough room to get out quickly, than sixteen and be packed in there like krill on a manta whale's baleen. Lukyan had argued against Katya being there, but she had insisted on going as the only one amongst them who had been to the command deck and knew how it was set out. Petrov had agreed and taken the furious Lukyan aside, talking quietly to him until Lukyan's rage subsided. "You can't protect her forever," she'd overheard. "It's what she wants to do." Lukyan had come back and stared at her for the longest time before saying she could go. Then he added that he was coming too and he'd tear the head off anybody who said otherwise.

"The plan is simple," Petrov told the crew around him. "We go in, deal with the guards, take their weapons, and then it will probably turn into a fire fight with the remaining troopers. An alert will almost certainly be called. When that happens, the other half of our number will make their way to the docks and secure a boat. We target the Leviathan, launch everything we can and then destroy the command stations so they cannot issue destruct orders to the torpedoes after we leave. We head straight for the decks in time to board the boat that has been commandeered for us. Any questions?"

There were none. Even to Katya, the plan seemed childishly simple. The best plans were always the simple ones, she'd heard. This was her chance to find out.

"Ready?" Petrov asked Olya. She nodded and hefted the carbine. "Good. You go right, I'll go left." The lift door opened.

The size of the FP-1's bridge awed Katya a little even now, but her attention was drawn to something else. Or rather the lack of something else. The bridge was deserted. The idea slithered through her mind like mercury on steel and came out of her mouth before the doors had even finished opening. "It's a trap!"

Petrov slapped the door close control but it didn't respond, overridden by the main computer. "Down!" he shouted. Olya wasn't listening; she was still following Plan B, unaware that they were being forced to come up with a Plan C. She stepped out of the lift and headed right. There was no guard there and she stood uncertainly for a moment, looking for a target. Somewhere over by the starboard hologram projector, there was a crack of a maser, and she sprawled onto the deck.

"Novgorods!" Lukyan roared the battle cry, and surged out of the lift like a torpedo from its tube.

"Pushkin!" shouted Petrov after him. "Don't be a fool, man!" Then he looked around at his huddled crew and realised that the only choice left to them might be whether to die fighting or trapped in that lift. "Novgorods!" he bellowed, running forward, the tiny maser pistol in his hand cracking repeatedly.

It seemed that the Yagizban had been expecting the escaped prisoners to behave rationally and surrender. There was a stunned silence that lasted the few seconds before a lucky shot from Petrov's maser caught a poorly concealed trooper in the arm and he fell screaming. Then the shooting really started.

Lukyan snatched up Olya's carbine and swung himself up against a wall behind a support stanchion. Using the small rifle as a large pistol he started laying down suppressing fire, giving the rest of the Novgorods a chance to scuttle out of the lift and to the cover of the nearest console stations.

Katya slid frantically across the floor until she reached cover. Petrov ducked down beside her, checking the charge left in the pistol.

"Not going quite to plan, lieutenant," said Katya as maser bolts cracked overhead. She wondered at her own apparent unconcern, as if they were playing a game. Maybe she couldn't take this seriously because she still wasn't quite used to the idea of people trying to kill her. It was a good state of mind, she decided. If she really accepted the danger she was in, she might never move again.

"No battle plan survives first contact with the enemy, Ms Kuriakova," he replied, ejecting the pistol's depleted cell and replacing it with a new one, fresh from the manufacturer's wrapper. Katya was going to ask him where he'd got it and the decided that she didn't care very much under the circumstances.

She looked over at Lukyan who was pushing himself as small as he could go behind the stanchion as a hail of maser bolts cracked and hissed off the metal. He saw her and shrugged, out of ideas himself. Katya smiled as bravely as she could manage and looked around. This was crazy, she concluded. There were nine of them altogether with only two guns between them. They should have had a contingency plan, but who could have guessed that they were heading into a trap? They weren't going to be able to shoot their way out of this. Either they surrendered or... what?

Katya wished that Kane was there with them; they could definitely have done with his infuriating habit of thinking off at tangents, seeing possibilities beyond the obvious. She made a mental effort and imagined him there, pinned down with the rest of them, and then she imagined what he might do, what ideas he might have.

He'd say that not only their plan, but their plan's objectives were no longer possible. Specifically the secondary objective of taking the bridge. That simply was not going to happen with them pinned down by any number of troopers...

"Give it up, Petrov!" shouted a familiar voice. "Don't get anybody else killed for no reason!"

...and the Chertovka. They were caught between the She-Devil and the deep black sea. But the primary aim had always been launching the attack on the Leviathan and perhaps *that*, at least, was still possible. Whatever they did, they had better do it quickly; the alarms had been blaring for the last minute and the rest of the Novgorods would already be on the way to capture a boat. They'd fight to the last ensign to hold it in the hope that Petrov's party would be joining them. For their sakes as much as their own, they had to get out of there.

"How do you think they knew we were coming here, Petrov?" Katya asked.

He took a moment to fire a couple of blind shots over the edge of the console they were cowering behind before replying. "Monitoring the lift system, they must have been. Looks like they did find we'd gone after all, but just played it quiet."

"So when they realised the lift was coming here, they just grabbed what troopers they could? That's what I thought, too."

Petrov nodded. "If they'd had more warning they'd have set up a crossfire across the lift door. We'd all be dead or recaptured by now." He looked at her seriously. "What's your point?"

"My point," she swivelled onto her knees and slowly poked her head up as far as she dared. The rake of the console's controls and the bulk of its monitor bank hid her from the trooper's guns but allowed her to examine what was there. Typical Enclave interface and, as the Enclaves supplied everybody else, that meant she was very familiar with the console's operation. "My point is that we don't need to take the bridge to open fire on the Leviathan."

She accessed the console and reconfigured it to the targeting protocols. The fire controls were locked, but only at a low level to prevent accidental launch. It took her less than a minute to bypass them.

The firing had trickled to a halt for lack of targets. "Petrov!" called Tasya again. "You're just delaying the inevitable. Your situation is hopeless. Surrender now and we'll go easy on you and your people."

Petrov was watching Katya with open admiration, not so much for her ability with the controls as thinking of doing this in the middle of a firefight in the first place. "Yes, okay," he called back vaguely, "I'll think about it. Give us a minute."

On the main holographic display, the Leviathan still surged through the waves towards FP-1. Suddenly a large red targeting marker appeared framing the Leviathan. "Target acquired," a computer announced.

Immediately there was pandemonium amongst the Yagizban. "What is going on?" demanded a voice Katya recognised as Major Moltsyn. "What the thunder is *going on?*"

"They've accessed the weapons systems, you idiot!" That was Tasya. "You! Lock them out!"

I don't think so, thought Katya. She'd already prioritised her console and forced a system lockdown across the weapons multi user protocols.

"I... I can't, colonel," she heard. "They've locked *us* out!"

Tasya again. Cold and very sincere. "If they fire, I will kill you." Suddenly Katya understood why they called her the She-Devil. On her console, a series of options she didn't understand came up. "What are *lanterns?*" she hissed at Petrov. "It says 'Lanterns – 10%' here."

"Torpedoes set to constant active sonar. They don't tend to last long but they light the target up like a phosphor worm for the rest of the torpedo spread. Set it to twenty per cent of the spread – we want the Leviathan to know it's being attacked."

Katya quickly upped the ratio to twenty, clicked through the next couple of screens and was met with "Ready to fire – enter authorisation code".'

"Uh-oh."

"What do you mean, 'uh-oh'?" asked Petrov. He raised his head far enough to look at the screen. "Ah. *Uh-oh*." He ducked back down again. "Listen to me, we're not sunk yet. That's not a security measure, it's just another failsafe to make sure weapons aren't fired accidentally. Go around it, through the system maintenance screens. Do you know how to get to those?"

"Are you kidding me?" said Katya, putting the request on hold and accessing the system maintenance screens. "Front end interfaces are for corridor rats. I can get around it."

I think I can get around it, she added to herself. It didn't appear that the Yagizban wanted to give her the chance. She was half aware of Petrov going flat on his belly and slithering off between the consoles before more of her attention was claimed by a new wave of maser bolts sizzling past her, cracking off bulkheads and supports. The attack came a moment later, troopers threading their way through the maze of consoles and abandoned seats at a run. Lukyan fired a scatter of shots into the middle of the Yagizban line causing a few troopers to dive for cover, but the ones close to the walls kept coming on. Then one right at the limit of the flank fell with a cry. Hardly had he vanished from sight behind a work station, than Petrov reared up, the fallen trooper's assault maser blazing off shots in a wild suppression pattern. Caught unawares from the side, a couple of troopers were hit and fell wounded. The others took cover and returned fire, but Petrov had already vanished.

"Damn you snivelling cowards!" It was Tasya, her fury almost incandescent as she swept through the clutter of stations and consoles, indomitable and unstoppable. Lukyan fired on her but her return fire was so accurate that he was forced to break the partial cover of the stanchion and seek more complete protection behind a processor bank.

"Weapons free," intoned the computer. "Launch in progress. Stand by."

The room seemed to freeze but for every face turning to the main display. On the holographic image, green crosses trailing short green dotted tails were squirming away from the circle labelled *FP-1* towards the arrowhead called *Lev*. Tasya looked at it for a long moment, anger and dismay working her features.

Then she saw movement and levelled her gun as Petrov rose, his rifle already aimed directly at her. Tasya was faster but Petrov was cooler, taking his time while her maser bolts fanned harmlessly around him. He returned fire, a three pulse burst, and she crumpled without a sound.

Then every console and all three displays in the place went dark. A moment later, they flickered back into subdued life, diagnostic data sliding across them.

Petrov was suddenly by Katya. "What did you do?" he demanded.

"Re-initialised their system. By the time it's up and running again, it will be too late to stop the torpedoes." She looked around at the dim flickering lights. "Can we go now?"

"Good time for it," agreed Petrov. He stood up and laid down a withering fire on the Yagizban, already in disarray from the reversal of the ambush and the loss of the Chertovka. Lukyan, a second lieutenant who'd taken Katya's pistol, and another who'd grabbed a carbine dropped by one of the injured troopers all joined in. The Yagizban weren't in flat retreat, but the FMA crew were able to force a pass to a secondary exit and went through at a run.

"Now what?" asked Lukyan from one side of the doorway as he laid down covering fire for the FMA withdrawal.

Petrov scattered some shots from his position on the other side of the door. "The docks. Let's hope and pray the other party were able to secure a ride out of here." As the last of their number ran crouching past them, Lukyan dragged the door shut and melted the lock with a welter of closely placed bolts.

They didn't trust the lifts to get them where they wanted to go and used the emergency stairs instead. They'd hardly got through the doors into the stairwell with its horizontal bulkheads separating each level when they found everybody just standing there. Petrov forced himself through the mass. "What's going on? They're going to be after us in a minute and they're not going to be taking prisoners!"

"Sir!" An ensign, pale and sweating stepped forward. Katya recognised him from the other group, the ones who'd gone to steal a boat.

Petrov regarded him with foreboding. "What's the news, ensign?"

"We couldn't get to the boat bays, sir! They were waiting for us. We lost Tobin and Keretsky."

Petrov nodded; it was only to be expected after the ambush in the bridge that the Yagizban would throw a perimeter around their boats. "So where are the rest of you?"

"Sir, we went the other way, towards the aircraft decks." The ensign smiled wanly. "I don't think they expected us to think about flying."

Petrov grinned wolfishly. "Tell me you've grabbed an aircraft."

The ensign nodded emphatically. "We've got a transporter, but they were hard pressed to hold it when I left to fetch you, sir. Mr Lubarin requests your company as quickly as possible."

Petrov looked up the well. "I'd be delighted to give him my reply in person." The Novgorods surged up the stairs, bristling stolen guns front and rear.

"They depend on their technology too much," Lukyan told Katya as they ran upwards. "They fight like children, terrified of being hurt."

The stairs seemed to go on forever, and Katya was too breathless to reply, although she was impressed that her uncle hardly seemed to be breaking a sweat. He was right, though. The Yagizban were badly coordinated and their response to the threat posed to them by a partially armed mob of Federal Marines had been piecemeal and ineffectual. A couple of troopers had stuck their heads out of a door on the stairs and fired a brace of wild shots before ducking back and locking it, duty done. Katya could see that the idea of having the Leviathan fight and win a war for them more or less by itself would appeal greatly to them. They'd had some structure and competence while Tasya had been in command, but without her they were a joke.

She felt ambivalent about Tasya's death. She was clearly very dangerous and would have been a significant part of the Enclave's war effort, with or without the Leviathan.

With her gone, she wondered if officers like Major Molt-syn represented their best. She hoped so; Moltsyn behaved like a middle-ranking bureaucrat, not a military man. Putting him into a uniform just looked like a good way to lose wars without the enemy even having to get out of bed.

On the other hand, she'd respected Tasya even if she hadn't actually liked her much. She would remember for the rest of her life the sight of Tasya – no, she hadn't been Tasya at that exact moment – she would remember the Chertovka, the She-Devil, leaping upon the deadly form of the Leviathan's drone. She'd never seen such an act of reckless bravery before, and doubted she would ever see its like again. Petrov had shown great courage in the bridge, but Tasya…. She was simply breathtaking. And now she was dead. Dead like Olya and those troopers and Tobin and Keretsky and who knew who else in this war that was stumbling into existence without anybody troubling to declare it. If they didn't stop this before it went any further, Olya's and the others only distinction would be that they were at the head of a very long list of the dead.

The stairs opened out into a staging area on the aircraft deck. A group of Yagizban troopers had taken cover behind packing crates and were firing steadily at a transporter like the one that had brought the *Vodyanoi* to the FP-1 platform. From the transport's open flight deck hatch and from behind its forward landing pylon, some little fire was being returned. It looked like the FMA team had only been able to steal a couple of guns.

A couple of the troopers saw Petrov's team heading for them and smiled, seeing only friendly uniforms and guns.

"Glad you lot finally got here," said one of them cheerfully, "if we set up a cross fire with you firing across from…" His voice trailed away as he realised that his "reinforcements" had their guns levelled at him and his comrades.

A nearby first aid box yielded a medical tape dispenser and Petrov didn't hesitate to dial it up to maximum adhesiveness before taping the captured troopers hands behind their backs. Taking their weapons, the FMA team, Katya and Lukyan ran across the open deck where they were enthusiastically greeted by the rest of their number.

"Does anybody actually know how to fly this thing?" asked Petrov when he'd got some hush.

"I do," said Suhkalev, stepping forward with an air of slight embarrassment.

"You?" Katya couldn't keep the disbelief out of her voice but, then, she didn't try very hard.

"I logged fifteen hours' flying time." He didn't sound defensive, just embarrassed still.

"Real flight or simulator?"

His voiced dipped. "Simulator. You need twenty hours before they'll trust you with a real AG flyer."

"This isn't a little reconnaissance craft, Suhkalev," said Petrov, "just remember that and don't try any fancy flying." Katya looked at him with surprise. He surely wasn't going to trust Suhkalev with all their lives? Petrov caught her look. "Submarines don't carry more than two air pilots for their flyers, Ms Kuriakova. Of ours, one died in the mines and the other is, *was* Tokarov. Fifteen hours in the simulator will have to do."

"We still have a problem," growled Lukyan. "How do we get this thing from here up onto the platform itself?"

Suhkalev had strapped himself into the pilot's position

and was quickly examining the controls. "On the elevator stage," he said without looking up. "But we don't need to use that if we can just get the platform hatch open. It's big – I think I can fly us straight from here and out without using the elevator at all."

"Can we do that from here?" said Petrov.

"No. That will be controlled from the deck flight control room. Over there." They followed the line of his pointing hand to a control room built into the wall some ten metres from the ground reached via an enclosed spiral staircase.

Petrov sighed. "Nothing's ever easy, is it? I'll get it."

"No," said Lukyan. "I'll do it."

Katya looked at him as if he were mad. "Uncle?"

Lukyan wasn't listening. He was trading the maser carbine for one of the more powerful assault versions and making sure it was carrying a full cell. "I won't be long," he said and climbed through the hatch. Katya looked to Petrov for support but he was busy going through the flight deck's controls with Suhkalev.

Lukyan was halfway to the base of the metal cylinder housing the control room's spiral staircase when he whirled at the sound of footsteps, his rifle ready. "Katya! Get back to the aircraft right now! That's an order!"

She skittered to a halt in front of him. "I'm coming with you."

"I gave you an order!"

"I'm not in the military and neither are you anymore!"

"Tokarov–"

"I don't think we can count anything Tokarov's done as being in the interests of the FMA, can we?"

Lukyan blustered for a moment while he thought of

another argument. "I'm your captain and you're my navigator. You take orders for me and I'm telling you to get back there!"

She glared fiercely back. "I quit! I resign my post!"

Lukyan paused, stuck for a reply. "I'll... I'll give you a *really* bad job reference."

They managed to continue glaring at one another for almost three seconds before Lukyan's face cracked into an embarrassed grin and he started laughing. Katya couldn't stay angry either and joined him. "That's the most pathetic threat I think I've ever heard, uncle."

"What else could I say? You're too old to have your allowance cut off." His laughter became subdued and he looked at her tenderly. "Sometimes, I really see my sister in you, Katinka. She could be mule-headed too."

"It's a family trait. Come on, we could have been there and halfway back by now."

They entered the cylinder and climbed quickly and quietly up, Lukyan leading with his rifle at the ready. After two and a half revolutions around the central newel column, they emerged into the control room. Lukyan immediately snapped the rifle to his shoulder and took aim at the person sitting there. "You," he snarled.

"Me," agreed Kane, affable as always. He was in one of the room's wheeled chairs at the far end of a long console that ran the length of the side overlooking the aircraft staging areas beneath a long window. He had his feet up on the console edge and seemed to have been waiting some time.

Katya stepped around from behind her uncle. "Are you going to make a hobby of turning up unexpectedly in places I'm heading for?"

"Ah," said Kane, "last time I was just somewhere you

were supposed to be, so it doesn't count."

"And this time?"

"This time I was waiting for you, admittedly. When you pulled that stunt on the bridge it was obvious you'd be looking for a way out. The Yagizban seemed very sure you'd try for the locks and threw most of their people down there. I selflessly said I'd take my trusty crew and guard the aircraft."

"We didn't see any of your lot, just a Enclave patrol."

"Yes, that was unfortunate. They wandered in when we were doing such a sterling job of guarding the place. What with me up here drinking horrible coffee and my crew in the *Vodyanoi* over at the emergency deployment locks just over there." He waved vaguely at the far side of the hangar.

"Hold on," said Lukyan slowly, "are you saying you were going to let us go? Us and the FMA crew?"

"No past tense about it, Lukyan Pushkin. I *am* going to let you and the Federals go. That," he pointed at the console, "is the control you're looking for, to open the flight deck. Goodbye and good luck."

"Why are you betraying the Yagizban?"

"I owe them no fealty. They've used me and my boat and my crew for the last few years. I used to think they were sincere in taking and holding the planet for Earth until such time as a new expedition from the home world could be organised. This whole Leviathan episode has put the lie to that – they just think they could do a better job of running the planet."

"And you don't think they could?" Katya asked as she walked to the console and casually snapped the control over. Outside, the massive hatch in the hangar's ceiling cracked open and the two halves slid ponderously apart, the whine of the motors driving them obscured by the thunder and gales outside.

"Oh, I'm sure they could. It's not a question of politics, Katya. It's about loyalties. Mine still lie a good few light years away. My crew are all Terran. We've talked it over and... we'll wait rather than put up with being lackeys to the Enclaves anymore."

Lukyan frowned. His gun hadn't drifted from Kane so much as a centimetre. "Wait for what?"

Kane looked steadily at him. "You don't think Earth has finished with Russalka yet, do you?"

The sliding hatch halves were now almost fully retracted and the storm lashed through. Curtains of rain poured down onto the hangar deck to swirl through gratings and into the bilges. Kane stood up slowly to avoid antagonising Lukyan's trigger finger and looked out of the observation window. "You had better go. As had I." He started to step away but something caught his eye and he moved back again. "Oh dear. That complicates things."

Katya looked down and saw troopers streaming onto the hangar deck, deploying to cover and securing as they went. Impossibly, they were led by...

"Tasya!" Katya went pale. "She's dead! We saw..."

Lukyan joined her. "So," he growled, "that fancy armour's not just for show." He took Katya's arm and headed for the steps.

"No! Wait!" Katya shook herself free and ran back to the console. On the communications board were the fin numbers for all the craft she assumed the Yagizban currently had available. She looked out of the window and then down the list until she found the channel for the transporter Petrov and his crew had taken. She selected it and spoke. "Lieutenant Petrov! This is Katya Kuriakova. Come in, please."

Almost immediately, the hail was returned. "Ms Kuriakova, what is your situation?"

"We can't get to you, we're cut off."

"We can..."

"No, don't try to rescue us. They want to kill you. The Chertovka's leading them."

There was a pause while this intelligence sank in. "Resilient, isn't she?" Petrov said finally.

"Get out of here. Right now! Get to FMA waters and tell them what's happening. Just go!"

"We can't leave you."

"Don't be stupid. Of course you can. You must. Don't worry, we have an alternative escape route." She looked at Kane, pleading. He smiled slightly at her and Lukyan and nodded. "Just go."

"What alter–"

The troopers opened fire on the transport. Maser bolts cracked off her hull.

"I'm not debating it, Petrov! Just go!" She snapped the communications link off. She turned to Kane, the confidence she'd had in the radio conversation evaporating. "Okay, Kane. How do we get to the *Vodyanoi* without being cut into pieces?"

"First, we wait. Let Petrov stay centre stage for a while longer." The three of them watched the transporter. It didn't move. "They *have* got a pilot, haven't they?"

"That boy, Suhkalev," replied Lukyan, watching the transport closely.

"Really? Oh." Kane seemed to be looking for something optimistic to add, and failing. "Oh."

SEVENTEEN

STORMY WEATHER

Petrov remained calm. "Take your time, Suhkalev. They can't penetrate the hull. Take your time and get it right." He did not voice his concerns that they might bring up weapons that *could* penetrate the hull soon; he didn't want Suhkalev to panic and crash the lot of them into the hangar wall at close to the speed of sound.

"I can do this," Suhkalev kept muttering to himself as he examined the controls, "I can do this." The sweat beading his lip did not lend confidence. "The lift controls are normal contragravity but, these," he waved at a display of inscrutably complex figures and status levels, "I don't know what they are. They should be the thrusters, but I've never seen anything like them."

Petrov thought back to the blue fire streaming from the engines of the transporter that had collected the *Vodyanoi* from the ocean. "They're Goddard units. Space manoeuvre drive, almost reactionless. Rediscovering how to build them is something else they didn't bother telling the FMA."

"You know how they work?" asked Suhkalev with pathetic hope.

"Of course I don't. The principle was lost during the original colonisation. Try and use the lift units to get us into the open air before engaging the thrusters. At least we won't have walls in front of us when you light them up."

Suhkalev visibly steeled himself and put his hand on the lift controls. As they wound up to power, the transporter jolted slightly on its landing-pylons. Slowly, the hydraulic shock absorbers extended as the aircraft lifted uncertainly from the deck. Almost immediately, one corner sagged lower than the others and the whole vehicle started to slowly drift to one side as it spun gently, if not actually out of control, certainly not entirely within it.

"What are you doing, Suhkalev?"

Suhkalev was barely listening. He was still chanting "I can do this, I can do this, I can do this," under his breath as he manually rebalanced the lifters, slowing the spin and angling the drift to take them under the open hatches.

Looking out of the cockpit window Petrov saw something to worry him. He walked back, keeping his balance by gripping the rails that ran along the ceiling for exactly that purpose until he was back in the crew disembarkation room aft of the flight deck. The remaining crew of the *Novgorod* looked up at him from where they sat cross-legged on the floor. All of them had weapons lying across their laps taken from the transporter's arms locker. They looked about as confident as Petrov felt. "They've brought up some sort of support weapon. I don't know what it is, but it's about two metres long and looks like it's shoulder-fired. Best shots to the door so they don't have an easy time using it."

Three Novgorods moved to the main external hatch, pleased to have something to do rather than sitting and waiting for Suhkalev to fly them into a steel wall.

The hatch slid open and the storm blew in. Suhkalev had managed to manoeuvre the transporter beneath the open hatch in the FP-1's topmost landing area and was now gingerly making it ascend. The rate of climb was slow and it would be almost a minute before they were hidden from the Yagizban troopers scattered around the deck below, plenty of time for them to score several hits. The *Novgorod*'s best surviving shots braced themselves against the door frame and took aim.

The Yagizban weapons team had been drilled in using the rocket launcher, they had been trained in maintaining it and its ammunition, they had even been trained in how to carry it in victory parades. Nobody, however, had ever shown them what to do in the event of the target shooting back. As the first maser bolts, fired more in hope than expectation of hitting anything, came raining down from the escaping aircraft, the weapons team dumped the launcher and scattered for cover.

Interesting, thought Petrov. *Once again they have the technology but they don't have the training, or perhaps the will to fight. They want their toys to take all the risks for them. That's a weakness.*

It was not a weakness shared by all the Yagizban, though. The Chertovka was living up to her name, throwing terrified troopers out of her path as she made a beeline for the discarded rocket launcher.

"A standard FMA reward bonus to whoever kills that woman," said Petrov.

Bonuses were handed out by the FMA with miserly tight-fistedness. Instantly, all three rifle barrels twitched onto the new target and started firing careful bursts. Petrov knew that the chances of hitting her at this range from a moving platform with what felt like half of Russalka's oceans pouring down on it were vanishingly small, but they only had to slow down her advance for the few seconds it would take the transporter to clear the lip of the hatch and get into the open sky.

Tasya was built of much sterner stuff than the rocket team, that much was clear. She zig-zagged from cover to cover, reaching the dropped weapon far too quickly for Petrov's comfort. She was down on one knee with the launcher tube over her shoulder and her eye to the targeting scope inside five seconds. A second after that, fire flared from the rear of the tube and a rocket zipped from the front. Petrov heaved his snipers back inside and slammed the door shut. "Brace for impact!" he barked at his crew. The command was usually applied to a submarine crew when a torpedo was about to hit or the boat was about to ram or be rammed. Petrov had never used it except in exercises and hoped they would understand what he meant by it in this situation. They seemed to, as they scurried for places where they could hang on if the transporter was thrown about. He didn't have time to make sure they were all safe, he was already throwing himself into the cockpit. He landed at full stretch, grabbed the supports at the back of the co-pilot's seat and shouted at Suhkalev, "Thrusters! Now!"

Suhkalev didn't need telling twice. They were still an agonising five metres short of the hatch, but he cut the aft lifters and the transport suddenly swung nose upwards. The forward lifters whined alarmingly as they tried to take the full weight of the transporter by themselves and their status displays flashed red. Suhkalev was aware of Petrov's grunt of surprise as he suddenly found himself dangling from the co-pilot's chair by his arms but didn't have time to pay him any more heed than that. Suhkalev reckoned he'd figured out the thruster controls. Now was the moment to discover whether he was right. Already the transporter was falling backwards, the forward lifters unable to take the whole weight.

I can do this, he thought, and opened the main thruster throttles.

From the control room Katya, Lukyan and Kane watched the transporter suddenly stand on blue columns of iridescent fire. "Down!" shouted Lukyan putting one great hand on the scruffs of Katya and Kane's necks and pulling them to the ground. As they hit the floor, the observation window exploded inwards. The room filled with the furious blue light and a million glittering shards of reinforced glass. Then, as abruptly as it had appeared, it vanished. Kane crawled rapidly to the console and activated a traffic control camera. The blue light of the transporter's thrusters were already fading into the stormy sky.

"They made it!" gasped Katya, her face filling up with a grin.

"Maybe," said Lukyan doubtfully. "Look. They're trailing smoke."

"And there should be two thruster flares visible," said Kane. "Tasya must have hit them with that rocket."

Katya's joy evaporated. "Can they fly on one engine?"

"I've no idea. Given it's Suhkalev in the pilot's seat, I'm astonished they can fly with two." He saw Katya's face. "I'm sorry, that was flippant. I don't know if they can fly on one engine."

Lukyan had gone to the shattered window and was

cautiously looking down at the hangar deck. "Firing their engines in here has caused a lot of damage. Casualties too. There'll be medics up here soon… Hmm, your friend the Chertovka has survived yet again, I'm sorry to say."

"*My* friend?" Kane and Katya chorused. They looked at one another.

"You shared a command with her, didn't you?" said Lukyan turning to Kane.

"Not really my choice. She was a condition of getting operational support for the *Vodyanoi* from the Enclaves. Oh," he nodded. "I see. You're trying to needle me. Sorry for not picking up on that immediately."

"Can we save the cat fight for later?" said Katya. "The area's full of troopers and they're bound to check on this room before long. Shouldn't we be leaving?"

"Too late," said Lukyan, looking out of the jagged frame of the observation window, "there are a couple of them coming this way now."

The troopers entered the control room to find a couple of administrators, one a huge man, the other a young woman. The woman lay amidst a dune of fragments from the destroyed observation window, the other administrator kneeling over her checking her pulse. One of the Terran mercenaries, the one who sailed with Colonel Morevna, was standing over them with an expression of great concern. When he saw the troopers, he implored them, "Please! She was caught in the blast when those Federals fired the engines! She needs a stretcher team immediately!"

The troopers gave the room a quick look over to make sure that none of the Federals had been left behind and left, assuring the mercenary they'd send one of the many medical teams that were now entering the hangar to deal with the injured from the gun battle and the obviously coldly calculated use of the transport's drives as weapons.

One of the teams was currently treating Colonel Tasya "The Chertovka" Morevna, who was submitting to their ministrations with very poor grace. "Damn them! Damn their eyes! Where did those cold fish learn to fly like that? Their pilots were supposed to be dead! Careful, you idiot!" The medic putting her broken arm in a temporary field cast muttered something nervous and respectful. Tasya turned her white hot attention to Major Moltsyn. "What's the situation with the Leviathan?"

"The torpedoes all detonated prematurely. They were intercepted somehow."

"It launched combat drones. That's obvious. Is it responding to hails?"

"No, colonel. We've lost it from sonar too."

Tasya's lips thinned. "It's activated its stealth systems." She shook her head. "Put all non-essential personnel on transports out of here, enact full evacuation protocols. That thing's going to attack and I don't know if we can beat it." She looked up at Moltsyn narrowly, daring him to ruin her day further. "Any good news, major?"

"A little, I think. Air radar followed the stolen transport for about twenty kilometres. Its path was erratic. Then it lost altitude, tried to climb and ending up pitching into the sea. It looks like you shot it down after all, colonel."

"Search units have been dispatched?"

"Of course. The ocean's very angry today, but their air search radar did not detect anything and one reported seeing something in the water that looked like a downed aircraft. It sank before they had a chance to relay pictures."

"I'd have preferred more solid evidence. Like Petrov's head on a spike." She unconsciously touched the closely grouped pock marks on her armour left by Petrov's maser bolts. "It will have to do for the moment. We have a larger and more immediate problem."

Across the hangar warning sirens suddenly wailed and red strobe lights flared into life. Moltsyn snapped his head to look. "What's that?"

Tasya followed his glance, curiosity hardening into suspicion. "An emergency launch from one of the… That's the *Vodyanoi*'s bay! Moltsyn! Who authorised that launch?"

"Colonel!" A trooper ran up, very conscious that he was the bearer of bad news. "The control room! We… There was an injured woman in there. We sent a medical team and…"

Tasya reared up onto her feet and turned on the trooper. "Spit it out, man! What's happened?"

The trooper looked at her as if he was expecting her to shoot him at any moment. "We went back to check on them and… They were tied up."

Tasya frowned. "The injured woman was tied up? What are you blathering about?"

"No, colonel! The medical team were tied with suture tape from their own supplies! The woman, the other administrator and one of the Terrans, they had gone. They had stolen the stretcher!"

Tasya's fury suddenly cooled, which only served to make her more threatening. "*What* Terran?" But she already knew. With all the medical teams around, two men carrying an "injured" woman on a stretcher would go unremarked, even if they were heading towards the boat bays rather than the exits. "Out of my sight," she said quietly and the trooper obeyed as quickly as he humanly could. She turned to Moltsyn. "Kane's turned. The *Vodyanoi* is no longer to be considered a friendly vessel. It is to be destroyed on detection."

"Shall we launch pursuit boats, colonel?"

"Launch all available warboats, but they're not going after Kane. He's tomorrow's problem. We have to live through whatever the Leviathan has for us first."

Kane leaned back in the *Vodyanoi*'s captain's seat like a king returned to his throne. "Take us out to about two klicks at one third and bring us about. Slow and steady, duck us under a good thermal layer. We're going to wait and watch developments."

"Kane." Lukyan looked at Katya and then back at Kane. "Kane?"

Kane looked up at him. "What will become of you? I don't know, Lukyan Pushkin. Not at the moment. We'll just have to see what develops, won't we?"

"Two thousand metres out from FP-1," reported the helmsman. "Bringing us about."

"I can hear launches," reported the sensors operator. "Boat launches." She paused listening intently. "Lots of them. Somewhere about forty."

"Forty boats?" Katya was aghast. "Warboats?"

Kane leaned forward in his seat. "Probably. Mostly copies of this one, I should think. Not quite as good, but numbers count for a lot. Can you track them?" he asked the sensors officer.

She shook her head. "Sorry, sir. They're running silent as quickly as they can. Everybody's playing hide and seek."

It was only to be expected; if the Leviathan saw them, it would kill them. A submarine battle is a strange mixture of tedium, terror and bewilderment, even more so than battles in other environments. It is perhaps the only battlefield where fortune *always* favours the cautious and firing first may be the worst thing to do. As a result, the best submarine commanders are cool, sanguine men and women who not only think clearly under pressure, but – just as importantly – think clearly when nothing is apparently happening.

Still, Kane may have been pushing the stereotype of the unflappable submarine commander when he produced an odd metal device; two thick metal discs with chamfered edges perhaps ten centimetres in diameter connected by a narrow axle around which a string was wound. Katya had never seen such a thing before and watched in fascination as it descended and rose on its string with little apparent effort on Kane's part. "What *is* that?" she asked finally.

"This? It's a yo-yo. It's just a toy."

"Where did you get it?"

"A little curiosity shop on Earth." The yo-yo rose quickly and slapped into Kane's hand where he held it tightly. "I bought it for my daughter."

The admission startled her slightly. She looked around for her uncle, but he had walked over to the navigation officer's position and was irritating him by reading the instruments over his shoulder. "You have a daughter?" She said finally just for something to say. As soon as she did, she realised how stupid a question it was, as if it were something he might be mistaken about.

Kane didn't seem to notice. He was looking intently at the yo-yo. Suddenly making his mind up, he carefully removed his finger from the loop at the end of the string and proffered the toy to her. "Would you like it?"

Katya almost asked what about his daughter, but something stopped her. Instead, she took it from him. "Thank you."

Her acceptance seemed to please him and he smiled the tired, sad smile she'd come to know. "It's all in the wrist action. There are tricks you can do with it, but I don't know what they are. You'll have to make some up for yourself."

The smile vanished as a low vibration thrummed through the *Vodyanoi*'s hull. "Sensors, what was that?"

"An explosion, sir, five degrees off to larboard."

Larboard? mouthed Katya to Lukyan.

"It's an old way of saying *port*," he explained, adding, "sometimes I think this lot have been playing 'Pirates' for too long."

A map of the area was flashed up on the main screen, the *Vodyanoi*'s position marked up at the centre. A flash mark indicated the direction and probable distance to the explosion. "The FP-1's been hit," said Kane. "I don't think the Yagizban are going to take that lying down."

He was right. A moment later a volume of sea to the southwest of the platform was swarming with torpedoes hunting with active sonar pinging furiously.

"There's a lot of ambient sound energy out there," said the sensors officer. "We may be detected, sir."

"Yes, we may be, but if we back off we may miss something important. Hold our position but keep us quiet, helm."

They watched as the bright flashing lights of the torpedoes ran around in search patterns for several minutes until, one by one, they flickered out without a single effective detection of the target, much less a hit. For five long minutes, they watched the unchanging screen in silence. Then another flash appeared. "That's a boat," reported sensors crisply. "It's bad, she's going down. I can hear bulkheads crumpling." Another flash. "Another boat's hit; she's…" Another flash, and another. The sensor operator swore under his breath. "It's a massacre out there, sir. Four hits. Five. One's limping, I think. No, another hit, she's been finished off."

Katya spoke to Kane, but couldn't take her eyes off the screen as new flashes appeared. "What's the *Vodyanoi*'s full crew complement?"

"Thirty-seven," replied Kane in a hoarse whisper, unable to tear his eyes away from the carnage being relayed to them as neat little symbols on a display screen.

"And the Yagizban versions?"

"The same." Another flash, another thirty-seven lives extinguished. "We have to do something. When it's finished with the boats, it will turn on FP-1."

"Good riddance," said Lukyan, but he flinched as a new flash appeared.

"I think you're labouring under a misapprehension if you think the FP-1 is purely a military facility, Lukyan Pushkin," said Kane, rage flickering in his voice. "There are family accommodations aboard. You just blithely wished 'good riddance' upon perhaps two hundred young children."

Lukyan looked at him aghast, his eyes widening. "What? I had no idea…"

"Well, now you do." Kane gestured hopelessly at the screen. "If anybody has any bright ideas, now would be a good time to share them."

There was silence. And then Katya said in a small voice, "Is the *Baby* still aboard?"

It felt strange to her, how her attitude to the minisub *Pushkin's Baby* had changed in only the space of a few days. Once she had regarded it as purely her uncle's, something that was always there. Then, when she had got her card, it had changed in her view into a place of work and she looked forward to knowing every kink and corner of her as well as Uncle Lukyan and Sergei did.

She stopped for a moment in the corridor leading forward to the salvage maw. "What's wrong?" asked Lukyan.

"Poor Sergei. He thinks we're dead." They started walking again.

Now, the *Baby* was the submarine that refused to die. The Leviathan had killed it and the *Vodyanoi* and her crew had resurrected it. Every time she saw it now, it was a faint shock. They stepped through the hatch into the sealed maw and Katya experienced the feeling again.

The *Baby*, for its part, sat patiently and awaited whatever they might ask of it. Katya walked to it and ran her hand over the curve of the hull. The urge to say "Good girl" to it was quite powerful. She looked over her shoulder at Lukyan and found him smiling.

"It's just a machine. Boats and ships have always been just machines for getting from one place to another. Yet we develop a... I don't know, a bond, I suppose. Life crawled from the sea back on Earth and, one way and another, eventually turned into us, but I don't think the sea ever really got out of our blood. Not even here."

Kane was checking the Leviathan's IFF identification module mounted on the *Baby's* side, nestled amongst all the other equipment she carried. "You have a poetical soul, Lukyan Pushkin," he commented without pausing in his work. "Just like your Russian ancestors."

Lukyan's smile faded. "I have nothing of Earth in me."

"Nonsense. Russian blood is far fresher in you than the lung fish blood you were waxing lyrical about a moment ago." Kane gestured offhandedly at Katya. "I gave Katya here the lecture on the importance of history a little while ago. I'm sure it's still burned into her memory and she can give you the benefit of my wisdom, if at one remove." He finally looked up to find both Katya and Lukyan glaring stonily at him. He sighed and went back to his work. "Yes, well. Perhaps we can work on the sense of humour before the sense of history." He resealed the unit and stepped away from it. "Okay, are we sure this is what we want to do? The chances are the Leviathan won't fall for this a second time."

"I wouldn't say it was something I *wanted* to do..." began Katya.

"We have to try," said Lukyan simply.

"We have to try," echoed Kane. He stood motionless as if listening to the words die against the metal walls. He nodded sharply, his mind made up. "We have to try." Katya noticed both men were looking at her. "Katya, Lukyan's the pilot. I'm going because I know the Leviathan. You're not needed. You should stay."

"Okay," said Katya. Both men visibly relaxed. Then she boarded the *Baby*. She was already strapping herself into the co-pilot's seat when Kane stuck his head around the open hatch, his expression perplexed.

"I'm sorry, did we just miss something then? I thought I heard you agree to stay behind."

"No. I was just agreeing that you'd done the decent thing and tried to talk me into staying behind. I've no intention of letting you two go off without me."

"Katya…"

She turned in her seat, her face tight with anger. "Do I *look* like I'm going to let you leave me behind? *Do* I?"

Lukyan pushed past Kane and went to take the pilot's seat. "You're wasting your time, Kane. I've seen that face before and you won't talk your way around it." He started strapping in. "Exactly like my sister. It's uncanny sometimes."

Kane accepted defeat philosophically. He climbed aboard and settled into the same passenger seat he'd taken the first time he'd been bought aboard the *Baby* as a prisoner. "It's the blood. Thicker than water. Blood will always out."

Strapped in, he slapped the hatch control and watched the door close and seal. The maw started to flood. Five minutes later they were clear of the *Vodyanoi*, moving slowly in the direction of the invisible battle being fought between the Yagizban warboats and the Leviathan.

EIGHTEEN
GETTING UP

The *Baby*'s sensors were nowhere near as sensitive as the *Vodyanoi*'s, nor was her computing power sufficient to create sonar maps of the same sophistication Katya had seen of the battle while they were still aboard the Terran boat. None of that mattered when you were actually travelling through the battleground, Katya thought. Her displays were full of explosions, cavitation noise, imploding compartments.

"I don't think they've managed to lay a finger on the Leviathan," she reported. "It's like fighting a shadow." Another flash on a display board, sound converted into light for easy viewing. "That was the FP-1. She's taking a real beating. She'll sink if the Leviathan doesn't cease fire."

Lukyan didn't comment. Instead he flicked the switch that activated the IFF unit.

Katya watched the green light on the Judas box cycle on and off, sending out an electronic lie to the Leviathan, that the *Baby* was its long lost combat drone six. "If it sees through this, Kane, what will it do?"

Kane considered. "If it was just the Leviathan, it would

ignore it. If it detected us, it would kill us without hesitation, now its list of enemies is so extensive. But it's not just the Leviathan. Its behaviour is moderated by Tokarov and I didn't know him well enough to be able to make any guesses."

"None of us did." Lukyan's voice was cold. "None of us. I still can't understand how a man could... do that. It's worse than suicide."

"No." Kane was quiet. "No, it's a lot like suicide. If Zagadko was still alive – or Petrov – they might have been able to predict his behaviour. Especially Petrov. He'd have made captain soon enough. Good judge of character."

They sat in silence. Katya had been trying not to think about the message the *Vodyanoi* had intercepted from the aircraft sent to hunt Petrov's stolen transporter. So Tasya had shot them down. They were all dead: Petrov, Suhkalev and all the others. She thought back to how it had been Petrov who'd tried to comfort her in his own distant fashion when she'd thought her uncle was dead. "I liked him," she said into the silence.

Another light flashed on her display, more insistent, brighter. At the same moment she realised what it was, the telltale pulsing tone started to sound through the hull.

"Torpedo!" called Lukyan. He was already pulling the steering yoke over and down. "Evading!"

Katya remembered the last time he'd done this, he'd trusted the Navcom to perform the evasion. Of course, on that occasion they were hit multiple times and almost died.

She felt the *Baby* pitch sharply and perform a corkscrew descent as Lukyan made for the next deepest thermal layer scattering noisemakers in their wake. Through the din in her headset, she could still plainly hear the fast pulses of the Yagizban torpedo's sonar and the hiss of its impeller motor until, abruptly, it stopped. The pinging ceased altogether and the hum of the impeller turned to a dying shriek even as it diminished in amplitude.

"There's something wrong with it," she reported. "I think it's sinking?" She checked for an IC resolution and it confirmed that the torpedo was tumbling into the depths. A moment later it exploded. She looked at the others. "I have no idea what happened there."

Kane looked around as if he could see through the hull. "I can make a guess."

Lukyan nodded and killed the *Baby*'s engines, neutralising their buoyancy so they coasted along for a few metres under no power. Katya suddenly understood.

"The Leviathan?"

Lukyan looked grim, and there was misery in his voice when he said, "Why didn't I try harder to leave you behind, Katya?"

"Where there's life, there's hope," said Kane. "They say that where I come from." He coughed. "Of course, they say all sorts of rubbish, but I think that one's true. While we live, nothing is certain. We walked out of the Leviathan once; perhaps we can do it again."

Lukyan was unconvinced. "And what if it just sinks us?"

"You're a cheerful soul, aren't you? Think about it; if it had wanted us dead, it would hardly have bothered stopping that torpedo. It saved us for a reason." They gripped the sides of their seats as the *Baby* was abruptly jerked upwards. "We're about to find out why."

"What exactly *are* those cables?" asked Lukyan as the Leviathan withdrew its grappling tentacles into the metallic hemisphere in the ceiling of the docking bay. A moment later, the chamber started to empty of water.

"Biomechanics. Biological principles applied to technology. I never liked it. I like my machines to look like machines." Kane patted one of the *Baby*'s structural ribs almost fondly.

Inside a minute the chamber had been pumped so dry it was hard to believe it had been full of water anytime in the previous hour. Without discussion, they cracked the seal on the minisub's aft hatch and clambered out. The exit door slid soundlessly open and they climbed the slight incline to reach it.

On the other side of the door, Kane stopped them and pointed at the floor by the hatch's edge. "There. That's been worrying me." Katya followed his finger and saw a quantity of dark powder. She started to bend to touch it, but he stopped her. "I wouldn't get it on you, if I were you. Too easy for some to get in your mouth and that wouldn't do you any good."

Katya stepped away from it, unsure. "What is it?"

"I had my suspicions when we were last here so I took enough for an analysis. It's a very, very fine powder made up all sorts of metals and metallic salts, some of them very heavy and very toxic, which is why it's not a good idea to risk ingesting it. Some very rare minerals in it."

"So what is it?"

"Soup," said Lukyan. "Dried out Soup from the ocean bed. Is that right, Kane?"

Katya thought back. "We detected the Leviathan in the middle of the Weft. There're lakes of this stuff there. It must have been lying in one. Maybe its airlock seal isn't as tight as it should be and some of the stuff leaked in." She shrugged. "Okay, it's interesting, but why should we care?"

Kane sighed in sharp exasperation. "Why should..? Katya, use your eyes. We're not *in* the airlock! How is it in the corridor but there's not a trace of it in the airlock itself?"

"Maybe there was but it washed out when it picked us up the first time," she replied sharply.

Kane opened his mouth and then shut it again; he hadn't thought of that. "That's possible. I'm just trying to understand why the Leviathan's been behaving so oddly, even before Tokarov joined with it. I thought perhaps the matrix of its synthetic intelligence had been contaminated with particles of Soup." He looked so crestfallen that Katya felt sorry she had snapped at him and even sorrier that she had shot down his theory. "I'm just trying to understand."

"If the airlock seal failed under the pressure," she offered, "maybe some other seal did too. Perhaps Soup did get in and poison the AI."

That cheered Kane up. "Yes. Yes, of course, you're right. If your idea's right, that doesn't mean mine isn't right too. Or at least, some of it."

Lukyan was eager to get on. "Some of it?" he grumbled. "There's more of it?"

Mistaking Lukyan's sarcasm for interest, Kane nodded. "Yes, I was also wondering if the trace of Soup was simply evidence that the airlock had been used after I left the first time and before coming back with you and Tokarov."

Lukyan's disinterest faded slightly. "Are you suggesting somebody might have come aboard and sabotaged the Leviathan? Who? When?"

"Why?" added Katya.

"Three excellent questions and I have a single answer for all of them. I don't know. It was just a thought. It just occurred to me that an accidental contamination would be more likely to cripple the Leviathan. What happened seems so..."

"Deliberate," finished Katya. She was beginning to think he had a point. "But we don't know who or how or why or when. You need motive, opportunity and method before you have a case, and you have nothing."

"No," he admitted, "I don't. Just an ugly sense of purpose behind everything that's happened. That's not much." He sighed. "Oh, come on. Let's get this over with." The three of them continued walking up the blank white corridor towards the interface chamber.

They paused at the door as Kane stopped them. "Do we have anything that, in poor visibility, might just possibly be mistaken for a plan? Once we're through that door, things might happen very quickly."

"Talk to Tokarov," said Katya. "We have to talk him around."

"I doubt there's much of Tokarov left, at least mentally. It's still worth a try. And if his personality has been completely destroyed, what then?"

"We kill him," said Lukyan.

"Uncle!"

"I'm sorry, Katya, I know that sounds cold. There's no choice, though."

"You can try killing him, but you'd be wasting your time," said Kane. "If the Leviathan has finished processing him, it will just be using his brain for extra storage space. If he dies, it's a nuisance to the Leviathan, but that is all."

Lukyan crossed his arms. "What, then?"

Kane looked uncomfortable. "Let's just see how it goes, shall we?"

"That's it then? If there isn't enough of Tokarov left to talk to, we don't know what we're going to do next?"

"In a nutshell, yes."

Lukyan shook his head. "We're doomed."

"Wars have been won on thinner plans than that," said Kane.

"Not as many as have been lost," retorted Lukyan. He stepped up to the door. "Not much point in asking if we're ready, is there?" He tapped the control and the hatch opened.

Some images are destined to stay in the mind's eye for the rest of one's life. Katya knew that, if she lived through this, what she saw in that room would haunt her in the moments before sleep and in the dreams that followed. She had braced herself for the worst thing she could imagine: Tokarov's mummified corpse caught in a paroxysm of agony forever perhaps, the moment of interface caught forever in tableau. What she actually found was far, far worse.

Tokarov was alive, but what a diseased impersonation of life it was. The interface chair had grown *into* him, the matter of the throne having grown hundreds, thousands of wiry cables like the grappling tentacles in the docking bay. The cables were thinner here, black and glistening in a foul oily fashion. The tips of the tentacles were all imbedded in Tokarov's flesh, latching onto nerve endings and muscle ganglion, hijacking his motor functions and devouring his reason. His pale skin seemed dark with the mass of tentacles, some as thin as threads, some as broad as fingers, that cut and penetrated and usurped and writhed his whole body. A hemisphere in the ceiling directly above the throne dangled yet more, vanishing into his ears, his nose and his eyes. Only his mouth had been left alone and they could all hear his ragged breathing even from the door.

Lukyan swore. Katya fought down the urge to vomit. Kane simply watched. He lifted his own hand to inspect it and Katya noticed several small crescent-shaped scars on him, the marks of the Leviathan's failed attempt to interface with him. She wanted to hate him for shirking this fate and leaving it to befall somebody else, but she couldn't. She didn't like to think what she might have done herself to avoid this hideous devouring.

Kane lowered his hand and, with infinite reluctance, took a step forwards. Instantly, a section of the chamber's ceiling dilated and the Medusa sphere descended on its stalk. Kane froze in midstep as several purple targeting dots appeared on his face and chest. He took a slow breath and said quietly to himself, "I'm not dead, am I? No? That's good. Stepping back now." He reversed his stride, but the sphere continued to target him.

"Kane, you're the only one who's been targeted. Katya and I are clear," said Lukyan in a measured, conversational tone. "That's different from last time."

"It seems personal," whispered Katya.

"I was thinking that myself." Kane looked down at the half dozen targeting spots that moved slowly across his chest like confused insects.

"You knew," said the Leviathan, but it was not the even tones of their last visit. The intonation was human. "You *knew*!"

"Of course I knew, Tokarov," said Kane directly to the human wreckage in the chair. "I warned you to stay away from that thing. I wish I'd known about your ulterior motive for staying behind. I'd never have agreed if I had."

"I can feel it. It's eating my mind." The Leviathan's voice – Tokarov's voice – was full of horror and, worse still, defeat. Katya knew he'd given up and accepted this terrible fate.

"Every time you express your personality, the Leviathan will monitor it as a malfunction, hunt down the section of your brain that generated it and... I don't know what to call what it does. Reconfigures it, I suppose." There was no catch in Kane's voice, but Katya was surprised to see a silent tear roll down his cheek. "I'm so sorry, Tokarov. If there was anything I could do, I would do it."

"I... No! Not me! The Leviathan doesn't trust you anymore." The machine voice modulated and cracked with emotions it had never been created to express. "The Yagizba Enclaves attacked. You are their ally. You are an enemy. You warned me. You are the only one who knows. You are a friend." The targeting dots shuddered around Kane as man and machine warred. "Kane is a real and present threat. Kane can help me. Kane is a category one threat. Kane has to... It fears you, Kane. It fears you!"

Kane looked up at the Medusa sphere. "Learnt about fear, have you?" He took another step back. "That's not necessarily a good thing."

"I know what you did, Kane. It's all in the Leviathan's memory. I know how you poisoned yourself to prevent interface."

Lukyan shot a hard glance at Kane, who was at pains not to return it. "Yes, well. Desperate times make for..."

"That was clever," interrupted Tokarov in the Leviathan's voice. "I wish I'd been as clever."

"Not your fault. Maybe I should have been more specific in my warnings. Anyway, you didn't have the resources handy." Kane slid his hand nonchalantly into his jacket pocket. When it came out again, Katya saw it cradled a pressure syringe. In its transparent barrel, a black liquid. She kept her face expressionless with a massive effort of will and returned to looking straight ahead.

"The Leviathan wanted to kill you. As soon as I... we detected the drone number six signal, it knew you were coming back and it wanted to kill you. Kane is a category... I confused it... supposed to make allowances during interface... follow my instincts even if it doesn't understand them... I didn't want you to die."

Where there's life, there's hope, thought Katya. She stepped forward. "Does it trust me?"

"You are unrecognised," said the Leviathan, before immediately adding, "You're a clever girl, you saved the *Novgorod*. Category one... category blue..."

As Katya walked slowly forward, she took the syringe from Kane's hand. He wasn't expecting the action and almost dropped it before she had it from him and concealed along the line of her forearm. He glared intensely at her as she walked past. "It could kill you in a second."

"Tokarov's doing everything he can to keep it off balance and sacrificing himself to do it. In a minute, everything he ever was will be gone. We can't waste that minute." She said it quietly as she continued to walk and wasn't even sure if Kane caught all of it. Perhaps, she wondered, she was just saying it to herself to root herself in the moment and the minute to follow.

She walked steadily, neither so slow that time was frittered away or so quickly that it might antagonise the

Leviathan despite its scattered priorities. She wondered how many targeting dots the Medusa sphere had painted on her: none or ten? She wondered if the sphere killed painlessly, or only silently. And, before she had time to wonder anything else, she was standing before Tokarov.

The interface threads, cables and tentacles flexed slowly as if connected to some great, ponderous heart, beating a thin ichor of machine hatred into Tokarov to replace his red, human blood. The tentacles running into his eye sockets must surely have destroyed the eyes and Katya remembered they had been a hazel brown once. She looked upon him unflinchingly, saw where his eyelids were rubbed raw from being unable to close but trying all the same, smelled the surgical scent of antiseptics and antibiotics the machine must be using to keep his body functioning until it had no further use for it, and felt the fear of an ebbing mind.

"Tokarov," she said gently. "It's me, Katya."

"I know," he half whispered, half sobbed through his own mouth rather than through the Leviathan. "I know. It can see you. Watching you."

A thought occurred to her and it seemed a ridiculous thought at first, but then she immediately realised that it wasn't ridiculous at all. For Tokarov at that moment, it might be the most important question anybody had ever asked him, so she asked it. "What's your name? I can't just call you Tokarov. What's your whole name?"

He sat silently. The tentacles imbedded in him shuddered slightly as if discomforted and suspicious. He opened his mouth and spoke, one word on each exhalation. "Pyotr... Grigorevich... Tokarov."

Katya nodded, as quiet and comforting as any nurse

at the deathbed. "Pyotr Grigorevich Tokarov. I shall remember you."

Then she stabbed him in the neck with the syringe. Her aim was good; the blunt end of the pressure syringe slammed up hard against his carotid artery and she kept her thumb on the dosage release until the whole chamber was empty.

She felt none of the sickness or self-loathing that she had felt so quickly when she'd shot the Yagizban trooper. That had been an impulse and the thought that violence lived so close to the surface in her was a terror to her. This though, this was an act of humanity.

Perhaps the large dose of Sin would kill him immediately, perhaps the rejection process would, perhaps the Leviathan would kill all of them in retaliation, Tokarov included. It didn't matter – there had been no choice.

The effect was instantaneous. Katya had seen deep ocean worms that shied from the touch of searchlight beams as if they were fire. The Leviathan's tentacles slid out of Tokarov as if his touch was poison. To the Leviathan, perhaps he was. In a great thrashing mass, the cables and tentacles and hair-thin threads withdrew and hung back, their tendrils waving in an unfelt breeze.

"Interface prematurely halted," said the Leviathan, any trace of Tokarov gone from its voice.

Tokarov slumped back into the throne, gasping violently. His flesh was a wreck, his eyelids had mercifully been able to close and Katya was spared the sight of the ruined sockets. But she'd seen that frantic clawing for breath once before: back in the mines when a crewman injured during the *Vodyanoi*'s attack had died. Katya knew he was going to die just as surely as that crewman, and that, just as surely, there was nothing she could do.

"I'm sorry, Pyotr," she whispered.

But there was to be no dignity in death here. A cable, thicker than the others, separated from the mass and snaked around Tokarov's neck. Before Katya could react, he was jerked into the air and thrown aside, nothing more than a failed component.

Katya saw him hit the wall with a horrible crack of breaking bone and took a step forward. Thus, she never saw the tentacle that hit her.

"New replacement selected," said the Leviathan. "Interface process initiating."

Katya felt the tip of the tentacle break the skin at the back of her neck, directly where it joined the skull. She felt it separate into roots and then into threads, penetrating muscle and bone. Even though she knew it was impossible, she felt it penetrate her brain.

Somewhere distant, she thought she heard screams and shouts; her uncle, Kane, perhaps even herself. Before she could wonder why everybody seemed to be so upset, the Leviathan was in her mind and, worse yet, she was inside its.

She saw it greedily access her memories, looking for intelligence, experience, tactics and strategies, human cunning and human guile. She felt it ransack her mind like a thief looking for valuables amongst family heirlooms valuable to no one but the owner. Each memory accessed flared into colours and smells and sounds as if it were yesterday. No, as if it were *now*.

...her mother came in to comfort her and she ended comforting her mother, her mother saying "This stupid, stupid war" until Katya said "Stupid war" and her

mother laughed or was it a sob and papa never came home again...

... she never liked her Uncle Lukyan, he was so big and he laughed too loud and here he was all quiet, his huge hands holding hers and saying, "My poor Katinka" and telling her something about an accident and how she would be living with him now...

... Sergei looking at the plot she had made on the practise table and scratching his head and asking, "Did you do this by yourself?" and showing Lukyan who smiled and said, "She's a prodigy, that one" and looking up "prodigy" and being proud...

"Let her go! Let her go, machine!"

"Pushkin! Careful, man! Look out!"

... feeling sick, stomach cramps and no one to talk to, Uncle Lukyan asking if she were well as if she just has a cold and no one to talk to and her mama dead these five years...

... being expelled from the Federal Cadet League for gross insubordination, in front of all the others, the shame and humiliation turning to hysterical laughter, the commander snarling "You're a disgrace, you'll never wear a Federal uniform!" and telling Lukyan and him just saying, "You've got all the training out of that programme that's worth having, plenty of civilian boats would be glad to have you"...

Something deeper, something in the shadows. An invasion? She thinks of the tendrils in Tokarov's flesh and the antiseptic and the thought gratefully takes up the theme. Not an invasion, a wound. Antibodies rallying against it. Burning out the infection. Whose memory is this? she wonders. Not mine. Tokarov's? Is that what another *person's memories are like? Disconnected images without context, ideas floating in vacuum. No, not that. The Leviathan? It must be, but why does it want to talk to me? What is wounded?*

Motion, a pressure at the back of her head. "You might kill her!" "It's not having her!" Not a pressure, a pulling, like when she used to wear a ponytail and Andrei Ivanovitch pulled it so hard she fell over backwards...

The agony was so exquisite, so far beyond anything she has ever experienced before, her only reaction was to open her eyes very, very wide. She had a momentary impression of Lukyan standing by her, a tentacle held in his fist, the end a tangle of fibres dripping... blood?

Then she collapsed and he grabbed her under one arm like he used to when she was young and they played monsters while her mother, Lukyan's sister, looked on and shook her head ruefully.

"Go, Pushkin! GO!" She heard Kane bellow as if every devil from every hell was pursuing them.

"Category one. Confirmed."

Katya heard a crack and Lukyan staggered. Then he straightened up and lumbered towards the exit, Kane running ahead of them. Another crack and then another, and another. Lukyan moaned miserably under his breath but kept running. Kane had reached the doorway and was unfolding something he'd had concealed under his jacket. As they neared, he raised it to his shoulder and it started making a very similar cracking noise. The agony was ebbing and Katya was now in a dull place of pain and distance. It took her a moment to realise that Kane's weapon must be Terran and that made her wonder if it was one of the laser small arms Earth was supposed to have. Then the similarity of the sound of the weapon to the sounds behind her sank in.

The Medusa sphere was firing. She wondered if she was being hit and the pain from being forcibly disconnected from the Leviathan was overshadowing the pain of laser wounds. Then Lukyan staggered again and she knew the truth of it. He was almost sobbing, not in pain but in desperation to reach the hatch before his strength failed, and she finally understood how important his promise to look after her he had made to the memory of her mother was to him.

Lukyan collapsed just a metre from the hatch, falling to his knees. Kane looked down at him and saw there was little life in him, but still there was hope. Kane flicked a control on the laser carbine and fired. From a stubby barrel beneath the laser emitter, a rocket propelled shell flew out, hissing past them and towards the interface chair. Kane threw the weapon down behind him and grabbed Katya, dragging her through the hatch. She looked back then and saw her uncle for the last time: all but dead, his eyes tired and glazing, his face pallid. She could see the smoke rising from his back where the Medusa sphere had rained laser bolts into him, and she could only guess at what kind of man could have carried on this long.

But she knew.

"Uncle."

He tried to speak but no sounds came. His lips moved and she thought he said, "Katinka." Then he reached forward, toppling as he did so. His hand slammed into the door control and the hatch slid shut.

Kane grabbed her by the shoulders and threw her to the floor at the same moment the fuse on the rocket he'd launched ran out. From the other side of the door, there was a ferocious concussion, a dull *whump* like a giant punching the wall. Instantly, alert sirens sounded.

Kane staggered back to his feet, collecting the laser carbine and stowing it away. "Rocket grenade. Nasty weapons, not really suitable for submarine actions. Blow down a bulkhead as soon as look at it." He listened to the klaxons. "I think it may have hurt the Leviathan quite badly. We should go."

She looked at him, dazed, then she shook her head. "My uncle," she said and walked unsteadily back towards the hatch.

"Lukyan's dead."

She stopped, staring at the hatch, willing it to slide open and Lukyan to jump through, safe and sound.

"He gave his life to save you, Katya. You know that. The sphere was firing on him right from the moment he released you. I've never seen anything like it." The hatch wasn't opening. Katya thought it would probably never open again. Behind her, Kane was still talking, his voice low and intense. "I'm going to honour him by telling anybody who'll listen about the bravest thing I ever saw, that I have ever even heard of. How are you going to honour him?"

She lowered her head. Then she turned and walked down the corridor towards the docking bay. "By living," she said quietly as she passed him.

They reached the docking bay a minute later. Kane went in first, his gun drawn in case the docking cables were set to attack. The hemisphere in the ceiling was quiet, though; it seemed the Leviathan had other more pressing concerns.

"How do we get out of here without the Leviathan's cooperation?"

"We override. This place has maintenance hatches and access panels very deliberately kept out of the areas that I had access to." He examined the apparently smooth wall, found a couple of shallow indentations and dug his thumbs into them. With agonising slowness, he unscrewed a small circular hatch.

Katya was pacing up and down. It wasn't fair that she should lose her last relative, and have him restored to her only to see him die. It wasn't fair that her father had died in the war. It wasn't fair that her mother had died in a stupid avoidable accident that wasn't even her own fault. "It's not fair."

Kane looked over his shoulder at her. "No," he answered. He turned back to his work. "It isn't. It never is."

"You don't know what it's like." She was getting angry with him, and she didn't want to. She needed to hurt him, but she didn't want to.

"What you're going through this minute? No, I don't. I don't know at all." He twisted a release control inside the hatch fiercely and, around them, the whole chamber started to reconfigure itself. The smooth wall panels slid back to expose pipes and girders and...

"Combat drones!" She waited for one or all of them to suddenly rise from their cradles and turn their destroying eyes upon Kane and her. Instead, they stayed utterly inanimate.

"They're inactive. I've put this chamber on maintenance cycle so the Leviathan can't access anything in here. Now if I can find the maintenance consoles... oh, wait." Another click and three sections of floor started to rise. "One of these will have launch controls. Check that one over there, would you?" Without waiting for confirmation, he moved to one of the control consoles still deploying itself and locking into place.

Keep myself busy, thought Katya. Plenty of time later for grief. Stay focussed. She went to the rising section Kane had indicated. It wasn't a console at all, she discovered when she reached it, but just a cover for a viewing porthole in the Leviathan's skin. She wondered briefly why it had such a thing, but then she looked out and all such questions flew from her mind. "Kane! Kane! Come here quickly!"

Kane ran to her side and looked down through the port. Beneath them was not the submarine darkness of the Russalka ocean. Instead, they could see waves crashing far, far below them. A moment later, clouds came between them and the water.

The Leviathan was flying.

NINETEEN

FALLING DOWN

"I hate flying," said Katya as she watched Russalka fall rapidly away from them. *Fine*, she thought. *Perfect*. "This isn't a submarine, is it?"

Kane raised his index finger in admonishment. "Now, I never actually *said* the Leviathan was a submarine. Not *just* a submarine."

Katya was only half listening. "This explains so much. Using lasers underwater is so incredibly inefficient. Tasya said it was a crazy way of arming the drones. Not if they were always meant to operate in the air." She looked up at Kane. He looked faintly embarrassed. "Or space. This thing is space capable, isn't it? It's a starship?"

"How did you work that out?"

"Every time you talked about how you came to Russalka, you said you were inside this thing. That doesn't really make sense unless there was no transporter starship carrying it. I actually wondered how big a ship would be needed to carry the Leviathan here and what happened to it after it finished its job. There's no mention of such a large Terran ship in the war records I've read. So there never was such a vessel. The Leviathan came here under its own power." She frowned. "Why did you never tell anybody? Why did you let everybody carry on thinking this was just a submarine?"

Kane sat down on one of the *Baby*'s outrider rigs and sighed. "I've been having doubts about the Yagizba Enclaves for a while. I was in no hurry to tell them that a starfaring battleship was about to hand itself over to them. Actually, that's not quite true. The Leviathan's stardrive is slag; they only work once. Still, it can reach space. The important thing was that it would have given the Yagizban control of the planet from orbit. I wasn't sure if they deserved that advantage." He scratched his nose. "I wasn't sure if anybody on this benighted planet deserves that."

Katya chose to ignore that last comment and looked out of the porthole again. "Why has it only chosen to fly now?"

"Because it's hurt. Its stealth systems work well underwater, not so well in the air or space, but I think its stealth must have been damaged by the explosion. Probably its hull integrity too. It uses a forcefield to lend its hull strength." He noticed Katya looking blankly at him. "A forcefield. It's... well, it's complicated. A projected energy field that exhibits some of the qualities of matter." From her expression, that was not a good explanation. He gave up. "All you need to know is that the Leviathan's skin is protected by a very powerful forcefield. It deflects attacks that actually reach it and, just as importantly, holds the hull together when it's under stress. It allowed the Leviathan to rest far deeper than a conventional boat's hull could bear. Between losing its stealth and its hull not being able to bear the same pressures, it feels vulnerable. It's running for high ground where it knows it can't be reached."

"Taking us with it."

"It has to prioritise its problems. We're probably pretty low in the list. It will use its damage control systems to fix itself up and then, when it's got a minute, it will kill us."

"I know. We have to get out of here." She looked down through the porthole. Russalka looked a long way away. "Any ideas?"

Kane walked over to join her and they watched the clouds become distant. "In a word, no." He cocked his head and admitted, "Well, one, but it isn't to get us out of here. Let me show you something." They walked to the console Kane had been studying. "The Leviathan uses two power sources. When it can get water, it uses simple electrolysis to break it down into oxygen and hydrogen, and stores the hydrogen."

"To use as fuel for a fusion power plant. Any boat much bigger than the *Baby* does that."

"True, but fusion doesn't give the large amounts of quick *I need it now* power something as big as this needs in, say, combat. Which brings us to the second power source." He tapped the display where a figure read 5.56Kg.

"So educate me. What masses 5.56 kilograms?"

Kane looked seriously at her. "Antimatter. It certainly didn't have that much when I left it. It must have been sitting at the bottom of the sea for ten years using fusion energy to make the stuff. Something else it's not supposed to do. If it had lost power to the antimatter containment field and it had come in contact with the side of its container... Katya, do you have the faintest idea what antimatter is?"

She shook her head. "I was hoping you'd tell me that."

Kane sighed. "Simply put, it's matter's evil twin. When

matter and antimatter come in contact, they obliterate each other, right down to the subatomic level. *Bang!*" Katya jumped. "Total conversion into energy! The amount of the stuff the Leviathan is carrying would produce a staggeringly huge explosion. It would have been suicide to destroy the Leviathan while it was still in the ocean; it would have caused a shockwave that would have travelled around the world wreaking untold damage. At least we can prevent that."

Katya looked curiously at the console readings. "How?"

"By making it explode up here where it won't do any harm. I can access the antimatter containment field from here, turn it off. A few minutes later it will decay to the point where the antimatter comes in contact with the matter wall of its container, and that will be that. The jig will be over for the Leviathan."

"And us."

"And us. Yes. What can I say? This always had the air of a suicide mission. All we can do is to try and protect Russalka."

Katya thought about it. Was it really such a loss, to give her life up like this? She had no family left. She had never really had any friends. It was a shame that the people down there would never know the sacrifice she made for them, but that was little enough compared to the lives that would be saved. "Why should you care, anyway? You're not even Russalkin."

"We're all human," said Kane simply. He gestured at the controls. "What do you say? Shall we?"

Katya nodded quickly, not trusting herself to speak. Kane reached for the controls, his hands hesitated above them momentarily, his fingers twitched once, then he tapped out some instructions. It took him less than five seconds to sign their death warrants. When he was finished, he stepped back.

"It's done. The Leviathan will try and run auxiliary power to the containment field, but I've put other demands on it. It will only delay the inevitable by a little while."

Somebody once said that the prospect of imminent death concentrates the mind. Katya looked around the chamber with all its exposed workings, units and equipment as a collection of entities for the first time instead of just a setting for her last moments. "What," she asked slowly, an idea starting to form, "is the pressure in low Russalkin orbit?"

Kane was surprised by the question. "The pressure? So close to zero to make little difference."

Katya walked over to the *Baby* and ran her hand over the hull. "The *Baby*'s rated down to four kilometres of ocean on her back. If she can stand that number of positive atmospheres, I'm sure she can bear no atmosphere at all."

Kane stood up very straight. "Are you suggesting we use it as an escape pod?" Katya nodded, but Kane shook his head. "Yes, we'll get caught in Russalka's gravity and re-enter the atmosphere, but we'd come down like a meteorite. We'd burn up."

"We have to be travelling fast to burn on re-entry." And she pointed at the combat drones.

Kane looked at them, understanding visibly growing in his face. "Use the drone's antigravity systems to neutralise most of the *Baby*'s mass? Like your *Novgorod* gambit?"

"Like my *Novgorod* gambit. I'm only ever going to have one bright idea in my life; I'm trying to get as much use out of it as I can."

"Don't do yourself down. If the drone's AG units were activated once we were inside the outer atmosphere, it would be like deploying drogue parachutes. We might just survive it."

"It's a plan. Re-energise the antimatter containment while we get this worked out and you can switch it off again when we're about to leave."

Kane's jubilant expression faded. "Ah," he said quietly.

Katya's own face fell. "You can't."

"If I could, so could the Leviathan. I had to lock out any attempt to reactivate it." He moved quickly to the console. "The Leviathan's doing everything it can to keep the antimatter safe, but it's losing. We've got fifteen minutes at most, probably less." He gestured hopelessly at the drones. "It would take that long to dismantle a drone to get the antigravity unit out and it would take at least two for us to stand a chance. There's just no time. I'm sorry, Katya, it was a good idea. Fate doesn't come much crueller."

Katya wasn't listening. She was already at one of the combat drones, opening its inspection hatch. "We're not finished yet. If we can't get the unit out in time, the whole damned drone is just going to have to come with us!"

She had the first drone's contragravitic system's fired up, before Kane got over his surprise. "I like you, Katya Kuriakova," he said finally. "You're mad, but I like that in moderation."

She was too busy wrestling the great cylinder – rendered almost weightless but still with all its inertia, out of its cradle and over to the *Baby* – to reply. She did notice that he wasn't helping, though.

She looked up from working on a second drone to see him opening a locker and pulling out a one piece suit, white and helmeted. "What's that?" She bent back to her work.

"EVA suit. Extra-vehicular activity, that is. A spacesuit." He pulled off his jacket and boots and started shrugging the suit on over the rest of his clothes. "Pretty good underwater, too."

"Is there one for me?"

"No, but you won't need one. You'll be in the minisub."

She stopped and looked suspiciously at him. "And where will you be?"

He pointed under the *Baby*. "Opening that hatch. It has to be done from the console. The chamber will have decompressed before I can get back so I'll need an air supply. The plan is I open the hatch, run over and come in through your minisub's dorsal airlock. You, meanwhile, sit tight in the pilot's seat and bring the drones online slowly as we start to fall through the atmosphere. Like it?"

"Not much, but I don't have anything better. When you've got that thing on, fetch me six connector leads from locker two and the tape gun in locker four."

"Aye-aye, captain," replied Kane and hurried himself into the suit.

Aye-aye, captain, thought Katya. *Your minisub's airlock. He's right; Uncle Lukyan never made a secret of his will. I own the* Baby. *I am her captain. My first command.*

She busied herself with the drone before the thought that the *Baby* might also be her last command had time to crystallise.

The *Baby*'s hull was pocked at frequent intervals with socket covers, each covering two sockets that allowed her to interface with equipment attached to her hull. The *Baby* had, at various times, mounted manipulator waldo arms,

extra light banks, cable laying gear, a specialised magne-
tometer array and a thermic lance. It was unlikely the
manufacturers had ever imagined her with two combat
drones strapped to her hull. Katya had been counting on
the drones complying with the same interface standards as
the *Vodyanoi*, which she had noticed used the types of
plugs and sockets that were Russalka standard. It made
sense; Russalka may have won its independence from
Earth, but the Terran technical conventions they'd inher-
ited were well tried and tested. There was little point in
changing things simply for a misguided show of independence from the old world. Even so, she gave an audible sigh
of relief when the connector cables snapped home at both
ends and the communication lights glowed, showing that
the *Baby* had successfully detected the drone's anti-gravity
units and could control them.

Kane looked at the web of metal tape that Katya had
created to clamp the drones in position to make sure the
aft hatch and the dorsal airlock were clear and accessible.
Satisfied, he hurried back to the console and checked the
state of the Leviathan. "How are we doing?" called Katya
as she stowed Kane's coat and boots into a locker.

"Just barely in time. Two minutes, I think. Get that
hatch sealed, we're doing it now."

Katya slammed that aft hatch and locked it shut, made
her way forward to the plot's seat and strapped herself in.
She checked the Judas box – all lights were green. "Just
you stay that way," she muttered.

Outside, Kane sealed his suit's helmet, made a quick
check that its life-support systems were working correctly, and turned his attention to the active console. The
antimatter containment was in a bad way. He guessed it

would fail in ninety seconds, perhaps even less. He pulled up the ship's operations controls and ordered the docking bay's hatch to open. The control flashed green and the hatch started to dilate. Somewhere a decompression warning sounded.

"Category one," said a voice in Kane's ear, so close he turned expecting somebody to be standing by him. It took him a moment to realise it was coming through his suit's communicator. A sense of great and immediate peril, even beyond the Leviathan's imminent death, overtook him and he started to run for the *Baby*. He was a metre away when the grappling cable snaked down from the chamber's roof and grabbed his leg. Suddenly he was dangling upside down over the *Baby*. He could see how wide the hatch had opened beneath the minisub and knew it must start falling slowly through in any moment. He reached and his hand barely touched the rail beside the dorsal lock before he was pulled still higher.

"Kane?" Katya's voice was loud inside the suit's helmet. "What was that? What's happening?"

Kane swung up and grabbed the tentacle-like cable. He tugged frantically, but it didn't budge a centimetre. "I... Unh! The Leviathan. It won't let me go!" He felt utterly helpless and allowed himself to flop limply like a rag doll in the cable's grip. "Sorry, Katya. You're going to have to make the descent yourself."

"No! No! I will not..."

"Out of our hands, Katya. For what it's worth, I'm glad I met you."

"Shut *up*! I'm not letting that *thing* have you!"

"Look after yourself, Katya. Don't think about me. You need to..."

The tentacle dropped him. He fell slowly; the chamber's artificial gravity had been deactivated when the hatch started to open. Even with only Russalka's gravity, weakened by their distance above it, he still hit the top of the *Baby* hard and rolled off it. As he lay stunned, he heard the Leviathan speak to him for the last time.

"Go."

Beside him, the *Baby* fell through the hatch, but all he could do was gaze up at the cable retracting lazily into the ceiling. Its voice... there had been something about its voice...

Suddenly, he realised his ride was leaving without him. He rolled over and pushed himself out after the *Baby*, shunting himself off from the hatch edge. It was little enough impetus, but just barely enough to catch up with the minisub. He grabbed one of the metal strips that secured the drones and then quickly transferred his grip to a stanchion rail running down beside the aft hatch before the sharp-edged tape had a chance to cut his glove.

"Kane! Speak to me! I can't see you!"

"I'm clear of the Leviathan. I'm hanging onto the *Baby*."

"You're clear? How?"

"I don't know." He looked upwards to where he could see the diminishing shape of the Leviathan between his feet, accelerating hard away from Russalka, away from them. In a moment, it was almost too small to see "It just... let me go."

"Can you reach the dorsal hatch?"

He laughed. "No. Not a chance. I'm only holding on with one hand. I can't move anywhere."

There was silence for a moment. Then Katya said, "Kane, even with the drones, the passage through the atmos–"

Behind them, the Leviathan exploded. For a moment, it glowed brighter than any sun as matter and antimatter combined in its heart and eliminated one another, changing directly to energy in the process. In an instant, the vessel, its huge but corrupt artificial mind and the bodies of two brave men were turned to plasma.

Kane was looking away and that saved his sight as the flash enveloped them, and made the cloud tops so far below turn to a rolling sea of white fire for achingly long seconds. Kane's helmet filled with interference as the communication frequencies were jammed by the brief burst of radiation generated by the explosion. Kane knew his suit would absorb it and that the minisub's hull would protect Katya. What he was more worried about was the possibility of debris raining across them and puncturing his suit.

Long seconds passed, but he was not perforated by a storm of metal particles travelling at hyperkinetic speeds.

This was small comfort. The re-entry into the atmosphere was still sure to kill him.

He heard Katya's voice penetrate and grow in clarity as the radiation died away. "Kane? Are you there? Did you say something?"

"I just said that today has just been one long round of jumping out of frying pans into successively larger fires."

"What? I don't understand you."

"I'll explain later." The *Baby* was starting to shudder as they entered the thickening atmosphere. Should there *be* a later, he thought. "Activate the drones, Katya."

"I already have. We need to get you in quickly. You won't be able to hang on during the turbulence."

Feeling the strain on his arm, Kane strongly doubted he would even last until the turbulence. "Don't worry about me."

"I've heard your brave farewell speech once, Kane. You're not dying today."

Kane's heart froze as he realised what was going through her mind. "*Do not open the hatch*, Katya! You *will* die!"

"What kind of idiot do you take me for?" He was never so glad to have somebody talk to him so contemptuously. "I've got an idea, but you'll have to be strong and hang on just for a minute. Can you do that?"

"A minute? I think so."

His arm burned with exhaustion. Even a minute seemed an eternity. He counted slowly to sixty to take his mind off the pain of the tortured muscles, deliberately losing count a couple of times and starting back a few numbers. He wondered what her plan was. He assumed the *Baby* might have a manipulator arm folded away somewhere that could hold onto him, but he couldn't see such an arm and, anyway, what would it be doing at the back of the minisub?

He was just about to ask Katya what the plan really was when he discovered it for himself. The aft hatch unsealed and started to open before him. His eyes widened; Katya was going to get herself killed to save him.

He knew it was already too late to try and stop her – the compartment would already have lost its air – now he had to think of some way to get inside and repressurise the *Baby* rapidly. A couple of plans flitted through his mind, but they foundered on the immediate fact that he was trailing from a plummeting minisub several kilometres in the air by the fingertips of one hand. Then the hatch finished opening and there was Katya, as grim as death.

As grim as death, but very much alive. Strapped over her face was an emergency respirator pack. She'd punched a small hole at the base from which the green oxygen-rich fluid was fountaining across her clothes. Through the transparent mouth piece of the LoxPak, he could see the stuff foaming violently as the oxygen boiled out of it in the very low pressure. She'd known enough not to try and use the breather as a simple life-support unit – the pressure difference between her lungs and outside could have been fatal. Instead she was letting it make a breathable atmosphere inside the mask, the gases making their way into her lungs under their own pressure while she just kept her mouth open. It would be like breathing at the top of a mountain, but it was breathing. Not for the first time, Kane was astonished by her ability to think clearly when danger threatened and time was short. He would have hugged her but for that small detail of trailing behind a plummeting minisub by the fingertips of one hand.

She reached out and snapped a lanyard loop around his wrist, drawing it tight with a reflexive tug. Then she braced herself against the hatchway and started to pull him in on the line, hand over hand. The flow of fluid stuttered and stopped. She was running only on the oxygen in her bloodstream now. Summoning up his every reserve, Kane reached forward with his free hand and managed to grab hers. She placed one foot on either side of the hatch so she was horizontal to the *Baby*'s floor and, screaming silently with a desperate rage, she straightened her legs. Kane was half through the hatch now. He used the hand with the line wrapped around it to grab the internal stanchion rail above the door and heaved himself in. It took achingly long seconds to clamber around so he could close the hatch without falling out again, seconds in which he knew Katya was suffocating. Finally, the hatch slammed shut and he released the automatic pressure valves Katya had disabled to prevent the minisub venting all its air in a vain attempt to repressurise a compartment open to space.

Air flooded in. Katya lay on her back hyperventilating, her colour an ugly blue. Kane cursed the slowness of the pressure gauge, tore open the medical kit and gave her oxygen directly from its emergency cylinder.

With a rapidity that surprised and relieved him, her colour and breathing returned to normal.

"Katya? Katya?"

Her eyes flickered open, but she could say nothing more cogent than "Nnnh?"

He levelled a finger at her. "Don't you *ever* save my life again." He didn't know whether his anger was mock or real.

Katya nodded slightly. "'Kay."

TWENTY

VENGEANCE

He had a nagging sense that he had overslept, but it felt so nice to lie there in his bunk. Maybe just another minute, then he'd get up. Just another minute. Maybe five.

"Lieutenant?" The voice was tentative, respectful.

"What is it, ensign?" he said. He didn't want to open his eyes, he had a feeling it would be too bright on the other side of his eyelids, and would give him a headache. Perhaps he already had a headache, he mused. His mouth felt dry, too.

"You're awake!" The relief in the voice was unmistakable.

Oh, dear. Was he meant to be on duty? That would explain why he felt so guilty for oversleeping. But why couldn't he remember going to bed in the first place?

He took a deep breath. "Tell Captain Zagadko that Lieutenant Petrov sends his apologies, and will be on bridge presently." Oh, he was in trouble now.

"Sir? Sir… Captain Zagadko is dead."

Petrov's eyes snapped open and he instantly regretted it. He'd been right; it was far too bright outside his skull. He tried to sit up but whoever had been talking to him took a gentle but firm grip of his shoulders and forced him back supine. "You shouldn't get up too quickly, sir. You took quite a knock."

It certainly felt like it. How could he have forgotten the captain was dead?

He looked around the room. He was lying in a sickbay, but of no boat or class he recognised. "What happened?" He looked up and recognised Officer Suhkalev. "I remember lifting from the Yagizban place – what was it? FP-1 – and then... not much. We were hit, weren't we?" Try as he might, the events in his memory just came to a ragged end and no amount of clawing after details seemed to help fill the blank. "Were we?"

Suhkalev nodded. "One engine took a missile. I lost control for a minute. You were hanging on behind me and, the next time I looked, you weren't there. You must have been thrown around in the manoeuvres and kissed a bulkhead. You were hurt. Hurt badly." Petrov reached up and found his head was bandaged. "We thought we might lose you for a while. I patched you up as best I could and..."

"*You* did?"

Suhkalev nodded again, slightly embarrassed. "The *Novgorod*'s medic was lost during the escape. I did a paramedic course. It didn't really cover severe head trauma, but luckily this place," he indicated the sickbay with a jerk of his thumb, "is well equipped. Lots of automated stuff."

"Where is 'this place' anyway? We're not still on the transporter, are we?"

"No, sir. We had to ditch in the ocean. *I* had to ditch in the ocean. We'd already detected the FP-1 launching pursuit craft and, if we didn't sink and drown, they'd have blown us out of the water anyway. The thing is, the transporter handling so badly even under one engine surprised me. It made me think." That slightly embarrassed smile again. "It made me think maybe the reason she handled like a manta whale in calf was maybe she was carrying something big and heavy in her hold."

The surroundings suddenly made perfect sense to Petrov and he settled back into his sick bed with a pleased smile. "This is a Yagizban boat? One of those *Vodyanoi* copies?"

"It was just sitting there in the belly. So we all got aboard, opened the transporter's ventral doors and swam out in this thing. The transporter sank like a stone after the hold flooded. The Yagizban interceptors must have thought we'd died in the crash or drowned in the sinking. They didn't drop depth charges or torpedoes or even sonar buoys. They just went home."

It didn't surprise Petrov. "They may have the toys, but they don't know how to play with them."

"We're making best speed towards FMA waters, but being quiet about it. There's always the chance they might send in search boats to look for wreckage and Mr Retsky thinks running into them at full speed or trying to get a message out could bring this trip to a sudden end. Another day and it should be safe to hail for FMA vessels."

"Mr Retsky is very prudent. Send him my compliments and... No, I'll tell him myself." He started to get up to Suhkalev's alarm.

"No! Sir! You're not fit to command yet! You'll..."

"My mother's not dead, Suhkalev. You can't have her job. Anyway, relax. I'm just going to show my face and then come straight back here. I want to congratulate the crew on a job well done. You, too. Now help me up." As he got slowly to his feet, he rested his hand against the bulkhead for support. He looked at the metal, patted it gently. "What's she called?"

"The boat? She doesn't have a name, sir. You know what they're like in the Enclaves; she's got a number. *YCV-K2301*, I think. Something like that anyway"

Petrov curled his lip. "*YCV-K2301?*" he said, disgusted. "What goes through their minds? How can anybody develop a sense of belonging to something called the *YCV-K2301*? No sense of esprit de corps, the Yagizban. Is she a good boat?"

"Your crew seem to like her. The general opinion is that she's not quite as nice as the *Vodyanoi* because she doesn't have Terran equipment aboard, but she's a good copy. Oh, the big difference is she doesn't have a salvage maw like the *Vodyanoi*. The bow's taken up with an extended weapons room. More fish, more tubes."

Petrov smiled a predatory smile. "I like her already. But that name's got to go."

"As senior officer it's your privilege to rename the prize, sir."

Petrov nodded slowly to avoid provoking his headache. If the Yagizba Enclaves thought they were going to have their surprise attack against the Federal settlements as planned, they were going to be bitterly disappointed. The counterstrike started now.

"Then take a note, Officer Suhkalev. As of this moment, the vessel formerly known as the *YCV-K2301*, taken in combat by the surviving crew of the RMV *Novgorod* and an element of the Federal law-enforcement fraternity on behalf of the Federal Maritime Authority, will now and henceforth be known as the RMV..."

He paused. He didn't even have to wait for inspiration; a name had already offered itself. The pause was his doubt about its suitability. Was it really an appropriate name for an FMA boat? A warboat should have a noble name, not what he had in mind. Then he thought of what the Yagizban had planned, their lying and treason, and he knew it was perfect. There would be no nobility in the next war fought in the seas of Russalka.

"...the RMV *Vengeance*."

TWENTY-ONE
EVERYTHING CHANGES

The *Vodyanoi* had drifted at a depth of two hundred metres, watching, waiting and doing very little else while the Leviathan mauled the FP-1. The crew had spent ten years learning pragmatism and they practised it now, ignoring the desperate distress signals from their sister vessels as the hulking killer-ship slid unheard and unseen through their midst, seeding death among the Yagizban boats with its combat drones. They listened as the battlefield grew quieter and quieter and they wondered how long it would be before the Leviathan sighted and destroyed them. Instead, the carnage halted abruptly. The Yagizban recalled their remaining forces and the great floating station had moved slowly away, listing badly in the water.

The *Vodyanoi* had started to cautiously follow, assuming that the Leviathan, invisible to their sensors, would be doing the same. Instead they had detected a massive disturbance behind them; almost seven million displacement tonnes of vessel surfacing at speed and tearing itself from the ocean top. They had released a camera buoy to the surface and watched the Leviathan fly upwards, upwards until it was lost in the boiling clouds.

For lack of anything else that they could do, they waited. Thirty minutes later, the clouds glowed white above them and the communication channels filled with random noise.

For lack of anything else it could be, they knew the Leviathan was destroyed, and that their captain was dead.

They were debating what to do next when, through the slowly clearing channels, they detected the transponder signal of the *Baby*. Triangulation showed it was not in the sea, but in the air. A *long* way up in the air. The most likely explanation was it had been blown free in the blast and was falling back to Russalka like an artificial meteorite. But it fell, and it fell and it fell and it took its own sweet time doing it. The camera buoy, coming back online after the radiation wave had temporarily silenced it, showed them the truth. The *Baby*, lightened to the point of almost no effective weight by the combat drones strapped to it, floating slowly towards the ocean, as slow as a soap bubble.

Finally, it touched down. The *Vodyanoi* was waiting for it.

When the minisub *Pushkin's Baby* finally reached Lemuria Station, it was ten days late. There was no fuss, no crowds at the locks when she arrived hungry for news of what had happened to her, not even anybody demanding to know where her cargo was. The official who processed her was new to the station and didn't know the local boats and masters, so nobody even asked about Lukyan Pushkin.

Katya Kuriakova signed the cargo – newly returned from the *Vodyanoi*'s stores – into the warehouse to await collection and left the locks for the station's commercial sector. With her went a passenger, a man travelling under false papers.

Now they sat in a small and almost empty coffee shop in the middle of the shopping area, watching people walk by and drinking real – and therefore expensive – coffee. Kane's treat.

"What are you thinking, Katya Kuriakova?"

She watched a mother argue with her children for a moment before replying. "Wondering how many of these people will still be alive in a year."

"Oh," said Kane. He drank a little of his cup. "You've become a fatalist."

"A realist."

"No, not necessarily. Things might not come to a full war. There's always the possibility of a cold war. Both sides bristle at each other, but nobody shoots." He noticed Katya's eyes upon him and shook his head in resignation. "No, they'll shoot. The FMA have been used to getting their own way for too long, and the Yagizban have invested too much to just step back. There'll be war." He drank a little more. "Nice coffee."

"Grown hydroponically. That's what it says in the menu. What will you do, Kane?"

"Me? Oh, I don't know. The usual. Make it up as we go along. We can start by selling off those combat drones. They can be reverse-engineered and, anyway, Terran components are always much sought after."

"Who will you sell them to?"

"Happily, there's two, so we can sell one to the FMA and flog the other off to the Yagizban. I know what you're thinking," he added quickly, "playing both sides off against the middle, but you're... actually, no, that's partially true.

The idea is that neither side gets an advantage over the other and we get ourselves some leeway, build some bridges. We'd like to stay neutral, but that will be impossible. People get into this 'if you're not with us, you're against us' mindset. It's shallow and inflexible, but that's what happens when people start thinking like a mob, and that's what happens in war. I can't say I'm looking forward to it."

"You won't live long on the proceeds from two combat drones."

"No. 'Honest, mate, lovely combat drone, one careful owner, fell off the back of an artificially intelligent battleship.' No, that won't set us up for life." He shrugged. "There's always piracy, I suppose. But what about you, Katya? What are you going to do? Are you going to sign up for the FMA? They'll be needing good officers."

Katya shook her head, smiling at a private joke. "The FMA isn't for me. I don't respond well to military discipline. I've got the *Baby* to look after now, anyway. Operating a minisub for conveyance and maybe recovery work will probably get me listed in a reserved occupation. I'll be more useful to them as a civilian than in uniform. I know that will cheer Sergei up; he hates the Feds." She closed her eyes and opened them again as a sharp pang of inner misery troubled her. "I have to tell him Lukyan's dead. They've been friends since they were boys." She steeled herself and put that where it belonged, in the future. "Anyway, yes. I've got the sub. I've got a business to run."

"You sound very grown up," said Kane, sadness in his voice.

"Of course I'm grown up. I've got a card somewhere to prove it." She patted her pocket, but it was empty. She laughed a small, bitter laugh. "I think it's still on the

Novgorod. That's a point. I'd better tell the FMA where she's lying. It shouldn't take long to get her seaworthy again and, the devil knows, they'll need every boat they can get."

Kane checked his cup. It was down to the dregs. "There's an alternative."

Katya looked up at him, mildly interested.

"We could go back to the locks, take the *Baby* back to the *Vodyanoi* and keep our heads down until this is all over. There are plenty of places to hide, plenty of small settlements who won't want any part of what's coming. You'd be welcome to join the crew."

"And why would I want to do that?"

"So you don't die."

Katya thought about it, but not for long. "No, Kane, I won't do that. I'll take my chances here."

Kane was unsurprised but felt he had to ask. "May I ask why?"

Katya thought longer this time, remembering what had happened to her, what she had learned, what she hungered to forget and never would. When she had her thoughts ordered and her mind clear, she replied.

"I don't like to be near you, Kane. People die near you. You go around wide-eyed and clueless as if you don't understand how these things could happen, and then, five minutes later, you say, 'Oh, well, that happened for this reason that I didn't bother telling you about until it was too late.' All this," she swept her hand across the tabletop, but the gesture encompassed the Leviathan, the FP-1, the Chertovka, the dead and the lost, "all this is *your* fault. You brought the Leviathan here. Then you abandoned it and just hoped it was a problem that would go away if you didn't think about it. But it didn't go away. Ten years later, it gets stirred up and you are *right there* when it happens. And what do you do? Nothing. You don't say a word. You didn't give Captain Zagadko enough information to fight it or even to realise he couldn't. You'd lost control of the situation and you couldn't even be bothered to tell us what that situation was. Why? You'd spent ten years hoping it would all just go away and it hadn't. What made you think it would just fade away now?

"And then it turns out you've been collaborating with the Yagizba Enclaves in treason. *Treason*, Kane! Without access to your boat, they wouldn't have been able to churn out copies. They've got a whole war effort based on technologies that *you* gave them! And now hundreds, thousands of people are going to die because of a war *you* helped start."

Kane was looking grey. "Katya, it's not…"

"No!" she spat at him. "Shut up! I liked Captain Zagadko. I liked Petrov. I liked Tokarov. I *loved* my uncle. Unless you can bring them back, then shut up. You have nothing to say to me." She wanted to cry but she would not, not in front of him. Later, she would discover that she could not cry at all and she would hate him for that too.

Kane sat silently, looking unblinkingly at his empty cup. Then he glanced up at the chronometer on the wall and back down again. "The *Vodyanoi* will be standing off the auxiliary locks by now. It will take me five minutes to get there, five minutes to get aboard, ten minutes to get out of the sensor cordon." He nodded in the direction of the corridor leading into the administrative area. "There's an FMA office just down there, first on the left. You can go and make a report there after you've finished your coffee. If you nurse it, it might last twenty minutes." He looked up but he couldn't meet her eyes. "Would you do that much for me?"

Katya didn't reply for a long moment. Then she said, "Go."

She didn't see his eyes widen as he remembered the last word of the Leviathan, and finally realised in whose voice it had been spoken.

Abruptly, like a man who'd forgotten something, he climbed to his feet and walked quickly away without looking back. Katya watched him until he turned the corner to the auxiliary facilities sector and was lost to sight. She sipped her coffee. It was cold and she couldn't taste it anyway.

It took her twenty-five minutes to finish her cup. Then she ordered another.

ACKNOWLEDGMENTS

All the Strange Chemists and associated lab rats, but especially Amanda Rutter, Marc Gascoigne, and Paul Simpson.

Sam Copeland, purveyor of splendid literary representation, silliness, and some of the most disturbing profile pictures on Twitter.

My wife and daughter, for putting up with my distracted mutterings about crush depths and baro-traumatic injury.

I'd also like to mention some SF writers whose work I read avidly in my school days, and from whom I think I learned a lot, both about science and storytelling.

Hugh Walters isn't a name that's much known these days, and that's a shame. I devoured his U.N.E.X.A. books about a UN-funded space programme.

Robert Heinlein is, of course, famous for books like *Stranger in a Strange Land* and *Starship Troopers*, but he was also writing YA novels long before they were called YA. I have especially fond memories of *Have Spacesuit – Will Travel* and *Podkayne of Mars*.

John Christopher (a pseudonym of Sam Youd) wrote the *Tripod Trilogy* in the late Sixties and, really, do yourself a favour and read these books. In so many ways they are the pathfinders for much of the YA science fiction and fantasy that was to follow.

ABOUT THE AUTHOR

Jonathan L. Howard is a game designer and the author of the Johannes Cabal series of novels. He lives with his wife and daughter near Bristol in the UK.

johannescabal.com
@jonathanlhoward

IF YOU COULD UNDO ANY DECISION IN THE MEREST BLINK OF AN EYE, WHAT WOULD YOU CHANGE?

SHIFT

KIM CURRAN

STRANGE CHEMISTRY

"It's like the best kind of video game: full of fun, mind-bendy ideas with high stakes, relentless action, and shocking twists!" – *E C Myers, author of* Fair Coin

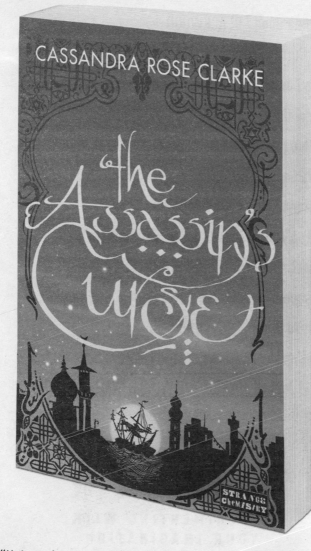

CASSANDRA ROSE CLARKE

the Assassin's Curse

STRANGE CHEMISTRY

"Unique, heart-wrenching, full of mysteries and twists!"
– *Tamora Pierce, author of* Alanna: The First Adventure

MORE WONDERS IN STORE FOR YOU...